WITCH QUEEN BOOK TWO

RITES OF PASSAGE

A.D. STARRLING

COPYRIGHT

Rites of Passage (Witch Queen 2)
Copyright © AD Starrling 2022. All rights reserved.
Registered with the US Copyright Service.
Third paperback edition: 2024
ISBN: 978-1-912834-28-0

www.ADStarrling.com
shop.adstarrling.com

Edited by Right Ink On The Wall

BRYONY CROSS NARROWED HER EYES AT THE teleconference display on the wall opposite her desk. "Are you being serious right now?"

Ephra Erwin, the High Priestess of the Houston coven, arched a perfectly manicured eyebrow. "Why, yes, Bryony. I'm not quite sure how you could have interpreted our request any other way."

Her brittle tone did not escape Bryony. Even though the High Council members were separated by thousands of miles, sitting in their respective offices spanning the East to the West coasts, the New York coven leader could practically taste the arctic front permeating the meeting. Armand Duprey, the current secretary, visibly swallowed a sigh.

Guilt flitted through Bryony at his harassed expression. Armand wasn't just a well-respected colleague and ally, he was also a close confidant of Barbara Nolan, the Chicago coven High Priestess and one of Bryony's closest friends.

Abraham Whitworth shifted slightly in his seat beside her. His jaw was tight and his owl familiar's normally limpid, yellow gaze glowed with a hint of heat. It didn't matter that the sorcerer had been the first to chastise Bryony for not scheduling the long overdue meeting before now. Abraham took any affront against the New York coven personally and the way the other High Council members were currently addressing her fell squarely under that category.

Bryony drummed her fingers on her desk, her own temper simmering beneath a veneer of civility. She knew she was at fault for not arranging this meeting sooner. But it wasn't exactly as if she'd been sitting around doing nothing this last month.

It had been two weeks since the Witch Queen prophesied to rule over the world of magic had awakened. Not only had Mae Jin saved innocent humans from being slaughtered by the demons the Dark Council had unleashed inside the hospital where she was working on the night her powers manifested, she had also gone on to fight the Sorcerer King's minions. Not to mention the modified demons he had placed in the ranks of a dangerous Russian crime gang creating waves in the city's underworld. The repercussions of her revival and the battles that had ensued were still being felt across New York's magical community and the city itself.

This had meant Bryony's coven having to field dozens of meetings with the U.S. Special Affairs bureau, as well as pacifying various local officials and the coven chapters of the neighboring towns who wished to know what their new queen's intentions were.

Mae's face rose before Bryony. She furrowed her brow.

She knew the High Council's disgruntlement had less to do with her tardiness at informing them about the crucial events that had transpired in New York and more to do with the fact that they believed her coven stood to gain the most by being the first to ally themselves with the Witch Queen.

They probably think we kept Mae Jin's existence a secret so we could benefit from her power and influence. A thin smile curved Bryony's lips as she met the probing gazes of the High Council. *Wait until they meet her.*

Mae Jin was not the Witch Queen nor indeed the woman Bryony had expected her to be. And she had never been more glad of that fact.

"Does this matter amuse you?" Gerard Mosele asked with a frosty grunt.

Bryony allowed her smile to widen, knowing it would only irritate the Orlando coven High Priest further. The magical community was a mostly matriarchal one and the heads of covens were witches by tradition. Few sorcerers held the title of High Priest. Only two occupied that position in the U.S.: Derrick Adlington, the leader of the Baton Rouge coven, and Gerard.

Of the ones abroad, the Sorcerer King was far and above the most notorious. As the head of the Dark Council, he was not just the unofficial sworn enemy of the wider magic community, but also Mae Jin's nemesis. For it was the Sorcerer King who had robbed her original incarnation of her birthright thousands of years ago, killing her mother and banishing her father Azazel to Hell.

The only thing stopping the magical societies of every nation from engaging in open warfare with the Sorcerer King was the Treaty of Argentheim, the accord reached at the end of the Middle Ages to stop the deaths of thousands of magic users on both sides of the divide.

"It does amuse me, to an extent," Bryony said. "The fact that you're asking me to command Mae to attend our next Annual Grand Meeting shows how asinine you're all being. One does not give orders to our queen."

Ephra bristled. There was a general darkening of faces across the board. Ice practically crackled across the speakers.

Armand pinched the bridge of his nose.

Only three Council members seemed to be paying no heed to unfolding events. Charlotte Brix, the Atlanta coven High Priestess, had her eyes firmly focused on her knitting. Raven Quinn, the L.A. coven High Priestess and the youngest witch present, was typing away furiously at her laptop, her hand occasionally straying to her iced latte. Derrick Adlington was perusing something on his phone, his expression somewhat bored.

"It's too soon for Mae to reveal herself publicly to our community," Bryony said curtly. "The Sorcerer King and the Dark Council may have gone to ground for now, but I have no doubt they're plotting something in the shadows." She lifted her chin. "It is our duty to ensure Mae's safety and that of her family until we know what his next move is. I've already told you what happened to her sister and grand—"

"What about her duty to us?"

The woman who interrupted her did so in a soft voice that still managed to grate on Bryony's nerves. Karin Everheart's gaze was steady as she observed Bryony over her steepled hands, the supercilious light in her pupils tempered by her fake smile.

Bryony met the San Francisco coven High Priestess's stare with a stony expression. "What duty are you alluding to?"

Penley, Bryony's black cat familiar, raised his head from where he'd been sunning himself on the windowsill. He jumped down, padded across the room, and leapt onto her thigh. Bryony stroked the cat absent-mindedly as he curled up on her lap, his presence and magic calming her ruffled feathers.

Karin waved a lazy hand. "I know many in the magic community have long held on to the antiquated belief that the Witch Queen is some kind of deity we must serve, but we need to move with the times. We cannot defer to this Mae Jin simply because of who she says she is. She needs to prove her worth to us." She paused. "She needs to serve *us*."

CHAPTER TWO

Ephra sucked in air. Charlotte's hands stilled on her knitting. Raven frowned at her laptop. A muscle jumped in Armand's jaw line. Even Gerard and Derrick stiffened.

The only one who didn't stir beside Karin was Linus Jarrett, the sorcerer standing in for the Phoenix coven High Priestess.

Heat flushed through Bryony. *Has Karin lost her mind?!*

She pushed her chair back and rose to her feet, Penley dropping to the floor with an anxious meow.

"Did I hear you correctly?" Bryony said in a dangerously quiet voice. "You want Azazel's daughter, the most powerful witch on this planet, to be a slave to the High Council? To *you?!*"

Her last words came out a roar.

Karin shrugged at her reaction. "Come now. Slave is a bit of an exaggeration. She will be in our employ." She smiled condescendingly. "Why, we'll even pay her a salary and call her queen."

A gnashing noise reached Bryony. A muscle jumped in Abraham's jawline where he stood by her chair. The sorcerer might have been antagonistic to Mae when she first came to the New York coven, but he'd had no choice but to acknowledge her, especially after witnessing her magic. Mae was one of their people now and he would gladly lay down his life for her even were she not the Witch Queen.

Bryony drew a slow, steady breath, the triumphant light in Karin's eyes telling her she'd fallen for the witch's bait.

Barbara was right. That woman's a snake. I can't let her rile me.

Charlotte spoke before Bryony could resume her argument.

"You seem to be forgetting something, Karin." The Atlanta coven witch had laid her knitting down and was looking steadily at the camera, her normally kind voice holding just a hint of steel. "The enemy of the magic community is the Sorcerer King, not the Witch Queen. Do not make a foe of the only one who can save us."

Karin's expression grew pinched, the color on her cheekbones broadcasting her irritation at the older witch's subtle admonition. Her lips curved, the motion more a smirk than a smile. "The *only* one who can save us? You don't seem to have much faith in the current generation of witches and sorcerers, Charlotte." She cocked her head to the side, confidence blazing from every line of her body. "I suspect we are infinitely more powerful than the people who last fought the Sorcerer King."

Abraham's eyes widened. The aide's expression told Bryony he was thinking the exact same thing as she was.

The San Francisco High Priestess was seriously deluded if she thought any of them had a chance against the Sorcerer King. From what they'd witnessed a few weeks ago, even his heir Oscar Beneventi could wipe out an entire coven with a dozen of his acolytes and demons if he so wished.

It had taken Mae's awakening for them to finally understand the reason for the immense power behind all the Sorcerer Kings that had existed through the ages. When one had the backing of an Archduke of Hell, there was little mere humans could do to stand in their path, even if they did possess magic in their souls.

Bryony had yet to reveal this singular truth to the High Council.

Ephra blew out a sigh, her frustration at the turn the meeting had taken clear. "Look, let's just meet the woman first. We can't rush through decisions that may affect the future of the entire magic community. Bring Mae Jin to the annual covenstead, Bryony. That's an order."

Bryony opened her mouth to protest. The screen went black.

She scowled. "Dammit all to Hell! I can't believe she cut me off!"

Penley twined around her legs, his magic warming

her flesh. She picked up the familiar and petted him, the motion soothing her nerves. A clink reached her ears.

Abraham was pouring her a brandy from the drink cabinet. The sorcerer paused, served himself a glass, and crossed the room to hand her the drink.

"That went well," he grunted.

Bryony's dark mood lifted as she sipped her brandy. Abraham had grown a lot more relaxed in the time he'd been working with her. Though he always showed her the respect she was due in public, they'd long since treated each other as friends in private. She hid a dry smile behind her glass. Four years ago, the very notion of drinking in her presence would have made the young sorcerer faint in horror.

A hollowness filled her chest, the matter at hand weighing her down once more.

"It could have been worse." She sighed. "I suspected they'd want to meet with her as soon as possible."

"Still, the Annual Grand Meeting is hardly the place for that," Abraham grumbled. "It'll be difficult to patrol with so many people around."

Bryony could see the cogs turning in the aide's head. They'd already made all the necessary arrangements to attend the covenstead in three days. He was no doubt calculating where to put Mae in the equation and whom to recruit to guard her.

They were both painfully aware that the Witch Queen was more than capable of taking care of herself. But the ongoing threat to Mae and her family was something the New York coven could not tolerate.

Bryony knew Abraham harbored the same regrets she still did about what had happened to Mae's sister Ryu and Ye-Seul Hwang, their grandmother. They hadn't anticipated the swiftness with which Oscar would try and take advantage of Mae's only weakness.

Her stomach twisted at the thought of Vedran Borojevic, the sixth Sorcerer King, and Barquiel, the demon and fallen angel who was once the ninth leader of the Grigori.

I won't let those bastards and their servants run amok in my city.

She looked at the clock. "Isn't Mae late? She said she'd be here by lunchtime."

"Noah called. Ryu is sick. Mae is covering for her."

Ryu was currently serving as the director of the Jins' family-run funeral home until they found a suitable replacement. Noah Tegner, Bryony's nephew, had been assigned to the protection team the New York coven had allocated to Mae's family after Ryu and Ye-Seul Hwang were kidnapped by the Dark Council. Though she'd been loath to lose Noah from the coven's security detail, Bryony could not deny that he was the best man for the job. Judging from the way her nephew talked about the Jins, he was pretty happy to be there too.

Bryony pursed her lips. *A little too happy.*

"Ask Violet and Miles to pick up Mae. They don't have class today."

Abraham gave her a shrewd look. "Admit it. You just don't want her coming here on the Vespa."

Bryony sniffed. "That scooter is a menace and we

both know it. She took me for a ride on the damn thing last week. It's a miracle she's survived this long without getting run over."

Abraham gaped. "Wait. Is that where you two disappeared off to that night?!"

Bryony waved a dismissive hand at his shocked expression. "We only rode around the neighborhood. I don't know why she doesn't just use the SUV we gave her. Any black magic sorcerer could pick her off that damn scooter."

"I'm sure Brimstone and Hellreaver would have something to say about that," Abraham muttered. "And you know she doesn't want to owe us anything. As much as it irritates me, I can see her point. She's still finding her feet in our world."

Bryony stared.

Abraham squinted. "What?"

"You've grown quite wise," she drawled.

The aide made a face. His cell phone buzzed with an incoming message. He checked the screen. "Looks like Vi and Miles read your mind. They're already there." Faint lines creased his brow. "They say it's gonna take a while. Apparently, all of Koreatown is at the funeral home."

CHAPTER THREE

Loud wailing punctuated by sobs echoed across the funeral parlor. Mae waited until there was a lull in the clamor before hurriedly launching into the eulogy.

"We are gathered here today to celebrate the life of Wang Ho-Nam, a much beloved grandfather, father, brother, cousin, and uncle."

She got five more words in before a high-pitched keen drowned out her voice. All eyes turned to the elegant, elderly widow in the traditional, black, silk *hanbok* adorned with pretty, white chrysanthemums bawling her eyes out in the right front row seat of the Fairhill Funeral Home. Kyo Seung Ho-Nam clutched her handkerchief against her lips and leaned heavily against her eldest son, the thin material barely keeping her sounds of grief at bay where the pair sat surrounded by the extensive Ho-Nam family.

A loud groan rose above her cries.

The widow twitched. She cut her eyes to the

woman seated in the opposite front row of the funeral hall, her mouth pressing into a thin line.

Jang-Mi Ye'un, Wang Ho-Nam's much younger mistress and the matriarch of his second family, released another whine, her triumphant gaze flitting to Kyo Seung. She gripped her expensive pearl necklace and sobbed loudly into her white silk hanky, her mascara streaking down her cheeks.

The air crackled with tension as the Ho-Nams and the Ye'uns glared at each other across the aisle, each family determined to be the loudest in the ritualistic lamentation that characterized traditional Korean funerals.

Mae swallowed a sigh. *Great. It'll be a miracle if this doesn't end in bloodshed.*

The guests packing the funeral hall seemed to share her opinion. They were staring unabashedly at the unfolding spectacle, their eager gazes swinging from one side of the room to the other. Everyone who was anyone in their close-knit community was here, including Myung Ki Son-Ha, Koreatown's chief gossip.

This was the funeral of the decade and no one wanted to miss it.

A faint sucking sound distracted Mae.

Ye-Seul was inhaling her orange juice where she sat on a padded chair in the private corridor that led to the back offices, the carton shrinking in her hands even while her rheumy gaze roamed the parlor with morbid interest.

Mae's mother stood behind Ye-Seul, arms folded

across her chest and a disapproving expression clouding her face. A *tsk-tsk* left Yoo-Mi's lips from time to time, the sound too low for anyone to catch but Mae. She had reluctantly accompanied Ye-Seul after the old woman insisted on attending the funeral and was now living through one of her worst nightmares. Drama.

Bianca Rhys, the mortician who'd prepared Wang Ho-Nam's body and who would be assisting Mae with the cremation, was lounging against the wall behind them, her goth make-up and dark outfit a sharp contrast against her short red hair and ivory skin. She blew gum and scrolled through a work tablet, making notes for the week ahead.

Luckily, all three were invisible to the people in the hall.

Mae sneaked a look at Wang Ho-Nam where he lay in the open casket beneath the flower-laden ceremonial altar holding his portrait. The old guy wore the serene expression of someone who no longer gave a shit about the theatrics being played out around him. She couldn't help but feel that he was watching the proceedings from Heaven with a big smile on his face and a middle finger shoved up at his loved ones.

Ah. To be dead and uncaring.

She became aware of a piercing stare from across the parlor. Mrs. Son-Ha's gimlet eyes were focused on her with a laser-like intensity. Mae tried not to squirm.

It never ceased to amaze her how much the woman knew about the private goings-on in their community.

She'd even clocked the New York coven's visits to her apartment, even though Mae lived miles from Koreatown, in Ridgewood. Mae had started to wonder if Mrs. Son-Ha was some kind of witch. She chewed her lip at that thought.

I'd know if she was.

Following her spectacular awakening as the prophesied Witch Queen of the occult world that had existed in the shadows of the more mundane human one since time immemorial, Mae could now sense magic in those who possessed it. She could even roughly see the locations of the witches and sorcerers who inhabited New York mapped out in her head like some kind of crazy GPS, a fact she had yet to reveal since it would more than likely freak them out.

But it wasn't just magic Mae was now able to detect. She could discern the demons who inhabited the souls of the unsuspecting humans wandering the city, as well as the men and women who had willingly embraced Hell's corruption.

There weren't as many of the fiends as there had been when she'd first come into her powers. A significant number had been affiliated with *Oniks*, the Russian crime gang whose influence had started to grow in the city's underworld a year ago.

Most of those demons and their human hosts had died at her hands and those of the magical and otherworldly allies who'd fought alongside her during the epic battle that had gone down in an abandoned factory on the Brooklyn waterfront. A fight that had seen the building reduced to its very foundations, with not a single brick or piece of metal left standing.

The missing structure and the gaping crater where it once stood were still baffling experts. Many were calling it the result of a freak incident of nature. No one had been able to answer the question of where several tons of masonry and steel had vanished to in the space of a single night, although some claimed they were now at the bottom of Upper Bay. Only the people who'd survived the fight knew the factory and its contents had been sucked into a black hole of Mae's making.

A chill coursed through her as she recalled the incredible things she had done, the role she'd been unwillingly thrust into, and the responsibility she now lived with every day.

Has it really only been two weeks?

Not only had she learned that she was the reincarnation of the daughter of the fallen angel Azazel and Ran Soyun, the first witch who ever walked the Earth and the woman whose family had given rise to the most powerful emperors to ever rule Korea, she had also come into possession of the familiar and the weapon that were once promised to Na Ri, the original Witch Queen.

However much she mourned the loss of her once normal life, Mae knew she had no option but to accept her fate and embrace her destiny. For none other than she could accomplish the task ahead. And that was to lead the world of magic and defeat the mad man and the demon who had wrought so much misery not just on her own family, but innumerable others.

It wasn't all bad, though. She had a lot of new friends and allies she wouldn't have met otherwise. People she trusted with her life. And she had Brimstone and Hellreaver. The bond between the three of them only grew stronger with time. And she wouldn't give that up for anything in the world.

CHAPTER FOUR

MAE'S FAMILIAR STIRRED WHERE HE LAY AT HER FEET behind the oratory podium.

Are all funerals like this?

The nine-tailed fox spirit was in his diminutive form, the aura of powerful, crimson magic that normally surrounded him when he manifested his true body curtailed to a faint, red light that occasionally flashed in his pupils.

"You mean the wailing?" Mae murmured. "Yeah, I'm afraid that's just a staple feature of traditional Korean funeral rites."

Ryu owes me big time for this.

Her sister was home with a cold and had begged Mae to take over the funeral ceremony that morning. Since she had yet to resume her mortuary assistant job at Grandview General, Mae had been splitting her time between helping out at the family business and learning more about the magical community from Bryony Cross.

The High Priestess had told her the New York coven was more than willing to take care of her every need and that she could quit her job at Grandview if she so wished. But that was something Mae wasn't ready to do. Not only because she fully intended to continue her surgical residency at some point in the future, but also because of Rose Blake's link to the place.

As far as the human world was aware, her best friend Rose had died during the attack on Grandview. Despite her remains never having been recovered from the wreckage and her grave at Union Field Cemetery bearing an empty coffin, the authorities deemed her deceased.

Only Mae and the magic world knew the truth. That Rose's body was now host to Barquiel, a fallen angel and Archduke of Hell. All evidence pointed to Barquiel having made an unholy alliance with the original Sorcerer King who killed Na Ri and Ran Soyun thousands of years ago. An alliance that extended to every Sorcerer King who had since followed.

A familiar rage danced through Mae as she called to mind the memories Na Ri had shown her on the day of her awakening. Memories of when the first Sorcerer King had attacked her people and her family.

It was by a sheer act of will and by focusing on her breathing like Brimstone and Na Ri had taught her that she managed to subdue the violent magic that would have escaped her core and made the funeral parlor shake on its foundations.

Though she did not hear her voice often these days, Na Ri was still alive somewhere inside her, her soul now fused with Mae's.

A lump formed in Mae's throat. The time Na Ri had spent with Ran Soyun and Azazel may have been short and ended with abrupt violence, but it had been filled with love. Just as Mae's life with the family she had been born into was.

Ryu's feverish face rose before her. Guilt darted through Mae. She suspected the stress of dealing with the Ho-Nams and the Ye'uns had finally gotten to Ryu. Her sister was normally as healthy as a horse.

I should have helped out more at the funeral home.

It had begun to dawn on Mae that she would not be able to split herself three ways once she started back at Grandview. The autopsy labs at the hospital were nearing the end of their refurbishment, having finally been released back to the hospital by NYPD following the end of their investigation into the attack. She couldn't hold on to her day job, help out at the family business, and unite the world of magic against the Sorcerer King and the Dark Council, like she was fated to do. Her chest grew tight.

Something had to give.

Oh well, I still have some time to figure things out. And I can always ask for their *advice.*

The faces of the two men who had entered her life in a dramatic fashion after she had awakened as the Witch Queen flitted across her inner mind. She bit her lip.

Nikolai Stanisic and Vlad Vissarion were as

different from each other as day was from night. And they had both started to lay claim to an equal share of her heart. Her face warmed when she recalled the kiss she'd shared with each man.

Brimstone's voice echoed inside her skull, his tone disapproving. *Are you in heat again?*

Mae narrowed her eyes. "No. And I'd be grateful if you'd stop reading my mind."

Brimstone sniffed. *I am not reading your mind. I can sense it in your magic.* He eyed Kyo Seung and Jang-Mi warily. *Those two women look like they're about to rip each other's throat out.*

"You're not wrong. This could very well turn into a bloodbath."

Hellreaver stirred where he lay in his medallion disguise under her dress shirt, his interest piqued. *Did someone say blood?*

"No!" Mae said hastily. "Now shut up and stay still."

The last thing she needed was for her demonic weapon to put in an appearance. She stiffened when she noticed Mrs. Son-Ha's stare.

Dammit. That woman is like a hawk when it comes to sniffing out trouble.

Hellreaver grew heavy around her neck.

Sure, the weapon sulked. *It's alright for the snake to steal the food offerings of a dead man, but I can't mention the B word.*

"What snake?" Mae snapped.

Several guests close to the podium glanced at her.

A sixth sense made Mae look over at the altar. Her eyes bulged.

Miles Nolan's familiar Millie was slithering her way across the dais, the boa constrictor's attention focused on the pear she evidently intended to snack on.

"Shit!"

The nearby guests startled and stared at Mae. Luckily, most of the funeral hall didn't hear her above the sobs and howls still punctuating the air. Mrs. Son-Ha's suspicious gaze swung from Mae to the altar.

Mae scanned the chamber frantically, relieved that normal humans could not see familiars. *Where the hell is that damn sorcerer?!*

Instinct had her checking out the corridor leading to the back offices.

Yoo-Mi stood frozen behind Ye-Seul, mouth open and left eye twitching. Ye-Seul was snorting into her juice carton, her cackles drowned out by the noisy crowd. Though Yoo-Mi and Ye-Seul did not harbor magic in their souls, they could see Millie; familiars possessed the ability to make themselves visible to the people they trusted.

Bianca was frowning at the pair. A little way behind the mortician, making desperate beckoning gestures at his boa constrictor, stood Miles, AKA a-soon-to-be-dead-sorcerer if Mae had any choice in the matter. His cousin Violet was beside him, her familiar Trixie perched on her shoulder. The rabbit had covered her eyes with her ears, clearly horrified. The witch, on the other hand, was wearing the sick smile of someone determined to enjoy this situation to the max.

The two sorcerers and the witch who formed part of the protection team the New York coven had assigned to Mae's family returned from patrolling the grounds and rocked to an abrupt halt next to Violet. Macabre fascination dawned on their faces as they watched the goings-on in the hall.

Miles caught Mae's glare.

I'm sorry! he mouthed.

Mae's eyes shrank to slits. A snicker drew her attention.

Brimstone was studying Millie with a grin, his bushy tail brushing warmly against her legs as it swept the floor. *This will be most amusing.*

Hellreaver tittered, the voices of the thousand demons who inhabited the weapon echoing in her head.

A headache throbbed between Mae's temples. She was contemplating forcibly removing Millie from the room with magic when one of Wang Ho-Nam's nephews jumped to his feet, yelled out some choice curse words, and threw a box of incense across the aisle.

It hit Jang-Mi in the head. The widow stopped mid-wail, her eyes rounding with shocked disbelief.

Kyo Seung sucked in air, sheer unladylike delight flashing in her pupils for an instant. Mrs. Son-Ha's jaw dropped open. Yoo-Mi let out a strangled sound. Bianca almost dropped her tablet.

A breathless stillness descended upon the hall.

"Great," Mae mumbled glumly. "Just great."

Loud yells exploded as the funeral descended into chaos, the Ho-Nams and the Ye'uns launching themselves across the room to attack one another.

Brimstone chortled.

CHAPTER FIVE

BRYONY TURNED FROM WHERE SHE'D BEEN LOOKING OUT over Central Park in the official meeting chambers of the coven, at the top of the high rise that housed its headquarters on Madison Avenue. The older witch did a double take when she saw Mae.

"What the devil happened to your face?!"

Mae winced slightly as she unhooked the chin strap of her helmet. She took it off, ran a hand through her hair, and blew out a sigh.

"I got punched by a widow."

Her black eye was already healing, courtesy of her magic. The one Violet had inflicted on Wang Ho-Nam's nephew when she'd inadvertently elbowed him in the face after jumping into the fray would not do so for days. Neither would the injuries meted out to the more challenging guests by the sorcerers and witch guarding her. As for the vicious back-kicks Brimstone had delivered to several of the attendees' legs while remaining invisible to their confused gazes, Mae suspected their visits to the hospital would reveal hairline fractures. She grimaced.

It's a good thing no one called the cops. I have Mrs. Son-Ha to thank for that.

It was the old woman who had finally brought the warring families to their senses and halted the fracas, her shrill voice piercing the clamor like some kind of godly herald. She'd barked out a tirade at Kyo Seung and Jang-Mi and marched the two matriarchs around the parlor to calm down frazzled nerves. She'd still been lecturing the widows when Mae left, having safely cremated Wang Ho-Nam and left Bianca in charge of dealing with the rest of the funeral arrangements.

Brimstone bristled at her side, the aura of magic around him pulsing dangerously. He finally let loose and transformed into his original form, his colossal head sending a chandelier swaying before he lowered it. A wind swept across the room as his nine tails vibrated with anger.

"How dare they strike you?! You should have let me bite their hands off!"

He gnashed his teeth, his pupils a bright vermilion.

"Calm down." Mae patted his flank, his fur hot under her touch. "It was an accident. No one was thinking straight. Besides, you can't just go around biting people's hands off." She stilled when she clocked the fox's mutinous moue. "Promise me you'll ask for my permission before you even contemplate doing something that crazy."

Brimstone turned his back to her and plopped his bottom on the marble floor, his giant frame radiating defiance and his tails polishing the floor in irritated sweeps.

Mae bit her lip. It was hard to keep a straight face when a fifteen-foot-tall demonic fox was pouting at you.

"Brim?"

The fox growled at her over his shoulder. *"You are my witch! I will defend you with my life!"*

Hellreaver grumbled in agreement.

"Look, I appreciate the sentiment. I truly do. But beating the hell out of a septuagenarian isn't exactly good for my reputation."

Bryony arched an eyebrow. "A septuagenarian did this to you?"

"She has a mean left hook."

A shudder raced down Mae's spine. *People are going to be talking about this funeral for decades.*

Footsteps sounded outside the doors. Miles and Violet came in, Millie hanging limply around her sorcerer's neck. The snake had received an earful from Miles while they'd still been at the funeral home and looked appropriately repentant. Trixie made comforting sounds at her friend from her perch on Violet's shoulder.

"You should have come in the SUV with us," Miles protested.

Mae rolled her eyes. "I got here before you, didn't I?"

"Anyone ever tell you that you ride like a madwoman?" Violet said sharply. "I almost ran three red lights trying to follow you. I'm surprised the fox didn't throw up."

"*I like the wind in my face,*" Brimstone grumbled. "*Besides, until you have ridden upon the back of a helldragon, you have not experienced true speed.*"

Mae made a face at that. There were times when she forgot her familiar's dark origins.

Violet stared up at the fox. "Why are you sulking?"

Brimstone sniffed. "*I would rather not talk about it.*"

Unease swirled through Mae as she studied Bryony. The older witch's features were set in hard lines that told her she was the bearer of news Mae didn't particularly want to hear.

"Why do I get the feeling your meeting with the High Council didn't go as planned?" she said warily.

"It didn't." Abraham marched out of Bryony's office and joined them. "They were a bunch of assholes."

He put away his cell, his face dark. His owl Shiloh swooped down from one of the chandeliers and landed nimbly on his shoulder. She hooted softly as he petted her head and blinked a welcome at Mae.

"You shouldn't call them that," Bryony admonished her aide, her tone not exactly forceful. "You realize they're all your elders? Well, apart from Raven."

"Raven?" Mae asked Violet.

"Raven Quinn. She's the High Priestess of the L.A. coven and the youngest witch to ever make the High Council. She's a tech genius who established her own start-up when she was sixteen. You've heard of *Ignis* right?"

Mae stared. "The company that invented that AI

chip that's in practically every digital device on the planet? The one that's worth billions of dollars?"

"Yeah, that one." Violet smirked. "Raven once locked Miles out of all his online accounts for a week."

"That was totally uncalled for," Miles protested.

Mae pursed her lips. "Did he make a move on her?"

Violet grinned. "He even bought her flowers."

Abraham gave Miles a pitying look.

Millie raised her head and hissed, her tongue flickering agitatedly. The familiar evidently thought any woman who refused her master was a complete moron.

Mae sighed. "Not that I really want to know the answer to this, but how were the High Council a bunch of assholes?"

Bryony and Abraham shared a guarded look.

Mae narrowed her eyes. "Spit it out."

Abraham rubbed the back of his neck. "They want you to come to our Annual Grand Meeting."

Violet straightened. "The national covenstead?"

"Yeah."

Mae's stomach sank as she observed their strained faces. "Why do I get the feeling none of you are particularly enamored with that idea?"

"We're not," Bryony said testily. "That's the worst place to introduce you to the wider magical community. There will be hundreds of sorcerers and witches there and some will undoubtedly have secret affiliations with the Dark Council."

Surprise jolted Mae at that.

"The Sorcerer King always knows what happens at

our covensteads," Abraham explained at her expression. "We've long assumed he has spies planted at every magical convention."

Mae's scalp prickled. She felt Brimstone and Hellreaver's disquiet through the bond that connected them.

"So, you're worried I'll get attacked if I go?"

"Yes." Bryony rubbed her forehead, looking weary all of a sudden. "From what Nikolai's contacts in Europe have told him, Oscar and his father are lying low." She met Mae's cautious gaze. "Things may have gone quiet in Budapest, but that doesn't mean the Dark Council isn't up to something. Nikolai thinks the same and so does Vlad. The Annual Grand Meeting would be an obvious place for them to set a trap for you."

Mae digested this with a frown. "Vlad's been looking into the Dark Council?"

"Whether we like it or not, he's involved in this fight," Bryony said. "His primary affiliation may be to the *Black Devils*, but he is a half demon half magic user, like you. His blood will always call him to battle. It's why he first approached the New York coven and the reason we've been working together behind the scenes these past few years to curtail some of the Dark Council's more nefarious activities in the city."

Vlad's handsome face and devilish smile flashed before Mae. The *Black Devils* heir acted like a carefree playboy most of the time, but there was no denying his instincts and his sharp intellect. Or how viciously good he was at fighting, his white, Bengal-tiger familiar

Tarang an equally daunting presence during their clashes with the Dark Council.

Mae had glimpsed the darkness that lived in Vlad's soul. A darkness that called to the demon blood within her. It was the reason she was torn between him and Nikolai, a man who possessed white magic similar to Ran Soyun's, despite being the scion of the Sorcerer King.

Darkness and light. Sin and temptation.

Somehow, Mae suspected she would still be struggling with this decision in the months ahead. Vlad had made it inherently clear he wanted to be the consort of the Witch Queen. Although Nikolai hadn't expressed the same wish openly, his competitive streak with Vlad and his not-so-subtle jealousy indicated he was similarly interested in the position.

Hellreaver stirred. *I sense burgeoning lust within you, my witch. You should just fornicate with the sorcerer and the incubus and get it over with.*

Brimstone growled at that suggestion. *They're not good enough for our mistress!*

Heat flooded Mae's cheeks. *No one is fornicating with anyone!*

Hellreaver spoke again. *Don't mind the fox. That fool is just being picky. Those two are your best options to release some of that sexual frustration you seem to be suffering from. Seriously, you need to let your hair down. All that pent-up desire is bad for your health.*

Hellreaver's vocabulary had expanded a lot since he'd awakened. In fact, he was starting to sound more like a regular New Yorker than a demonic weapon that was thousands of years old.

Mae scowled. *That's it. I'm banning you two from watching TV.*

Hellreaver groaned in protest.

What did I do? Brimstone objected, his tails thumping the floor agitatedly.

"Why is your face red?" Violet asked Mae curiously.

"Because I'm bonded to two idiots," she snapped. "Anyway, when and where is this Annual Grand Meeting?"

"It's in three days," Bryony replied somberly. "In Philadelphia."

Mae stared. "*What?!*"

CHAPTER SIX

Sweat trickled down Nikolai Stanisic's temple as he pressed his hands against the belly of the figure lying on the gurney. The man screamed and arched his back, muffled voice underscored by the screech of the demon clinging to his soul and skin blanching where he fought the leather restraints holding him down.

Nikolai focused, his heart thumping heavily against his ribs. *Just a little bit more!*

A grimace twisted his mouth as he drew on the white magic coursing through his veins. Though it didn't exactly cause him pain, he could feel an unpleasant tugging in the middle of his body. He knew it was because the fiend was trying to feed off his energy.

Exorcisms suck.

Alastair's eyes blazed where he perched on Nikolai's shoulder, the crow familiar amplifying his powers.

A dark, twisted shape finally emerged from the body of the possessed man. Nervous murmurs broke out among the New York coven members and the soldiers supervising the purge. Though it wasn't the first time they'd witnessed this in the past few days, it still made them skittish. Nikolai could hardly blame them. He wasn't thrilled about what he was seeing either.

At least they're not the ones touching the damn thing.

He clenched his teeth, gripped the writhing shadow trying to escape his magic, and wrenched it free of the possessed man's soul.

The man bowed off the bed, his breath locking in his throat on a guttural rasp. His eyes rolled back in his head. He groaned and jerked fitfully, a sliver of blood trickling out the corner of his mouth despite the gag stopping him from biting his tongue. He collapsed back down on the gurney, body drenched in sweat and chest heaving.

The army medics and coven healers standing by rushed over to him, the group giving Nikolai and the agitated, ethereal form spitting and growling in his hold a wide berth.

Nikolai turned, walked over to the glowing rings scored in the floor of the chamber, and squatted in the center of the magic circle. The runes warmed his skin as he pressed the demon's intangible soul against the cold stone.

"I banish you back to the place where you came from. *Begone, fiend!*"

The demon shrieked, the sound echoing painfully in his ears and reverberating off the soundproof walls. The corruption making up the creature's soul disintegrated into inky specks that soon faded in the brilliant, pale light that was his magic.

Nausea churned Nikolai's stomach. He swallowed down bile, his vision swimming for a moment.

"That's enough for today," someone said coolly.

Nikolai turned his head.

FBI Special Agent Alicia Calvarro straightened where she leaned against the wall, the scythe-shaped silver medallion on her leather necklace gleaming for a moment where it lay on her chest. She ignored the wary looks the soldiers and coven members cast at her, crossed the room, and offered him a hand.

"Are you okay?"

Nikolai nodded weakly and took the agent's hand, the quiver in his limbs telling him he'd overdone it. The room spun dizzyingly as she pulled him to his feet. He blinked and swayed.

Alicia steadied him with a firm hand, her fingers cold where they clutched his arm. An anxious squawk left Alistair. The bird's wings fluttered worriedly against his cheek.

"It's okay, Al," Nikolai mumbled.

Alicia smiled faintly and scratched the crow's head. "He really is like your mother."

Alastair crooned and butted her hand in a friendly gesture. He recognized the FBI agent's true nature and was not afraid of her.

Faint lines marred Alicia's brow as she looked at the bright rings around them. Though she was from Hell, Nikolai's magic did not harm her. As Thod, the Queen of Soul Reapers, she could navigate the world of the dead and the living at will, although she'd been spending most of her time on Earth lately.

"Ten exorcisms a day is your limit. You should avoid doing more than that unless you want to drain your soul magic dry."

Nikolai had to concur with her warning.

It had been a week since he'd started helping the innocent men and women he and the New York coven had rescued following their battle with his brother Oscar and the demon Barquiel in Brooklyn. The people he was purging of possession had been taken up by fiends against their will, victims of his father and the Dark Council's dire experiments aimed at creating modified soldiers of Hell.

It was Alicia who had suggested to the coven and the U.S. Special Affairs bureau that Nikolai try and exorcise them.

"These people will go mad and ultimately die because of the demons riding their souls," the Soul Reaper queen had told Bryony and General Rutger Cooke bluntly. They'd stood in a ward in the private U.S. army facility on Staten Island where the ones they had saved that fateful night lay groaning and screaming, magic and drugs the only things stopping them from fully transforming into the monsters dying to escape the prison of their flesh and skin. "There is a way to help them."

Mae had appeared as full of misgivings as Bryony when Alicia had claimed that Nikolai's newly awakened white magic could rid the men and women of the fiends eating them from the inside out.

It was Mae who had broken the spell the Sorcerer King had engraved upon Nikolai's soul when he was a child, an act that had allowed her to locate the sorcerers holding her sister and grandmother prisoner in the city. The spell was borne not just by him and Oscar, but by all Dark Council members from the time they were initiated into his father's court. It was a way to mask their black magic from detection, especially in combat situations.

Undoing it had almost killed Nikolai. It was thanks to Mae that he'd survived the process, although she'd always insisted it was his will to survive that had saved him.

Neither of them had anticipated that the side effect of that deed would be the ability to fully tap into his powers for the first time since he was a child.

Accessing the magic he'd inherited from his mother without the shackles that had long bound him meant he could now draw on ley lines, a gift that looked like it would fast become a hindrance. According to Alicia, he was the first human in centuries to be able to tap into the magic seeped in the very bones of the Earth.

He'd been able to sense the preternatural energy humming beneath his feet ever since he was little, a fact his mother had made him promise never to reveal to anyone. He'd even managed to use a ley line briefly when he'd performed the *Aura of the Moon*, the scrying spell that had revealed New York city as the location where the Witch Queen would awaken.

Has it really only been three weeks since that night in Paris?

So much had happened since then. Things that he was still trying to process. One fact had become crystal clear during his recent clashes with his brother Oscar and the demon who inhabited Rose Blake's body. He was now a walking target for the Dark Council, just as Mae was.

Instead of killing him like he'd thought they would, Oscar and Barquiel had wanted to capture him. Not just because he'd managed to perform the *Aura of the Moon* and *Soul Storm* on his own. But because he'd broken the binding ritual Barquiel and the Sorcerer King had concocted to entrap Mae.

Not once, but twice.

And now my father probably knows I can draw upon ley lines too.

Bryony had wondered if it were the possibility that Nikolai could unlock this particular skill one day that had kept him alive in his father's court all this time. He shivered as he thought of the hellish years he had endured under the Dark Council, always waiting for the one wrong move that could end his life.

In a way, the spell his father had engraved in his soul had protected him from whatever grim fate would have awaited him had he managed to manifest that aptitude while still at his mercy.

Alastair shifted nervously, his claws sinking into his flesh when he sensed Nikolai's unease.

If my father gets his hands on both me and Mae, this world is doomed.

The memory of the kiss he'd shared with the witch the night she'd broken the spell binding his soul sparked through Nikolai's mind. His chest tightened. He could not deny that he was attracted to Mae, just as Vlad Vissarion was; the incubus had made his intentions ruthlessly clear since his first meeting with Mae. Truth be told, Nikolai believed those two had more in common with one another than he and Mae did, especially since they were both descended from demons.

Still, he could not extinguish the hope that had ignited inside him. The only thing he had ever wanted in his life was to escape the clutches of his father and avenge his mother. And now, he wanted something else. The love of a woman he likely did not deserve.

The doors to the basement chamber clattered open, startling him and scattering his troubled thoughts.

A young sorcerer Nikolai dimly recognized from the local coven stormed in, face pale and expression haunted. A golden retriever and a cat stopped next to the man. The dog lowered his head and pressed his body against the sorcerer's leg, his whimpers echoing across the room.

"Please." The sorcerer's voice broke as he locked gazes with Nikolai, his eyes full of despair. "Please, help my sister!"

A woman struggled violently in his arms, her teeth exposed as she snarled at him past her gag. Her skin was scraped raw where she'd fought the ropes binding her and her pupils kept flickering from black to the sulfurous yellow common to demons.

Her eyes flared when she caught sight of Nikolai.

CHAPTER SEVEN

A COUPLE OF SOLDIERS RUSHED IN AFTER THE SORCERER and grabbed his shoulders.

He shook them off furiously.

One of the coven witches hurried over to him, brow furrowing and voice a low hiss. "Gregory, you know you're not allowed in here! Your sister's exorcism isn't scheduled for another two days!"

The sorcerer's chin quivered, his anger vanishing as quickly as it'd appeared. "She doesn't have two days, Rita. She'll die if she doesn't get purged right now!"

A soldier undid the safety on his gun. "Look, pal, the lady said it isn't her time yet, so—"

"Wait," Nikolai ordered. "Let him go."

His skin itched as he observed the faint aura of darkness bubbling above the possessed woman's head, his gaze unblinking.

Is that what Mae meant when she said she could detect bedeviled humans?!

Alicia was studying Gregory's sister with a thoughtful frown.

The sorcerer barged past Rita and the soldiers, his cat familiar and the dog keeping close to him. "I'm begging you. I'll do anything you want me to do. Just save Agnes!"

A low sob was wrenched from his chest as he fell to his knees before Nikolai and Alicia, tears streaking down his face. The dog sat on his rump, lifted his head to the ceiling, and let out an agonizing howl.

Nikolai's throat closed up.

"You don't have to do this," Alicia told him warily. "This wasn't your fault."

Nikolai shuddered, face locked tight. "Everything that happened in New York was my fault." He turned to the Soul Reaper queen. "Will you help me?"

Gregory drew a sharp breath, hope lighting up his eyes as he looked wildly from Nikolai to Alicia.

Alicia blew out a sigh and rubbed the back of her head. "Don't say I didn't warn you."

Relief loosened the knot in Nikolai's belly. "Thank you." He cocked his head at the sorcerer. "Put her in the middle of the magic circle."

Gregory climbed to his feet and hurried over to the glowing runes, the golden retriever and the cat at his side.

Rita cleared her throat. "Are you sure this is a good idea?"

Her companions and the soldiers looked similarly uneasy.

Nikolai studied the figure Gregory placed on the ground. "We won't know until we try."

Alicia followed him to where the possessed woman arched her back and kicked her heels on the stone floor, determined to escape her brother's hold.

"You'll have to pin her down," Nikolai warned Gregory.

The sorcerer swallowed and nodded, determination hardening his face.

Nikolai pressed a hand to the crow on his shoulder. "You ready, Al?"

Alastair nuzzled his cheek, his eyes blazing.

Nikolai knelt on the ground next to Agnes. He inhaled, laid his palms on the bedeviled woman's belly, and concentrated. Air whooshed above him. Startled gasps echoed around the basement chamber. He didn't have to look around to know that Alicia had changed into her reaper form.

Magic flooded his veins and warmed his blood as he focused his powers deep within Agnes's body, seeking out the corruption rotting her soul. Blackness danced against his fingertips a moment later.

It took a single heartbeat for him to realize they were in trouble.

A horrendous roar ripped through the chamber, causing several soldiers and a witch to cry out in alarm. Agnes's mouth split impossibly open from ear to ear. The whites of her eyes shifted to an ominous obsidian.

"Shit!" Nikolai grated out. "Alicia! This doesn't feel like a regular demon!"

"That's because it isn't." Bone clinked against stone

as the Soul Reaper queen landed next to him. "That's a ghoul."

Nikolai could feel Agnes's soul flickering weakly in the center of the dark miasma fighting his magic. He knew instinctively that the only thing stopping the young woman from fully transforming was sheer will.

"Talk to her!" he urged Gregory.

"What?" the sorcerer mumbled, his horrified gaze riveted to the monster trying to take over his sister.

"She can hear you! Just talk to her!"

Tension tightened Nikolai's shoulders as he poured his magic into Agnes's body. The ghoul shrieked, the sound making his eardrums throb.

Gregory jerked. He started speaking to his sister, his voice low and urgent.

"Lock those doors," Alicia ordered the nervous soldiers watching them, light from the magic circle catching on the edge of her dark scythe. Her pupils flared crimson as she looked over at the coven sorcerers and witches. "Shield us. Nothing comes in and nothing gets out of this circle."

They nodded and took up position around the glowing ring, faces ashen. A haze formed on the periphery of the runes as they engaged their magic.

The air trembled where Nikolai's powers clashed against the hellish energy throbbing from the monster clinging desperately to his host. A wave of lassitude swept over him. He sagged and blinked sweat from his eyes. Dread curdled his stomach.

His magic core was nearly depleted.

"Al!" he cried out, fear raising the pitch of his voice.

The crow squawked. Power seeped into Nikolai's body as his familiar's soul merged fully with his own. The ghoul's shape came into focus.

Now!

He gripped the wisps of corruption twisting around his fingers and ripped the monster out of Agnes, his mouth open on a harsh shout. The creature materialized with a stench that made him gag. Gregory twisted to the side and vomited.

The dark, hideous, crooked form shivering above Agnes's now limp figure focused on her brother. A pair of ochre spots flashed in the shadowy mass as it started to thicken. It reached for the pale-faced sorcerer.

Nikolai let go of the ghoul and cast Gregory and the two familiars beside him out of the circle with a blast of magic. The monster halted abruptly at the edge of the runes, an outraged growl emanating from his solidifying body as his talons missed his intended victim by a hairbreadth. His evil eyes turned to Nikolai. He lunged at him, his movements blisteringly fast.

An inky blade sliced the air and ripped through the ghoul before he could reach Nikolai, pinning him to the floor. The monster screeched, spectral claws raising sparks as he raked the stone inches from Nikolai's legs.

"I can't hold him for long," Alicia warned where she hovered above the monster. "I can kill him, but he'll rip you to shreds if I let go now." Redness filled her orbits. "Drop the spell and get out of here!"

Nikolai's pulse raced. He lowered his brows. "I've got a better idea!"

CHAPTER EIGHT

HE SLAMMED HIS HANDS ON THE GROUND, CLOSED HIS eyes, and sent his magic into the Earth, his heart in his throat. The white lines that made up his power appeared in his mind's eye, jagged lightning racing through dirt and rock.

Where is it?! There's gotta be one close by!

He was beginning to wonder if the facility was too far from the center of New York when something pulsed weakly in the darkness deep beneath Staten Island.

There!

Nikolai reached for the branch ley line, sought out its core, and drew on the incandescent magic within it. Brightness filled his and Alastair's souls. The floor shook beneath them.

The ghoul's shrieks transformed into screams of pain.

Nikolai opened his eyes. He blinked.

The magic circle was now a column of dazzling

brilliance that almost blinded him, the radiance it cast shooting straight through the concrete ceiling.

Fuck! I hope that's not visible from outside!

Tremors shook the basement, plaster dust raining down and sparking against the barrier. He squinted and made out the monster's struggling shape in front of him.

Alicia swore as the creature slipped free of her scythe. Nikolai braced himself, his watch transforming into his double-bladed spear in the blink of an eye.

The ghoul shot past him, the creature's will to survive evidently stronger than his intent to kill them. He smashed into the walls of the radiant pillar with a violent thud, a prisoner of Nikolai's white magic.

Alicia moved as the creature started raking the barrier with his claws. Nikolai grabbed the Soul Reaper queen's dark robe and shook his head.

"Don't. He's dying."

The ghoul's crooked body was fragmenting into dark blobs that hissed and evaporated in the light bathing him. The monster vanished a moment later, the only evidence that he was ever there a rotting smell that soon faded.

A deathly hush descended upon the chamber.

Alicia drifted down beside Nikolai, her body taking on a human appearance once more. "Well, that was fun."

Someone groaned behind them. They turned.

Agnes's eyes were open, her pupils dark in a rim of blue. She twisted her head with agonizing slowness and met their gazes, her own blind as she stared at something only she could see.

"The key! Don't let them get the key!" She gagged, her throat working convulsively. An object fell out of her mouth and clinked onto the stone. "Please…guard this…with your lives…"

Her voice withered away. She went limp, body sinking into the ground and eyes fluttering closed.

"Agnes!"

Gregory banged on the magic barrier, agony distorting his features. The dog howled and scratched frantically at the pale wall.

Nikolai touched the runes he'd etched into the floor and retracted his spell. The pillar of light winked out, the shadows at the edges of the chamber coming to life once more. Gregory rushed to his sister's side ahead of the army medics and coven healers.

Alicia walked over, picked up the item Agnes had regurgitated with a tissue, and cleaned it. It was a small, antique, bronze skeleton key.

"Is she…" Gregory gulped and gripped Agnes's hand, "is she going to be okay?"

"She's just unconscious," Alicia said absentmindedly as she studied the key.

"Are you sure?" Gregory mumbled.

Alicia lifted her head and made a face. "Look, kid, I would have eaten her soul if she'd been dead." This caused several soldiers to blanch. She noticed Nikolai's expression and shrugged, unabashed. "What? It's the truth. And, FYI, the guy was right. His sister would have died by sundown if you hadn't exorcised that ghoul."

"Thank—thank you!" Gregory stammered at Nikolai, his gaze swimming with gratitude.

"It was nothing," Nikolai murmured awkwardly.

His legs trembled with exhaustion where he stood, Alastair drooping weakly atop his shoulder. It had been this way the other time they'd tapped into a ley line source too. Though the power it gave them supercharged their souls, the hangover from the magic-induced high was all the more extreme. Nikolai studied his shaking fingers uneasily.

We have to find a solution. Otherwise we'll be sitting ducks for our enemies every time we access a ley line.

Alastair made a soft, concurring noise on his shoulder.

Alicia brought the skeleton key over.

Nikolai's scalp prickled at the sight of the ornate details etched into the metal. "May I?"

She handed it to him. Heat scorched his palm when it kissed his skin. He sucked in air, his eyes widening.

Alicia tensed. "What's wrong?"

"This thing has magic in it," Nikolai mumbled.

Rita's head whipped around from where she'd been tending to Agnes. "What?"

Nikolai ignored the witch, his attention focused on the object in his hand. It was difficult to ascertain exactly what it was he was feeling. That the key possessed magic of some sort was undeniable. He just couldn't tell what kind it was.

Mae might know.

He observed Agnes uneasily while the medics and healers checked her over under Gregory's watchful gaze, the young woman's warning echoing through his mind.

"What was that about?"

Alicia arched an eyebrow. "You mean the ghoul?"

Nikolai made a face. "Well, yeah, that too." He frowned at the skeleton key. "I meant this."

"I have no idea."

He hesitated. "That's the first time I've seen a ghoul."

"It's rare for one to possess a human." A calculating look dawned on Alicia's face as she scrutinized the unconscious woman and the dog carefully licking her face. "Maybe I should look into it." She met Nikolai's troubled stare. "See if this was just a coincidence or another one of Barquiel's diabolical plans."

He nodded, grateful.

The chamber doors slammed open, metal clanging violently against concrete and making them all jump. Jared Dickson appeared at the head of a group of frowning, uniformed men and women.

"The heck was that, Lisha?" the Immortal snapped.

Nikolai blinked at the nickname.

Alicia's jaw set in a hard line. "You were in the building?"

A guilty look darted across the NYPD Lieutenant's face. "Yeah."

The Soul Reaper queen propped her hands on her hips and narrowed her eyes, her pupils flashing crimson. "Then, why didn't you come and help us, asshole?!"

"I was busy," Jared retorted.

"Busy eating a sandwich?!" Alicia snarled.

Jared did a surprised double take. "How'd you know?"

"There." Nikolai pointed helpfully at the corner his mouth. "You've got some mayo."

Jared wiped away the evidence with an irritated swipe of his hand.

Major Bianca Schuman headed over to Nikolai and Alicia, her sharp-eyed gaze flitting to Agnes. She was General Cooke's aide and had been left in charge during his absence, Cooke having gone to Washington to report to the White House and the Pentagon about the incident in New York.

"Mr. Stanisic, Ms. Calvarro." She dipped her head at them curtly.

"Just call me Alicia."

Schuman stiffened. "That would seem… disrespectful considering who you are."

Alicia cocked a thumb at Jared. "That asshole disrespects me all the time."

Jared made a face.

Schuman glanced uneasily at the NYPD Lieutenant. "Well, he *is* descended from a you-know-what."

Alicia's expression darkened. "Uriel must be laughing his ass off wherever he is. I'm gonna have a word with that damn archangel some day."

Schuman's eyes glazed over slightly at the casual mention of the biblical figure that had given rise to the

Immortal races that walked the Earth. She recovered her composure and leveled a hard stare at them.

"Would one of you care to explain what we just witnessed through the cameras? And that beam of white light that shot straight through this facility's rooftop?"

Shit! It did go all the way through the building. Nikolai sagged. *Bryony is gonna be so pissed.*

Alastair let out a comforting croon.

"That light was Nikolai's magic." The Soul Reaper queen shrugged. "As for the other stuff, I haven't got a clue. Well, apart from the ghoul. That's one nasty creature."

Nikolai grimaced and scratched the back of his head. "Same."

Schuman's mouth pressed into a thin line. Her gaze dropped to Nikolai's hand. "Is that the object she coughed up?"

Nikolai curled his fingers over the key. "Yes. We'll look into it."

Schuman squared her shoulders. "Maybe you should give that to us."

"It's a magical item," Alicia intervened. "I doubt your people would know what to do with it."

The atmosphere in the room grew fractionally cooler.

"Still, it's the property of the U.S. Special Affairs bureau," Schuman countered with narrowed eyes.

"I'm afraid not," Jared interjected. "The coven cut a deal with the U.S government. Anything magical is their domain."

Schuman looked like she was about to say something when Rita spoke.

"Mr. Dickson is right, Major." The witch joined Nikolai and Alicia. "I have strict instructions from Bryony Cross that anything deemed to be of an occult persuasion will remain under the jurisdiction of the New York coven."

A frustrated frown darkened Schuman's face.

Nikolai cast a grateful glance at Rita before staring at the key.

I need to show this to Mae ASAP.

CHAPTER NINE

YULIY VISSARION'S FIFTEEN-THOUSAND-SQUARE-FOOT Brooklyn mansion was not so much a home as it was a fortress. It was also a statement of strength. As the leader of the most powerful *Bratva* on the East Coast, the Russian crime lord needed to demonstrate the power he wielded. Nothing did this more than a multi-million-dollar, glitzy manor house in one of the most expensive zip codes in New York.

Vlad slowed his midnight-blue, custom-fitted Bentley convertible to a stop at the end of a private road in Mill Basin. He drummed his fingers impatiently on the leather steering wheel as he glanced at the cameras above the towering, metal gates set in the steel-reinforced, concrete wall surrounding the estate.

He'd been summoned to the mansion by Yuliy. Not that that was an uncommon occurrence. After all, he was the man's heir. It was just exceedingly rare for his uncle and adoptive father to pick up the phone and call him himself.

A metal post sprouted from the ground next to his car. The top flipped open when it reached the car's window, revealing a small, black cube that was the latest in identification software. A thin, red light shot out of it and scanned Vlad's face in a grid pattern. A computerized voice issued from the device seconds later.

"Please identify yourself."

"The Great Pretender."

The A.I. went silent for a moment. "Error."

Vlad smiled. "The hottest incubus in New York."

The A.I. was having none of his shit. "Error. You have two more attempts before security is alerted."

"Is there a problem, boss?"

Milo, the newest member of his security detail, had wound down the window of the SUV behind the Bentley and was leaning out, a concerned expression on his face.

"Get back in the vehicle, kid," the stony-faced man in the driver's seat said gruffly.

"But boss looks like he's struggling with the—" Milo protested.

"He's not struggling with anything," the other man muttered. "He's just trying to piss off that computer."

Vlad grinned at Ilya in the rearview mirror. His oldest serving bodyguard was used to his shenanigans.

Tarang growled where he sat in the passenger seat of the Bentley. He hated the A.I. with a passion and had even attempted to eat it once. Vlad stroked the Bengal tiger's head before turning to the voice box.

"It is I, your demon lord."

"This is your final attempt," the A.I. said superciliously.

Vlad rolled his eyes. "You seriously need a sense of humor transplant." He grew serious. "This is Vlad Vissarion."

The A.I. beeped a haughty acknowledgement as it finally matched the distinctive voice signature associated with his name. The black cube and the post retracted into the ground. The gates rolled open, well-oiled hinges barely making a sound as they unveiled a cream driveway.

Vlad rode up the winding access, Ilya and Milo following in the SUV. A sprawling, three-story mansion shielded by trees appeared atop a shallow elevation. The white-concrete and glass manor overlooked extensive, terraced gardens and an artificial, pebble beach with a private marina and a helicopter landing pad. Tension knotted his shoulders as he pulled up on a circular forecourt with a marble fountain.

It had been hard to judge his uncle's tone over the phone. Not that he'd expected anything else. Yuliy hadn't made it to the top of the *Black Devils* by giving away his hand so readily. Still, a small voice at the back of Vlad's head told him he wasn't going to like what his uncle was going to say to him.

Call it his demon instinct.

The guards patrolling the estate dipped their heads

respectfully at him when he stepped out of the Bentley. Vlad glanced at the other vehicles parked in the grounds.

Great. The Three Stooges are here.

He masked his irritation behind a neutral expression and headed up the marble steps rising to a pair of wide, bronze front doors. Tarang followed, his tail swishing languidly around Vlad's legs.

Milo and Ilya stayed with the other guards.

The entrance opened before Vlad reached it. A man in his fifties stood in the doorway, his crisp, white shirt and charcoal suit hiding the gun under his armpit and the knife strapped to his ankle. Gustav Luchok was Yuliy's secretary and had been Vlad's tutor and nanny when he was growing up.

The older man bowed respectfully. "*Molodoy master.*"

Vlad made a face. "I told you to stop that young master crap ages ago. You used to wipe my ass, for Christ's sake."

"And what a fine ass it's turned out to be," Gustav murmured.

Vlad chuckled and embraced the poker-faced man. He stiffened a moment later. "Are you feeling me up?"

"Just checking to see if you've still got the Ka-bar I gave you for Christmas." Gustav patted the outline of the sheath on Vlad's lower back before pulling away, his eyes warm with affection. Lines furrowed his brow as he studied Vlad's figure. "You should come home more often. You look like you've lost weight."

He scratched Tarang's head absent-mindedly as the tiger rumbled out a greeting.

"The only ones who think I need to put on weight are you and Lena. I'll grow fat if I visit every week."

As if summoned by his voice, Lena Dubravac appeared out of nowhere, her gray hair pinned back into an austere bun and her dark dress swishing around her legs. Though well past retirement age, Yuliy's main housekeeper was still sprightly and ran the *Black Devils* leader's various properties around the world with an iron fist. She'd also helped bring Vlad up, back when they'd still been living on their isolated estate in Russia.

"I made apple pie," Lena murmured as Vlad leaned down to kiss her cheeks. Her tone turned sharp. "I would have prepared your favorite lunch if I'd known you were coming."

Tarang bumped her leg with his head and purred out a hello. Her expression softened. She tickled the tiger under the chin.

Though Gustav and Lena were distantly related to Vlad, they didn't possess magic in their souls. They'd known Tarang since the familiar was a cub and had always been able to see him.

Vlad arched an eyebrow at Lena. "What happened to the outfits I gave you for your birthday?"

Her mouth curled. "You mean those monstrosities even my whores wouldn't wear?"

Vlad sighed. He kept forgetting Lena once ran one of the most notorious high-end brothels in Moscow in her heyday. The place hadn't just provided alluring female and male escorts to the city's most powerful governments officials, it had also served as an information network for the *Bratvas*. A place where deals were made and bribes passed hands.

"They're not monstrosities. They're from Yves St. Laurent. And they're the current fashion for ladies of a —" he waved a vague hand, "you know, certain age."

Gustav winced.

A thin smile stretched Lena's mouth. She patted Vlad's face gently. "Say that again and I'll put razor blades in your apple pie, *moya lyubov'*."

Vlad grinned. "I love you too, *totya*." His smile faded as he looked past the pair to the corridor leading to the east wing. "Is he in his study?"

"Yes." Lena's eyes grew flinty. "He's got company."

"How long have they been in with him?"

"Two hours."

Vlad cracked his knuckles and glanced at Tarang. "Let's go rescue *dyadya*."

The tiger growled out an approval.

"I'll make a fresh pot of coffee," Gustav murmured diplomatically.

Vlad's gaze swept the ultra-modern contours of the manor and the minimalistic decor as he and Tarang headed over to Yuliy's favorite room in the whole place. Having grown up the eldest of five children in a cluttered two-bedroom apartment in St. Petersburg, his uncle loved open spaces and clean lines.

Though Vlad had spent several years at the mansion when they'd first come to New York, he very much preferred his penthouse in Chelsea. Set atop a redbrick industrial warehouse that had been turned into an upscale apartment building, which he'd bought outright, it was bright and airy and more than big enough to accommodate the eclectic collection of antiques he'd amassed from his travels across the world.

A low murmur of voices reached him as he neared the study. Tarang made an irritated sound when he picked up the scents coming from the room.

The *Black Devils* generals were not his favorite people in the world.

"Don't eat anyone," Vlad warned the tiger.

Tarang gave him a hurt look.

Vlad knocked and opened the door.

THE MEN LOUNGING ON THE CONTEMPORARY Chesterfield leather sofas in front of the open fire looked around when he walked in.

"Gentlemen," Vlad greeted with a relaxed half-smile.

Arseny Maximov, Ustin Larionovich, and Zacharin Yaroslav grunted out greetings, their expressions guarded. Their gimlet eyes swept the area around Vlad. Though they couldn't see Tarang, they knew he was there. They'd witnessed what the familiar could do the first night Vlad gave in to his dark side and let his demon magic loose.

Yuliy's study was decorated along the same clinical lines as the rest of the mansion, the only splash of color the vibrant, red, Diaspro wall with rich black and cream veins framing the fireplace. The Sicilian marble had been shipped over from the mountains of Custonaci when the property was being built and had stirred much interest amongst city officials when it went through customs.

"Take a seat," Yuliy said gruffly around his cigar.

He sat at his neat, white-granite desk, his gaze on the paperwork in front of him.

Vlad observed the smoke curling around his uncle's face with narrowed eyes. "I hope that's filtered. You know what the doctors said about the state of your lungs."

"The state of my lungs is no business of yours, boy."

"It is if I'm gonna have to spoon feed you and change your diapers in your old age," Vlad retorted.

The three generals' faces turned disapproving.

"You should show more respect for your father," Maximov growled.

Yaroslav looked over at Yuliy. "I told you you should have whipped him when he was a kid." He met Vlad's cold gaze, his mouth a sneer. "Nothing like a bit of lashing to make impertinent boys submit to their elders."

Vlad tried not to curl his lips. Everyone in the *Black Devils* knew of the dungeon Yaroslav kept for his own private use in the sex clubs he owned. The young men he would keep there for days on end were mostly from families who owed debts to the *Bratvas* and were selected by the Russian crime lord to spend the night with him in exchange for clearing their parents' dues. A few came to his bed willingly, hoping to get a helping hand up the ladder and a better position in the syndicate.

By the time they left Yaraslov's red room, not only

were they covered in bruises and their eyes dead, they would often end up addicted to the drugs he pumped into them to make them more compliant during sex and spend their best years serving as male prostitutes for the *Bratvas* and Yaraslov's clubs in exchange for their next fix.

"No one is whipping anyone," Yuliy muttered, his attention still on his paperwork.

Larionovich looked like he was about to say something. Yuliy cut his eyes to him briefly.

They all knew he had never raised a hand to Vlad.

A memory flitted through Vlad's mind then. He suppressed a grimace.

Well, except for that one time, when I broke my mother's favorite hairbrush.

He'd been six when it'd happened and hadn't been able to sit for the rest of the day after Yuliy spanked him for smashing the hairbrush during a temper tantrum. It had taken Lena icing his bottom for the redness and swelling to finally settle enough for him to get to sleep that night.

It was the one and only time Yuliy had ever taken a hand to him.

The next day, his uncle had brought Tarang to their home, the cub rescued from a passing traveling circus.

Vlad had often wondered if it was fate that had caused him to grab his mother's hairbrush and hurl it to the floor that day. Because Tarang had turned out to be the perfect match for him as a familiar, something that wouldn't become apparent for several years.

"These all look in order," Yuliy told the three

generals. "I'll sign them and send them over tomorrow."

The men nodded and rose. They brushed past Vlad, their animosity rising fractionally. Tarang snarled at them as they headed out of the room. The door closed with a click.

Yuliy sighed and took off his glasses. "You need to try and get along with them. I'm not going to be around forever to keep the peace."

The pale scars on the backs of his uncle's hands didn't escape Vlad's attention as he watched him pinch the bridge of his nose. Yuliy had literally fought his way through the ranks of the *Black Devils* and was missing a kidney and two toes as a result. The older men in the syndicate who used to visit their estate in Russia had often regaled Vlad with tales of Yuliy's exploits, much to his uncle's dismay.

It had never been Yuliy's intention to involve Vlad in the *Bratva* life. If anything, his uncle had wanted to keep him as far away from a life of crime as he possibly could. It had been Vlad's decision to take over the mantle of Yuliy's heir, after he killed the man his uncle had chosen as the next leader of the *Black Devils*.

Kaspar Petrovich's face swam before Vlad's eyes.

It's funny. Even after all these years, I still don't regret ripping that bastard's heart out.

Vlad subdued the memories from that dark day and focused on his uncle. "You look tired, *dyadya*."

The unease he'd been experiencing all morning grew ten-fold at the hard look Yuliy gave him.

"That's because my heir is gallivanting around New

York with a witch instead of taking care of my business."

Vlad's skin prickled. *Shit. So this is about Mae.*

That the infamous Witch Queen from the prophecy long whispered about in the magical community would turn out to be an aspiring surgeon and mortuary assistant from Queens had surprised every sorcerer and witch he knew, including the usually unflappable Bryony Cross.

Truth be told, Vlad hadn't paid much heed to the Witch Queen's story and the blind hope her forecasted resurrection engendered in those who wished to defeat the Sorcerer King and his Dark Council. It wasn't his business and he had zero interest in getting involved in their fight. Though he'd reached out to the covens after his magic awakened, his interactions with them over the years had very much centered around fighting the growing darkness in the underworld he inhabited. A darkness only he seemed to sense and that he'd finally convinced Yuliy would have a huge impact on not just the *Bratvas*, but the entire criminal network.

Though many altruistic souls wished for the demise of all crime syndicates, it was a fact of life that they were essential tools that governments often relied upon to control the more abhorrent transgressors in human society.

Tarang plopped his head on Yuliy's lap and huffed, impatient for his attention. Yuliy's face lightened as he patted the tiger.

He sat back in his chair and reached out to the familiar. "Hand."

Tarang lifted a giant paw and placed it nimbly in Yuliy's palm.

Yuliy rubbed the tiger's scruff briskly. "Good boy. Now, play dead."

Tarang dropped to the floor, rolled onto his back, and went deathly still.

"It's a good thing Brimstone can't see you," Vlad told the familiar dryly. "That fox would laugh you out of town."

Tarang rumbled a protest and rolled onto his front, abashed.

CHAPTER ELEVEN

YULIY GRUNTED. "IS BRIMSTONE THE NAME OF THAT nine-tailed beast?"

Vlad went over to the fire and plopped down on a couch. "Yeah."

Yuliy rose, crossed the study, and settled on the opposite sofa. Tarang curled up at the older man's feet and propped his head on his front paws, his mesmerized gaze on the flames crackling in the hearth. He'd been fascinated by fire ever since he was a cub, probably since it was the closest thing on Earth to his and Vlad's crimson magic.

The door opened. Gustav wheeled in a serving tray with coffee and apple pie, and steak for Tarang. He excused himself and vanished.

Vlad finished his cake and coffee in record time, almost beating Tarang as the latter wolfed down his meat. One thing he did miss about the mansion besides the people he loved was the food.

He polished off his spoon, set it down on his plate,

and sat back with a sigh. "I'm glad she didn't put razor blades in it."

Yuliy squinted. "Did you do something to piss Lena off?"

"I called her old."

Yuliy rolled his eyes. "You have a death wish, boy."

A warm feeling swept over Vlad as he observed the older man. Many assumed his childhood had been mired in violence and blood. Little did they know that that was as far from the truth as one could get. Though his beginnings had been ridden with misfortune, his life with Yuliy, Gustav, Lena, and eventually Tarang had been filled with nothing but happiness.

A comfortable silence fell between them. It ended with his uncle's next words.

"The main syndicate wants the witch."

Ice filled Vlad's veins. Tarang lifted his head and looked at him warily, sensing the change in his mood.

"What do you mean?" Vlad said, his heart hammering against his ribs.

Yuliy leaned against the backrest, his face inscrutable. "Someone recorded what happened two weeks ago at that warehouse. The video has been circulating among not just our men, but the *Bratvas* in Europe too." His uncle paused. "Let's just say Mae Jin's power has impressed the people at the top. They are now believers in magic. And they want in on the action."

Vlad's stomach churned. *I'm gonna find the asshole who recorded that video and slice him up!*

He clamped down on the trepidation slithering through his mind.

"They're believers? After all this time?!" He couldn't keep his burgeoning anger from seeping into his voice. "You're telling me those fuckers refused to help us when I told them about *Oniks,* but suddenly they've seen the light? What a load of bullcrap!"

The air trembled with a faint, crimson mist as his incubus power slipped from his control for an instant. Tarang whined and rose from the floor. The familiar padded over and brushed his body against Vlad's legs.

Vlad sank a hand in the tiger's fur. He met his uncle's enigmatic gaze, tension a taut band across his shoulders.

"What are you not telling me, *dyadya?*"

A tired smile stretched Yuliy's mouth. "I still don't know if your ability to read my mind has to do with your demon magic or not."

"It doesn't," Vlad said impatiently. "I have good instincts. And they're currently telling me—" He stopped, realization dawning with an abruptness that almost made him gasp. "They're afraid."

Yuliy stayed silent.

Vlad fisted his hands, knowing he was on the right track. Tarang let out a protest. He uncurled his fingers from the tiger's flesh and patted him guiltily.

"They think Mae has allied herself with the *Black Devils* through me," he said between gritted teeth. "And they don't want that to happen because they presume it will make us the strongest *Bratva* in the world. Those bastards in Moscow want that power for themselves. That's what this is about, isn't it?!"

His furious words rang around the study.

Yuliy stood up and came over to Vlad. He pressed a comforting hand on his shoulder and stared into the fire.

"I promised Katarina that I would always protect you. And I have, since the day you were born from her dying body. But this is different. This is bigger than me, my child." A far-away look came over him. "Maybe it's because I'm growing old, but there are days when I can almost feel her presence. It's as if she's waiting patiently for me to join her beyond the veil that separates the world of the living and the dead."

Vlad closed his eyes at the mention of his dead mother. He had never known her, yet her existence continued to haunt his everyday life, like an invisible Sword of Damocles hanging over his neck.

He knew Yuliy had never blamed him for Katarina Vissarion's illness and her eventual demise. Even the magic that had skipped several Vissarion generations and made Katarina one of the most powerful witches in Russia had been unable to stop the progress of the insidious cancer that had spread through her bones.

No, the one his uncle held responsible for his beloved sister's death was the demon who had seduced Katarina shortly after her diagnosis and abandoned her to her dire fate, her pregnancy hastening her death as the incubus child within her consumed her magic.

Still, every picture, every recording Yuliy, Gustav, and Lena had captured of Katarina's final months on this Earth had only ever shown the love she bore for her unborn child and no sign of any resentment for the monster inside her. Her hands almost never left her growing bump and her voice was always soft and sweet while she crooned lullabies she must have known she would never be able to sing to him after he was born.

"This situation has the potential to upset the long-established balance between the *Bratvas* of the West and the East," Yuliy said somberly. "No one wants to see a war." He looked at Vlad. "Just bring Mae Jin to the table. That's all I ask of you."

Vlad shuddered. He knew he couldn't refuse his uncle's request. The face of the woman he was about to betray flitted before his eyes.

Mae had stirred his frozen heart from their very first meeting. He didn't know if it was because both their fathers were demons or because their magic was similar. Quite frankly, he didn't care. He just knew one thing. He wanted her.

Vlad's chest grew tight.

I'm sorry for dragging you into this, Princess.

CHAPTER TWELVE

Mae parked her Vespa outside her apartment, turned the engine off, and sat still for a moment, the evening air cooling her face. It had been a long day and the last couple hours hadn't made it any easier.

Coven politics is exhausting. I don't know how Bryony does it.

Though she'd attempted to absorb the information the High Priestess and Abraham had relayed to her about the people she would be meeting in Philadelphia, her mind hadn't been fully engaged with the topic. The fact that a certain Sorcerer King and an Archduke of Hell could be plotting to capture her again had proven to be mighty distracting. She could already tell her first covenstead was going to be a major pain in her butt.

Brimstone jumped off the Vespa. *Do you want me to eat them?*

Mae climbed off the scooter. "You can't go around eating every witch and sorcerer who annoys me."

Hellreaver spoke up, his tone hopeful. *We can try.*

Mae's mouth became a thin line. *I am bonded to a pair of bloodthirsty lunatics.*

Hey, we heard that, Brimstone protested.

She unlocked the side entrance around the corner from the old cinema in Ridgewood and headed up the flight of stairs at the end of the dimly lit corridor beyond it. Her apartment was on the second floor of the building, right above the main theater. An early 20th century brownstone, it boasted exposed brick walls, parquet flooring, and a crooked layout she'd fallen in love with the very first time she'd seen the place.

Mae opened her front door and was greeted by the sound of running water coming from the main bathroom. She paused in the hallway, her keys poised above the tray on the console table. Nikolai had already dropped his set there.

It still felt strange having the sorcerer in her personal space. Though Vlad had grumbled plenty about the fact that his main competition for Mae's affection was now living under the same roof as her, he'd grudgingly acknowledged the safety net Nikolai presented. With his white magic now unleashed, the sorcerer made a powerful foe against the Dark Council and an ideal live-in protector for Mae. Not that she needed protecting.

To her surprise, Yoo-Mi hadn't objected to Nikolai renting the spare room in her apartment. If anything, she'd seemed relieved. Remorse clenched Mae's belly. Though she didn't show it, her mother was still shaken by what had happened to Ryu and Ye-Seul.

Mae's gaze shifted to the men's boots arranged with military precision on the shoe rack against the wall. One good thing about having the sorcerer around was that he was a neat freak and the apartment was now universally spotless.

That guy would make a great housekeeper.

The bathroom door opened just as she passed it.

Nikolai appeared amidst a cloud of vetiver-scented steam. He was bare chested and had his head down, his hands busy rubbing his wet hair with a towel.

Mae tried not to stare at his six-pack and the water droplets clinging enticingly to his tanned skin and sharply defined muscles. Her treacherous gaze followed the seductive trail of dark hair arrowing down his taut belly to the top of his low-hanging sweatpants and the deep V of his obliques. Heat flooded her face. She swallowed. Hard.

Wow, Brimstone said dully. *You're practically drooling.*

Shut up.

Nikolai looked up and froze when he noticed their presence. His pupils dilated. "Oh. I wasn't expecting you back so soon." He stared. "What happened to your face?"

"A widow happened to it. And my meeting with Bryony was shorter than usual."

Mae dragged her gaze from his body and headed into the living area, her skin prickling. Her attraction to her tenant was getting out of control. She blamed it on the fact that she hadn't had sex in months. It didn't help that her trusty vibrator, Bob, had met an untimely demise a few weeks back and she still hadn't bought a replacement for him. Her cheeks grew even hotter.

It felt wrong somehow with Nikolai in the apartment.

Hellreaver's words from earlier that afternoon danced through her mind, bringing with them a flurry of torrid images involving the sorcerer and an incubus with devastating sexual charms.

Mae chewed her lip. *Damn that demonic weapon and his asinine suggestions.*

Hellreaver snorted in his sleep.

Alastair squawked a hello to them from his perch on the windowsill overlooking the main road, his intelligent eyes gleaming. He took flight and landed in front of Brimstone. The two familiars butted heads gently in a ritual greeting.

Nikolai overtook Mae on his way to the refrigerator, his footsteps silent on the floorboards. "I was going to make spaghetti. You hungry?"

Mae's stomach rumbled in response.

"I'll take that as a yes," he muttered.

The other bonus of having Nikolai live with her was that he was a great cook. As good as Vlad. Compared to them, her skills in the kitchen could best be described as dubious, with a high probability of food poisoning.

She stilled at the sight of the jagged scar running diagonally across the sorcerer's back. It was her first time seeing it. The skin was puckered, as if it hadn't healed properly. Anger sent heat flushing through her body.

"You can probably heal it. You know, with your white magic."

His brows knitted together. "Does it bother you that much?"

Mae blinked.

"No!" she blurted out. "I didn't mean it that way."

A tense silence fell between them.

Nikolai's shoulders loosened. "I know. I'm sorry, it's just…it's still a sore subject." He sighed. "Why don't you have a shower and change? It won't take me long to—" He stopped and narrowed his eyes at the top shelf of the refrigerator. "What the hell happened to the ground beef I was defrosting?"

They turned to Brimstone, their stares accusing. The fox avoided their eyes.

"Do you have something to say?" Mae asked coolly.

What? the fox said defensively. *I was peckish.*

She flashed an apologetic look at Nikolai. "I'll order pizza."

"Fine," he grumbled. "FYI, the rate at which we're ordering takeout, we're gonna pile on the pounds."

Mae studied Nikolai's perfectly toned body surreptitiously. There wasn't an ounce of fat on the man and they both knew it.

Brimstone grinned. *There's something you both can do about those pounds*—ouch! He glared at Mae. *What'd you step on my tail for?*

"To stop you from putting stupid ideas in his head," she muttered.

Nikolai glanced suspiciously from her to Brimstone.

Why? It's not as if he can read my mind. Brimstone sniffed. *Besides, the bird thinks he's keen to do the dance of the two-headed beast with you too.*

Mae's stomach clenched. *He does?!*

She looked at Alastair. The crow squawked and groomed his feathers, oblivious to the racy thoughts filling her mind.

I'm joking. Brimstone chortled. *That crow is as innocent as they come.*

Mae flipped a middle finger at Brimstone and stormed toward her bedroom.

"What'd you say to her?" Nikolai asked the wheezing fox.

By the time she'd showered and changed, Nikolai was wearing a T-shirt and their order had arrived. Mae's stomach gurgled loudly at the smell of garlic and cheese permeating the apartment. She joined Nikolai at the dining table and pulled out a chair.

A piece of pepperoni flew in front of her face and landed next to her hand just as she sat down. Hellreaver whizzed past her and hoovered it up. She frowned at the mess around Brimstone and the weapon where they were scarfing down their extra-large servings of pizza.

"How come you guys barely spill a speck of food at my mom's house and yet here you act like total pigs?"

Your mother's a scary woman, Brimstone said.

Mae arched an eyebrow. "And I'm not?"

There are pink bunnies with halos on your pajamas, Hellreaver said helpfully.

Mae glanced at her outfit. "There's nothing wrong

with my pajamas. They were a gift from Ryu." She scowled. "And they're cozy."

"Ryu needs to rethink her clothing choices for you," Nikolai grunted. Lines creased his brow. "On the other hand, better her choices than that damn incubus's."

Mae's eyes glazed over slightly. She still had the lingerie Vlad had gifted her for one of their outings a few weeks ago, the night they'd trashed a strip club. The scraps of lace and silk fitted her to a T and made her look like a sex goddess. She shivered.

She could only imagine what he would gift her as nightwear.

"How did your day go?" she muttered to Nikolai distractedly.

"Funny you should ask. I've got something to show you."

He wiped his hands on a napkin, rose, and went into the hallway to grab his leather jacket. He was fishing something out of his pocket when he froze.

A horrible smell was filling the apartment.

That wasn't me, Hellreaver protested.

Goosebumps broke out on Mae's skin. She stood slowly, her gaze sweeping the room. "Nikolai?"

The sorcerer was staring at the window opposite him. "Fuck!"

Glass smashed all around them. A horde of monsters stormed the apartment in a foul miasma of decaying flesh.

CHAPTER THIRTEEN

THE CORRUPT POWER OF HELL WASHED ACROSS MAE AS the creatures lunged toward her.

"Hellreaver!"

The weapon flashed across the table and slammed into her hand, metal warming her palm. She swooped beneath the claws flying toward her face, roundhouse kicked the fiend who'd attacked her in the gut, and sliced the head off another. The monster's ochre eyes dimmed. His skull bounced next to her feet, the unholy radiance of his pupils blinking out. By the time his body hit the floor, he was human once more.

"What the heck are these things?!" Mae shouted as she blocked strike after strike, the misshapen creatures' claws raising sparks where they met Hellreaver's blades. The aura of darkness crowning the monsters' heads and enveloping their bodies was so thick, it was almost solid. "They don't look like regular demons!"

Brimstone growled beside her, hackles raised and

pupils aglow as he amplified the energy within her soul.

Nikolai blasted two of the monsters surrounding him with spheres of white magic and stabbed another one in the eye with his spear, Alastair similarly focusing his powers where he crouched on the sorcerer's shoulder. "They're ghouls! I met one for the first time today!" His alarmed gaze locked with Mae's across the apartment. "They must be after the key!"

She elbowed a monster in the face and front-kicked another in the groin, Hellreaver taking chunks out of the creatures attempting to disembowel her. "What key?!"

Nikolai bunched up his jacket and lobbed it at Mae. "Here! Guard this!"

The garment sailed above the ghouls. Their heads snapped around as they followed it with their creepy, yellow stares. One of the fiends leapt and snatched the jacket from the air before Mae could grab it.

"Shit!" Nikolai cursed as the monster made for a gaping window. "Don't let him get away!"

Brimstone transformed into his nine-tail spirit form. He sprung, his jaws opening to gargantuan proportions a second before he devoured the ghoul and the jacket in a single bite.

The creature's screech cut off abruptly. The other monsters faltered, ochre pupils flaring with wariness as they studied the demonic fox's monstrous appearance.

"You've never done that before," Mae mumbled numbly.

"Please tell me you can bring my jacket back up," Nikolai said, pale faced.

"*Fear not,*" Brimstone growled. "*I'm only guarding it.*" He spat out some human bones, burped, and snarled in disgust. "*Hellreaver, do not eat these fiends. They're bad for your health.*"

I kinda feel queasy already, the weapon whined.

"You shouldn't have had that third pizza," Mae admonished.

Her shoulders tightened as she watched the monsters observing her with raw hunger. The ghouls were surrounding her and Brimstone where they stood back-to-back in the kitchen.

"You said you met one of these things today?" she called out to Nikolai.

The sorcerer's knuckles whitened on his spear where he stood braced inside a ring of monsters in the living room. "Yeah. Alicia helped me get rid of him!"

Mae started spinning Hellreaver above her head, the power that dwelled within her warming her blood as she drew upon it. "How?"

"She pinned him down while I used a ley line and isolated him within a column of white magic. It destroyed him!"

"Think you can do that again?"

Nikolai's expression grew awkward.

"What?" Mae asked.

"I can. As long as you don't mind the roof of this building lighting up like the Fourth of July."

Mae blinked. "Oh, wow. Is that what happened? Those military guys must have been thrilled."

"They were ecstatic," Nikolai said glumly. "I'm sure Bryony will have something to say about it once Rita tells her."

Mae tensed. She felt a dark energy growing around them. The aura of corruption wreathing the ghouls was thickening.

How are they doing that?!

"*I don't know,*" Brimstone grumbled.

Power pulsed from the monsters, an eerie wave that rattled china and glass and made Mae's stomach roil. Shadows filled the apartment. Her eyes widened.

What the—?!

The ghouls attacked.

Brimstone roared, the sound so powerful it pushed back the creatures before they could reach her. It was all the time she needed.

Magic blasted around her, a red haze that lit up the gloom. Mae levitated off the ground, body vibrating with power and hair rippling wildly around her head as she twisted Hellreaver faster and faster.

"*Wind Fury!*"

A crimson whirlwind swirling with inky currents erupted in the center of the apartment, magic arcing from the weapon in her hands to the rapidly spinning funnel. She'd discovered using Hellreaver helped her focus the spell on a more defined area during her practice sessions with Bryony and Violet.

The air trembled as the tempest sucked at the ghouls, dragging them across the ground and lifting them off their feet. The monsters shrieked and fought the pull of the magic storm, to no avail.

"Now!" Mae barked at Nikolai.

He dropped to one knee, pressed his hand against the floorboards, and started chanting an incantation. Sweat beaded his forehead as the words fell from his lips. A ghoul lunged out of the violent squalls and clawed at his arm. Alastair squawked in outrage as red lines bloomed on Nikolai's flesh. The sorcerer gritted his teeth, his spell never faltering even as he bled.

Mae scowled and cast Hellreaver across the room. The weapon sliced the ghoul's arm off clean at the wrist. The monster hissed and fell back. Hellreaver twisted around and hovered defensively in front of the sorcerer.

A circle formed under the tornado holding the ghouls prisoner, white lines that flickered before solidifying. The creatures screamed, their terror evident as they grasped their impending fate.

The sound made Mae's ears throb.

A dazzling pillar exploded above the magic ring, Nikolai's power so blinding she had to shield her eyes. She ended *Wind Fury*, her pulse pounding.

There was no need for her spell anymore.

The ghouls' uncanny screeches tore the air as they started disintegrating, their bodies breaking into dark blobs that hissed and evaporated inside the blazing column of light. They were gone in less than a minute, the only signs they were ever there the blood splashed across the apartment and the fading reek of their presence.

A noise came from behind Mae. She whirled

around where she hovered in mid-air, crimson magic bursting into life at her fingertips.

A ghoul had hidden inside a closet and was attempting to sneak out of the kitchen through a broken window. His path had unfortunately crossed that of an incubus with a raging bloodlust.

Vlad's eyes glowed a pure vermilion as he climbed inside the apartment and grabbed the creature by the throat. He snapped the ghoul's neck and threw him at Tarang, his face icy. The tiger caught the monster and ripped out his throat. Blood splashed onto Vlad's trousers. The incubus was oblivious to the stains, his hot gaze watching until the monster grew still.

Tarang dropped the creature's now human remains and retched up a gory chunk of tissue, stringy flesh and bone dangling from his jaws. He whined and pawed at his tongue. Concern darkened Vlad's eyes as he landed beside his familiar.

"Tarang?!"

"*It's alright,*" Brimstone reassured. "*They just taste nasty.*"

The fox came over and rubbed a tail against the tiger's flank. Tarang relaxed.

Vlad straightened and glared at Nikolai. "What the hell happened? I saw a white beam above the building when I was driving here, then all the lights went out."

Mae peered out the closest window. The road was dark. In fact, the entire block was pitch black. "Shit. Bryony is gonna kill us."

Not if that Abraham guy gets to us first, Hellreaver said glumly. *That sorcerer has anger management issues.*

Brimstone huffed in agreement.

Nikolai joined Mae and stared out into the night, his face pale.

"This didn't happen at the facility on Staten Island."

A worried sound left Alastair. The crow flew down onto the windowsill.

Mae's stomach fluttered nervously as she observed Nikolai's pinched expression and his familiar's dull feathers.

"Maybe it's because that place was built by the army?" she suggested.

"Or it could be your white magic gets stronger the more you use it," Vlad murmured.

She hadn't thought of that.

Mae pursed her lips. "He's got a point. You did feel more powerful tonight."

Nikolai's eyes flared. Color stained his cheekbones. Brimstone snickered. Tarang joined in.

"Are you guys done?!" Mae snapped at the familiars, face flushing.

Vlad muttered something under his breath. He indicated what was left of the monster. "What *is* that?"

"It *was* a ghoul," Nikolai said curtly.

He crossed the room, white light blooming at his fingertips.

"Wait." Mae went over to them, the disquiet she'd experienced during the fight hardening into a conviction that chilled her to the bone. "Don't destroy the body."

Nikolai gave her a puzzled look. "Why not?"

"We need to analyze it." She squatted next to the

corpse and carefully peeled the dead man's eyelids open. "Didn't you feel it? When we were fighting them just now?"

"Feel what?" Nikolai asked.

"They're not normal."

The sorcerer frowned. "Of course they're not normal. They're ghouls."

Mae shook her head. "I don't mean what they are. It's what I sensed inside them."

Nikolai and Vlad's faces grew tight.

"What did you sense?" Vlad asked stiffly.

Mae hesitated. "Magic."

Surprise rounded their pupils.

"*Mae is right,*" Brimstone said. "*I detected it too. It was faint but it was there.*"

Nikolai blinked. "Wait. Is that why I can see their aura?"

Lines creased Vlad's brow. "You saw it too?"

Mae's pulse quickened. "You mean, you guys picked up those ghouls' auras?!"

Nikolai dipped his chin, a muscle twitching in his jawline. "I asked the coven people who were at the facility today if they'd noticed it and none of them had. Alicia was the only other person who saw it."

Mae chewed her lip. *Is it because they're a different type of demon? But then, why is it only these two who can—*

I believe your connection with these two men is changing their magic cores, Brimstone said gravely.

Surprise jolted Mae. *What?!*

It's not necessarily a bad thing, the fox mused. *If anything, they should count it as a blessing. It means your soul has recognized them as potential mates. Speaking of magic, this appears to contain one such object.*

Brimstone gagged and retched, his throat working convulsively.

Nikolai's jacket fell from his jaws amidst thick flecks of drool.

"I don't think you can dry clean that," Vlad told the sorcerer dully. He squinted at Mae. "What happened to your face?"

CHAPTER FOURTEEN

AGNES KEEVAN BIT HER LIP AS SHE OBSERVED THE GROUP
at the foot of her infirmary bed.

"Are you—?" She stopped and swallowed, her voice
quavering. "Are you here to arrest me?"

Gregory Keevan's fingers tightened on his sister's
knuckles, his face pale. Her dog familiar huffed
worriedly by his side.

"No one's going to arrest you." Major Schuman
glanced at Mae and Nikolai, her expression neutral.
"Ms. Jin and Mr. Stanisic are here to ask you a few
questions."

Her gaze skimmed over Vlad where he leaned
casually against the wall next to the door, her face
darkening for an instant. Having a Russian mafia
prince inside a U.S. army facility was evidently rubbing
her the wrong way.

Shock widened Gregory and Agnes's eyes.

"You're—you're the Witch Queen?!" Gregory

stammered. His gaze dropped to Brimstone. "Then, that's—?!"

"Yeah." Mae scratched her cheek lightly. "Just call me Mae."

The coven healers in the room exchanged nervous glances.

Mae saw Vlad smirk out of the corner of her eye. He'd told her she should get used to being revered. She swallowed a sigh and sat on the edge of Agnes's bed. Brimstone plopped down next to her, his tail swishing across the floor.

"I know you've been through a lot," she told Agnes quietly. "And you may not wish to revisit what the Dark Council did to you. But it would really help us if we knew what happened to you."

Agnes hesitated before nodding, determination brightening her gaze. "I'll tell you everything I remember."

The witch started talking, faltering at first. She spoke of how she'd been walking home three weeks ago after a shift at a clinic that catered to magic users, when a van pulled up beside her and a group of men had dragged her into the back. Her dog familiar had bitten two of them before they'd injured him and left him behind.

"The next thing I knew, I woke up in this underground facility." Agnes shuddered. "To be honest, it was more a cave than anything. From what I glimpsed whenever they opened our cell, there were a lot of people being kept prisoner on several galleries.

Our jailers barely fed us and pumped us full of drugs to keep us docile." Her face grew haunted. "Every day, they dragged some of us out and took us to this—this room. It was on the lowest level of the cave and had a white door. There was this weird antiseptic smell whenever it opened. Like it was some kind of lab or hospital operating room. Half the people that went in there never made it out alive. Those who did became... monsters."

Mae's skin prickled unpleasantly at the witch's words. An image of the first demon she had ever met and slayed flitted before her eyes.

Was it like that for him too? Or did he go into that room willingly?

"Did you ever see someone who looked out of place?" Jared asked in a hard voice. "Someone who wasn't a magic user and might have been a scientist?"

Mae glanced at the NYPD lieutenant as he stepped forward, a frown on his face. He'd told them that the Immortal Societies had suspected for some time now that one of their own was working with the Dark Council to make modified demons. As well as being the Immortals' liaison with the U.S. Special Affairs bureau, Jared had been assigned the task of finding out who that person was and bringing them in.

Agnes clutched the sheets. "I—I did. The day they took me into that place. They gave me a powerful sedative so I wouldn't fight them. I couldn't make out the details of the room. But I remember him. A man in a white coat. He strapped me to a table and injected me

with that strange serum. He…he looked like an angel."
Tears bloomed in the witch's eyes. She wiped them
away angrily. "He told me I would be okay. That it
wouldn't hurt." Her voice broke. "He lied. When that
woman opened that rift and forced that thing into my
body, I wished I were dead."

Gregory's face crumbled. He stroked his sister's
back and gave her some water to sip, his eyes
glistening.

Mae's blood had turned to ice. "Woman? Can you
describe her?!"

Agnes blinked at her urgent tone.

Nikolai pressed a warning hand on Mae's shoulder.

"Was she blonde? Pretty, with gray eyes?" he asked
quietly.

Mae's pulse quickened as she fished her cell out of
her jeans and brought up a picture of Rose Blake.

She showed it to Agnes. "Was this her?"

Agnes's eyes grew round. "Yes!"

Mae's chest tightened. Brimstone whined and
pressed his flank against her leg.

"Who is she?" Agnes asked tremulously.

"She was—" Mae paused and clenched her teeth.
"She *is* my best friend. Now she's possessed by
Barquiel, an Archduke of Hell."

Agnes drew a sharp breath.

Schuman shifted, her unease plain to see despite her
impassive face. Even though they'd been dealing with
Immortals and magic users for decades, the idea of
Heaven and Hell and their respective inhabitants

actually existing didn't seem to sit well with the U.S. government.

Agnes wavered before reaching out and touching the back of Mae's hand. "I'm sorry."

Mae shook her head, her throat tight. "Don't be. I'm going to rip that asshole's heart out and shove it up his ass if it's the last thing I do."

Brimstone growled in agreement. Gregory and Agnes gaped. Schuman stared.

A snort left Alicia where she stood beside Vlad.

The incubus smiled. "That's the spirit."

"Do you remember anything about the object you gave me yesterday?" Nikolai asked Agnes.

Mae fished the skeleton key out of her T-shirt where it was hanging on Hellreaver's necklace and showed it to the witch. They'd decided it was the safest place to keep it for the time being.

Agnes paled at the sight of the key. "Oh."

"You told us to guard this with our lives." Nikolai narrowed his eyes. "I take it this opens something important. Something the Dark Council wants access to?"

Agnes rubbed her forehead. "My memories after I became that—that *thing* are still hazy." She paused, her expression hardening. "All I know is that the monster I became was one of the creatures tasked with the safekeeping of that key. I overheard Barquiel and Oscar Beneventi mention that it was crucial to helping them achieve their goals."

Nikolai stilled at the mention of his half-brother.

"And you have no idea what those goals are?" he asked roughly.

It was Mae's turn to lay a calming hand on the sorcerer's arm. "I'm sure Agnes would have told us if she knew."

Nikolai clenched his fists, regret flashing on his face. "I'm sorry."

Agnes shook her head. "No. I'm just frustrated I can't help you more. You saved my life."

Schuman crossed her arms. "So, the coven is nowhere near figuring out what this thing does?" She indicated the key with a sharp jerk of her head. "Maybe you should let us take a look at it."

"You won't be able to do anything with it." Mae rolled the key between her fingers, frustration gnawing at her. "This thing has a powerful spell on it. One I still haven't figured out." She made a face at Schuman. "Besides, unless you want ghouls tearing into your people, I suggest you leave it with us."

Schuman's eyebrows knitted together. "What do you mean?"

One of her aides whispered in her ear.

The major's pupils flared. "Wait. That freak accident in Ridgewood last night was you?!" She glowered at Jared. "Why wasn't I informed about this?!"

The Immortal rubbed the back of his neck awkwardly. "Because I took care of it."

He cast a faintly accusing look at Mae.

She grimaced.

It was thanks to Vlad's quick thinking and Jared's assistance that they'd managed to avoid the attack on the apartment making headline news that morning. Because the power had gone out in the neighboring blocks, they'd cooked up a story about a freak explosion on a nearby powerline causing the apartment windows to blow in. The incubus had added an element of truth to the narrative by blasting a hole in a transformer unit on the junction next to the building. Luckily, the cinema had been almost empty at the time and the ghouls' screams had gone mostly unheard.

By the time the cops and the fire engines turned up, all evidence that a deadly battle had unfolded inside Mae's apartment had been cleansed, courtesy of Vlad's phone call to one of the *Black Devils'* clean-up crews. The speed with which the silent men and women had turned up and their efficiency at scrubbing all the blood and gore from her place had sent a chill down Mae's spine.

It was obviously not their first rodeo.

Jared had been quick to take over the case once it was determined the exploding transformer had not been an act of vandalism. As for her windows, Vlad had sent a company out that morning to replace them.

Mae's shoulders grew tight. They had a meeting with Bryony in an hour. She'd hoped she would have more to tell the High Priestess after speaking with Agnes. But, bar some cryptic clues, they were nowhere near figuring out the nature of the skeleton key or its place in the Dark Council's schemes. She came to a decision and gazed at Agnes.

"I have three questions for you."

Agnes dipped her chin. "Go on."

"You said that scientist injected you with a strange serum. Any idea what it was?"

"I—no." The witch frowned. "It was dark and kinda oily. And it caused the most excruciating burning when it hit my bloodstream." Agnes's knuckles whitened on the sheets. "I know this is gonna sound weird, but it felt…alive."

She looked blindly at them, her eyes full of the pain she'd lived through.

The hairs rose on the back of Mae's neck. *Alive?*

"I'm sorry I made you remember that," she told Agnes apologetically. "Second question. This key." Mae lifted the skeleton key. "Do you know what it opens? Were there any clues you might have picked up from the Dark Council members who were in that cave?"

Regret darkened Agnes's gaze. "I'm afraid not."

Mae bit back a sigh. Gregory stirred in his chair, his expression uncomfortable. She could tell he was concerned about her line of questioning and its impact on his sister's fragile state.

"Last question. I want you to think very carefully about this. The people who were successfully possessed by ghouls. The ones that didn't die in that white room. Were they all magic users, like you?"

The coven healers in the room sucked in air.

"Oh," Alicia murmured, her face clearing.

"What?" Schuman said suspiciously.

Jared looked equally puzzled.

The color drained from Agnes's face. She clamped a hand to her mouth.

Gregory straightened in his chair. "Agnes?"

"You're right," Agnes mumbled shakily, her gaze never leaving Mae. "I didn't realize it until now! They were all sorcerers and witches!"

Mae scowled. *Bingo.*

"I have a final request. Can I have a sample of your blood?"

CHAPTER FIFTEEN

"ARE YOU SURE?" BRYONY SAID, HER VOICE STRAINED.

Mae drummed her fingers on the armrest of her chair, her unease unabated. "That's what she said."

Nikolai and Vlad looked similarly troubled where they sat in the meeting chambers at the top of the New York coven headquarters. Bone crunched as Hellreaver and Tarang chomped into their steak where they lay beside Brimstone.

Mae observed Vlad from under her lashes. The incubus still hadn't told her why he'd come to her place last night. Judging from the guarded looks he kept flashing her way when he thought she wasn't looking, she knew he was hiding something.

They'd left Jared negotiating with Schuman at the army facility on Staten Island, the Immortal doing his best to pacify the irate U.S. Special Affairs Bureau representative. Alicia had stayed back to support him.

Mae could comprehend Schuman's dissatisfaction to an extent.

So far, the U.S. government's involvement with the covens didn't appear to have benefited them in any significant way. Not as much as their alliance with the Immortals had, from the information Jared had let slip. The technology and science the Immortals had contributed to human society over the millennia had gone mostly undetected by ordinary folks. It was only recently that the governments of the world had begun to realize how much they owed the descendants of Uriel for humankind's advancements.

What was more intangible were the atrocities the covens had protected normal humans from ever since the Sorcerer King defeated Azazel and started to exert his influence over the world several millennia ago. There were no monuments to the thousands of sorcerers and witches who had died while protecting mankind from black magic. No national holidays to celebrate their lives and their sacrifices. No concrete proof any of it ever happened.

That fact upset Mae. That the world had carried on spinning while remaining oblivious to what Azazel, Ran Soyun, and their descendants had done for them didn't sit well with her.

Now that I'm here, things are going to change. I will not have the world overlook the contributions magic users make to keep it safe from those who wish to destroy it.

Na Ri's voice shivered through her mind, her past-self echoing this conviction. Mae recalled the anger and determination that had flooded her mind and body upon her awakening. Feelings that had belonged to Na Ri and were now hers. She clenched her hands.

She was beginning to understand Na Ri's outrage.

Bryony's brittle voice distracted her from her dark thoughts.

"Does this mean the Dark Council has been targeting magic users in the city without our knowledge?"

"It would seem so," Nikolai said grimly. "They're experts at making people disappear. Many of the people we rescued from that warehouse weren't from New York, so I'm not surprised the disappearances went undetected by your coven."

This information did little to reassure the High Priestess.

Abraham came through from his office, a tablet in hand. "I've made a list of all the victims at the facility on Staten Island."

Bryony straightened in her chair. "And?"

A frown furrowed his brow as he scrolled through the display. He looked up and met their tense stares. "Agnes Keevan was the only magic user among them."

Mae traded a confused glance with Nikolai.

"The ghouls we fought last night were magic users," she said adamantly. "I have no doubts about that and neither does Brimstone."

The fox growled out his assent and licked his chops, the enormous dish of black bean beef before him now empty.

Abraham's brows knitted together. "So, how come there weren't more of them at that warehouse?"

Silence followed his question.

"I reckon they made a mistake," Vlad said slowly.

They stared at the incubus. Brimstone raised his head.

"I don't think Agnes was meant to be there," the incubus explained. "The ghouls must have been part of another experiment, separate from the ones that created modified demons like Antonovich and Sobol. I think the Dark Council slipped up and accidentally brought her with them."

"That would make sense," Mae murmured. "Her ghoul didn't manifest during that fight."

The incubus is likely right, Brimstone said.

"Then why are they using those monsters now?" Abraham's voice was edged with frustration.

"They must have something to do with that key," Nikolai said.

"I agree. Agnes told us she was one of many ghouls whose principal task was to keep it safe." Mae furrowed her brow and fingered the skeleton key where it lay against her chest. "Our priority should be to stop the Dark Council from getting their hands on this thing until we figure out what it's for." She looked at Bryony and Abraham. "By the way, are the remains of the dead guy from my apartment here?"

"Yes. His body is in the cold storage facility in our infirmary." Bryony studied Mae curiously. "What do you intend to do with him?"

"I want to take a closer look at his magic core. Well, that and other things."

"Wait," Abraham said numbly. "You can do that?!"

The doors of the meeting rooms opened before Mae could reply. Violet and Miles barged in, Jared in their wake.

"I can't believe we missed all the action," Violet grumbled. "Why didn't you call us?"

Mae sighed. "We were busy."

"You could have messaged," Miles told Nikolai accusingly.

Nikolai narrowed his eyes. "Like she said, we were a tad occupied. You know, monsters from Hell?"

Mae looked past Jared. "Where's Alicia?"

"She decided to take a trip home to investigate the origins of those ghouls." The Immortal shuddered. "Better her than me."

Mae wrinkled her nose. "Oh."

Alicia's human appearance meant she often forgot who the FBI agent really was.

I wonder if she'll meet Azazel this time.

According to the Soul Reaper queen, no one in Hell had seen her father for centuries, Na Ri and Ran Soyun's deaths having apparently driven him to the depths of despair. The last time he was spotted, he'd been making his way to the lowest levels of that dimension, a place devoid of light and hope.

Bryony cleared her throat.

"By the way, Mae," she said carefully. "Have you told them yet?"

The High Priestess cut her eyes to Nikolai and Vlad.

Mae's stomach sank. *Shit. I totally forgot the most important thing about yesterday!*

"I, er, haven't had time," she mumbled guiltily.

Vlad's tone cooled a fraction. "Tell us what?"

Nikolai's expression hardened.

Mae knew this wasn't going to go down well with either of them.

"I've been summoned to the Annual Grand Meeting, in Philadelphia. The, hmm, High Council insisted on my presence there."

A deathly silence befell them.

"Is it me or did the temperature in the room suddenly drop?" Miles muttered to Violet and Jared out the corner of his mouth.

Nikolai rose to his feet, a scowl darkening his face. Vlad's eyes shrank to slits as he uncrossed his legs and followed suit.

"You're our queen," the incubus said icily. "You answer to no one."

"Exactly," Nikolai said between gritted teeth.

Penley jumped onto Bryony's lap. The witch sighed as she stroked her familiar. "We all know that. But I'm afraid coven politics means Mae has to make an appearance at the covenstead."

The air around Vlad trembled with a wave of demonic magic. "I can always take care of that problem. Permanently."

"You can't go around killing everyone who pisses me off," Mae protested.

"I can try," Vlad ground out.

"Seriously, between you, Hellreaver, and Brimstone, I'm gonna get a goddamn ulcer," Mae grumbled.

An expression she didn't care for darkened Nikolai's face.

"I'm coming with you," the sorcerer stated.

"What?" Abraham snapped. "Hell no!"

Mae's belly clenched as she watched the stubborn light brightening Nikolai's eyes. "I don't think that's a good idea. You have a lot of enemies there. Besides, Bryony hasn't formally revealed the truth about your powers to the High Council yet."

Nikolai flicked a dismissive hand. "It's not like we're gonna be able to keep it a secret forever."

"By the sounds of it, you'll have many enemies there as well," Vlad told Mae mulishly. "He's right. I'm coming too."

Abraham pinched the bridge of his nose. "I'm starting to get a headache." He turned to Bryony. "Please, stop them."

Bryony ignored the aide and steepled her hands. She observed Nikolai and Vlad shrewdly above her fingers. "If you accompany us, it will be under the aegis of my coven. Which means you'll have to obey my orders."

Abraham swore. He twisted on his heels and stormed into Bryony's office.

"Where is he going?" Mae asked warily.

"To have a drink," the High Priestess said dismissively. She narrowed her eyes at Nikolai and Vlad. "So, what say you?"

The two men glanced at one another.

"We can obey orders," Nikolai said with a shrug.

"Sure," Vlad murmured. "Whatever you say."

Mae swallowed a groan. The gleam in Nikolai and Vlad's eyes told her otherwise. Judging from Bryony's skeptical stare, the witch wasn't buying their bullshit either.

"Why don't I go take a look at that sorcerer's remains?" Mae said to break the tension.

CHAPTER SIXTEEN

To Mae's utter lack of surprise, Abraham led them to the basement.

It must be part of some unspoken code.

What is? Brimstone said.

The lift opened on a brightly lit corridor.

Mae pursed her lips. *Dead bodies and basements.*

Well, they are *closer to Hell that way.*

Mae sighed. *Thanks for that unpleasant reminder.*

She studied the shadowy passages branching off the intersections they crossed. They were lined with steel doors sealed with magic.

"That's the coven's arsenal," Vlad explained at her curious expression.

"Arsenal?"

"Weapons, grimoires, potions." Nikolai shrugged. "Things they'll need if they have to fight a battle."

"Do I even want to ask how you two know this?" Abraham said darkly over his shoulder.

Vlad smiled. Nikolai kept quiet.

They'd insisted on coming along despite her protests. Jared had returned to his precinct, Miles had gone off to a lecture, and Violet had elected to stay upstairs with Bryony.

Mae pondered the two men's words with a faint frown. *To think all this stuff's been happening and most of the city's not even aware of it.*

Her eyes widened when they reached the infirmary. It was a large, modern space divided into three bays and a row of cubicles. She spotted two operating theaters and a handful of treatment rooms lining one of the walls. Mae could tell no expense had been spared to equip the place.

"I think you do this place a disservice calling it an infirmary."

Abraham's chest puffed out slightly. "You think so?"

She smiled wryly. "Yeah."

It was clear just how much the sorcerer cared for his coven.

He's a nice guy once you peel away his prickly exterior.

You're right, Brimstone mused. *He reminds me of that creature.*

A hedgehog?

A cactus.

Mae made a face. *That's a plant.*

Hellreaver spoke. *You obviously haven't seen the ones where we come from.*

Mae shuddered. *And I don't want to after that statement.*

"By the way, why do you even need an infirmary?"

"A magical fight produces the kind of injuries that

would raise eyebrows in a regular hospital, so sorcerers and witches generally prefer to get treated by their covens," the aide said. "Most coven healers are licensed healthcare professionals who work both sides of the divide, in the human healthcare system and ours. Anything that can be done in a hospital, we can do here."

His statement sobered Mae. She wondered how often the infirmary had been filled to capacity following clashes with the Dark Council, all while she and ordinary humans went blissfully about their lives. Luckily, the place was currently empty, bar the medical witch on duty. Abraham introduced them to her and explained what Mae wanted to do.

The witch appraised her with a guarded look, the guinea pig on her shoulder twitching his whiskers curiously. "Where would you like the body?"

"One of the operating rooms would be great."

The witch wheeled out the remains of the dead sorcerer from the cold storage and brought the body into the first room.

"Have you performed an autopsy yet?" Mae asked.

The witch shook her head. "We don't normally carry out autopsies."

"Mind if I do one?" Mae lifted the duffel bag she'd brought with her and placed it on a counter. She'd gone past Grandview General that morning and snuck into the autopsy labs to 'borrow' some equipment.

The witch glanced uneasily at Abraham.

"Bryony said to give her carte blanche," the aide confirmed.

The woman shrugged. "Knock yourself out."

Mae laid out her instruments on a tray before turning to the table where the body lay. She eyed the dead man for a moment before placing a hand an inch above his belly. She closed her eyes and took a deep breath.

Magic swirled in her veins, warming her blood.

"What's she doing?" the medical witch whispered.

"Examining his magic core," Abraham murmured.

The witch sucked in air. "She can do that?!"

"Apparently, yes," the aide said, troubled.

Mae shut them out and focused. Goosebumps broke out on her skin an instant later. Her suspicion had been correct.

The dead man's core was smashed to pieces.

From the faint traces of magic that still lingered on the twisted fragments, it had happened at the time of his death. She frowned.

Is that from Nikolai's power? Or did being possessed by a ghoul render it fragile?

A light flashed weakly in the darkness of her mind. Mae's pulse stuttered.

There was something else there. Something she hadn't expected to feel. Her breath shuddered out of her when she opened her eyes.

"What is it?" Nikolai said nervously.

"His core is broken."

Surprise jolted the others.

Mae clenched her teeth. The spell she was searching for finally came to her, the words rising from the seemingly endless magical archives buried in the depths of her consciousness.

"*Soul Conjure.*"

The corpse trembled. A cracked, pale orb rose from the body, the light flickering agitatedly. It settled down when she clasped it gently in her hands.

Mae's throat constricted. She could feel all that the dead man had been in his life as she held the last fragments of his soul, from the good he had done to the shameful secrets he had kept. But more than anything, she experienced his final, wretched moments in this world, when his will had become subservient to the entity that had taken control of him. Crimson magic bloomed on her fingers.

She lifted the ethereal orb and pressed her lips to it. "Be at peace."

It flared for a moment before slowly vanishing. Tears blurred Mae's vision, the sorcerer's relief and gratitude carving a scar on her mind as his soul finally departed this world. She clenched her teeth.

I will never forgive them for what they did to him. To Agnes and so many others!

A heavy silence befell the room.

"Was that his soul?" Vlad said quietly.

Mae nodded jerkily, not trusting herself to speak yet. She put on a gown, gloves, and splash shield and lifted a scalpel from the instrument tray, her movements stilted.

Brimstone spoke. *Calm yourself, my witch.*

Mae met the fox's wise gaze across the room. She inhaled and forced her body to relax. Hellreaver hummed softly against her chest. She traced the weapon with her fingers, grateful once more for the bond that linked the three of them.

She was conscious of Nikolai and Vlad's stares as she made the first incision. She concentrated on the task at hand, her fingers moving with practiced ease as she dissected the sorcerer's body. The low whir of the bone saw echoed across the tiled walls when she cut open his skull a short while later. It didn't take long for her to expose his brain.

The hairs rose on the back of her neck.

The dead man's pineal gland was enlarged, just like the one she'd discovered in Antonovich, the *Oniks* member she'd performed an autopsy on the night Grandview General was attacked. Except the sorcerer's was all dark and deformed. Vlad and Nikolai came closer as she carefully extracted the lump of tissue from the man's brain.

"Is that what you found inside Antonovich?" the incubus asked in a hard voice.

"Yes." Mae held the black nodule up to the light and scrutinized it with narrowed eyes. "And also no. His wasn't this color."

The nodule glistened.

Mae squinted. *Wait. Did something just move in there?*

Brimstone bolted onto all fours next to Tarang. His hackles rose and his eyes flashed crimson.

Mae, get away from that thing!

She looked over at the familiar, puzzled. "What's wrong?"

The air throbbed with a wave of corruption. Mae's

pulse spiked. Dark strands shot out from the gland and coiled around the forceps in her hand. She jerked and dropped the instrument.

"What the—?!"

The nodule bounced on the floor. The inky tendrils swarming it darted under her gown and latched onto her foot. Mae swore, ripped the covering from her body, and stamped on the black threads.

They flattened before coalescing into an amorphous, black mass that wrapped around her shoe. The shapeless lump writhed wickedly as it attempted to pierce the thick material.

"Shit!"

Mae called on her magic and hardened her skin a second before the tendrils reached her flesh. The blob stilled when it sensed the intangible barrier now protecting her body. It sniffed the air with its threads and started crawling up her leg, leaving greasy trails on her jeans. Bile flooded the back of her throat.

Power thrummed around Vlad and Nikolai as they closed the distance to her, their familiars at their side and their weapons in hand. Brimstone got there first, the fox reaching her in a single spring.

He skidded across the tile floor, sank his teeth into the squirming mass, and tugged.

It's going for your soul magic!

Hellreaver transformed and dropped, the weapon's blades slashing and chomping on the corrupt shape. The thing stretched and recoiled from the fox and the weapon's claws and teeth, but did not tear.

Yellow magic erupted on Abraham's fingertips and in his owl's eyes.

"Sound the alarm!" he barked at the medical witch.

The woman nodded jerkily and hit the panic button on the wall.

Brimstone snarled in frustration. His body swelled into his full nine-tailed form, his giant shape towering above all of them and his massive head brushing the ceiling.

The medical witch gasped.

Brimstone doubled down on his efforts to rip the throbbing entity from Mae, Hellreaver assisting him with renewed tenacity. Vlad and Nikolai joined them, swords and spear arcing repeatedly through the air.

Their efforts proved fruitless.

Fear had Mae's heart slamming against her ribs. She knew the siren blaring through the building would soon bring reinforcements. She also knew it would be too late to stop whatever this thing was from doing what it intended.

Understanding dawned in a flash that made her draw a sharp breath. Dread formed a heavy pit in her stomach.

"It's looking for another host!"

"What?!" Nikolai snarled, horrified.

Mae discarded her face shield and stripped off her gloves. Magic flooded her bloodstream, bringing a rush of heat to her skin.

A spell. I need a spell that can protect our magic cores until we can trap whatever the heck this is!

CHAPTER SEVENTEEN

A susurration drifted through Mae's mind above the clamor echoing in her ears. She froze. Letters rose from her subconscious, forming words of power.

It was Na Ri who whispered them to her.

Mae inhaled, raised her hand, and shouted out the first part of the incantation. *"Soul Shield!"*

Fire sparked from the points of power in her heart and her belly. It ignited her flesh and bones and sizzled through her veins, a tide of pure magic. A crimson sphere exploded in the middle of the room, bathing everything in a red light. Dazzling, pale lines bloomed into life on the translucent surface, forming complex runes that she could feel more than read.

Mae's heart lurched. *That's white magic!*

She exchanged a stunned look with Nikolai.

"What is that?!" Abraham yelled, gaze locked on the pulsing globe.

Mae looked at the black shape on her leg. The thing had stilled, as if it sensed danger. It started moving again, the speed of its ascent confirming what she'd begun to suspect. She scowled.

I knew it! Agnes was right! This thing is sentient!

It is?! Brimstone ground out.

Let me eat it! Hellreaver growled.

Mae's pulse thrummed in alarm. *No! I don't know what it could do to you, Hell! We can't take that risk!*

Hellreaver grumbled in protest.

She ignored him and said the second part of the spell Na Ri had shown her. *"Multiply!"*

The red and white orb she'd brought forth split several times over under her command.

Mae barked out the last part of the spell. *"Guard!"*

The spheres shot across the operating room. They vanished inside everyone, including all the familiars. Mae shivered as the one within her formed an impenetrable fortress around her and Na Ri's merged souls.

Nikolai pressed a hand to his belly, his expression stunned.

Abraham and the witch in charge of the infirmary traded a dazed look.

Vlad's pupils flared crimson. "Is that you?!"

"Yes," Mae said grimly. "That spell should keep this thing from attacking our magic cores!"

She hesitated as she prepared to unleash more of her magic. *I can't just destroy this thing. We need to analyze it!*

A scarlet wave exploded around Vlad. Nikolai brought forth a brilliant, white globe. Their power warmed Mae's flesh as they reached for the corrupt mass, Abraham in their wake.

"Don't kill it!" she warned.

"What?!" Vlad snapped.

Nikolai glared at her. "Why the hell not?!"

"I need to figure out what it is!"

"Are you insane?!" Abraham hissed. "That thing's trying to eat you!"

"It can't hurt me," Mae insisted. "Trust me!"

Abraham glowered at her. "Dammit!" The aide's eyes and those of his owl familiar glowed gold as he drew on his magic. "*Contain!*"

His spell formed a yellow sphere around the dark, roiling mass. The thing quivered furiously as the aide wrenched it free from Mae's body, trapping it inside the globe.

Abraham's knuckles whitened. "It's resisting my magic!"

The medical witch barked out the same spell, her powers manifesting a blue sphere around Abraham's where it floated in mid-air. The black mass continued to fight its makeshift cages, its attempts to escape distorting the spells holding it at bay.

"*Contain!*" someone barked from their right.

Green radiance blossomed on Bryony's hands as she stormed inside the chamber, her spell enclosing Abraham and the witch's inside a complex, multi-layered lattice. Penley's eyes shone the same color as his mistress's where he perched atop her shoulder. Violet rushed in with Trixie. A purple cage formed around the prison as she repeated the incantation.

The amorphous shape throbbed and writhed against the barriers restraining it. A crack appeared in Abraham's sphere.

Mae's stomach lurched.

Nikolai's pupils flashed white. "Al, we need to draw on a ley line!"

The crow flapped his wings and squawked.

"No!" Panic made Mae's voice harsher than she intended. "That's going to drain your soul magic! Besides, I want this thing alive!"

Nikolai scowled. "I can contain it!"

"This would make it your third time in under twenty-four hours accessing a ley line!" Mae gnashed her teeth. "I saw what happened to you and Al last night! Don't pretend it didn't affect you!"

He flinched. Bryony stared between the two of them, her somber expression telling Mae she'd grasped her meaning.

Remorse shot through Mae at Nikolai's hurt look. *I don't have time for this right now!*

She focused on the spell Abraham and the three witches had manifested, the power she had been born to wield analyzing and copying it in an instant.

"Contain!"

A crimson sphere twice the size of the others exploded around the corrupt mass and its prison of spells. Mae's skin prickled.

The dark shape continued to struggle within it.

It's only a matter of time before it breaks through that. There's gotta be another way. Think, Mae! What could put this thing to sleep?!

The answer struck her like a bolt of lightning.

"Of course!" she mumbled. "Ice!" She glanced dazedly at the others. "We need an ice spell!"

Violet's jaw set in a hard line. "I've got one." The witch planted her feet wide and raised both hands. "*Ice Cage!*"

Purple magic bloomed around her hands. Mae's breath misted in front of her face as the temperature in the operating room plummeted rapidly. White crystals formed around the spheres. They merged, forming a thick layer of ice.

Mae's lips thinned. *That's still not enough to quell its power!*

She moved, crimson magic detonating around her with enough force to push the others back.

"No!" Vlad barked.

He gritted his teeth and tried to draw closer, Tarang struggling in his wake.

Nikolai's shout echoed in Mae's ears, his voice and Alastair's squawk full of dread. "Don't, Mae! *Please!*"

Mae gripped the magic prison with both hands and squeezed her eyes shut, her hair fluttering wildly around her. The spells sizzled against her skin, stinging her. She sensed Brimstone and Hellreaver's presence at her side a heartbeat later. The bond connecting them brought goosebumps to her flesh as the power of three amplified her magic exponentially.

The structure of Violet's spell formed in her mind, the symbols aligning themselves neatly before her inner vision. It took but seconds for her to deconstruct it and create a stronger, more indomitable formula.

Brimstone growled, his demon soul bolstering her own.

Mae's eyes snapped open. *"Ice Fortress!"*

Whiteness exploded at her feet. It spread, covering the floor and the walls of the operating room in a flash. A thick prison of frozen air and water formed around the magic spheres. The corrupt mass within them slowed, growing sluggish. It stopped moving when *Ice Fortress* formed fully, trapping it inside a solid cage from which there would be no escape.

Mae fumbled and almost dropped the cube as gravity took effect.

Damn! It's heavier than I thought it would be.

CHAPTER EIGHTEEN

Vlad snatched the ice block from her grip and dumped it on the operating table.

"It's okay," Mae mumbled at his angry expression. "The cold put it to sleep."

This only seemed to enrage the incubus. *"Just because you're the Witch Queen doesn't mean you're invincible!"*

Mae flinched. Tarang's head drooped, his shoulders hunching as his master's wrathful words echoed around the chamber.

A horde of sorcerers and witches stormed the operating room, magic shining at their fingertips. They staggered to a stop when they sensed the mood and looked around awkwardly.

"Er, is it over?" one of them asked nervously.

The medical witch hushed him.

"I hate to agree with Vlad, but that was really reckless, Mae." Bryony approached her, face pale. "We should have gone with Nikolai's idea and gotten rid of that thing with his magic."

Mae's heart sank. *Was what I did truly that crazy?*

The High Priestess's face softened. "I know how powerful you are. We all do. But there are times when a queen's subjects' wish to protect their monarch is as strong as their queen's desire to shield them from harm."

Mae deflated at that. Brimstone shrank to his small fox form and nudged her hand with his head, a low whine escaping him. Hellreaver shifted back to the pentagram medallion before returning to her neck, his weight heavy.

"No," Nikolai said in the tense silence. "Mae's right. This is our only clue as to what the Dark Council could be up to. Destroying it would have been foolish."

Relief loosened the tightness in Mae's belly. She gave the sorcerer a guilty look. "I'm sorry. About shouting at you. I was worried."

Nikolai blew out a sigh. "I know." He raked his hair with a hand. "I was going to talk to you and Bryony about it today."

"Are you struggling to access ley lines?" Vlad asked roughly.

Nikolai shook his head. "On the contrary. It's getting easier. But it comes with a side effect Al and I didn't anticipate. We're pretty much defenseless immediately after tapping into one. It only lasts a minute or so, but that's too long in the midst of a battle."

It was Oscar who'd inflicted the wound on Nikolai, on the night they'd engaged in the Trial of Blood, a competition where a Sorcerer King would force his children to fight to the death to determine who was the strongest among them. The last child standing would be deemed his heir and go on to inherit the evil sorcerer's powers when the next king needed to take the throne. Though long banned by former Sorcerer Kings, Nikolai and Oscar's father had revived the practice in recent years.

Mae knew the Dark Council would have had healers who could have tended to Nikolai's wound. Except they had chosen not to.

That's something else I won't forgive those bastards for.

Nikolai studied her with a faint frown as he opened the refrigerator. "Are you okay? You look like you're about to murder someone."

"Yeah." Mae forced her face to relax. She hesitated. "Does it hurt?"

"Does what hurt?"

"Your scar."

His eyes flared with surprise. His face grew shuttered the next instant.

"Not really," he said dismissively. "It's more numb than anything."

Mae couldn't help but feel a little hurt at his reserved tone. She'd thought the stuff they'd been through together meant he trusted her. She chewed the inside of her cheek.

"What?" Nikolai grunted.

Bryony observed Nikolai with an unreadable expression.

"There may be a solution to that problem," she said curtly.

Nikolai blinked, startled.

Hope fluttered through Mae. "There is?"

"Possibly. We'll know more at the Philadelphia covenstead." Bryony paused. "The Council of the Moon will be in attendance."

Mae's breath caught. Nikolai grew deathly still.

His mother had belonged to the Council of the Moon before she'd caught the Sorcerer King's eye and been forced to leave her coven to enter into a relationship with him.

The medical witch indicated the frozen block of ice nervously. "Not that I want to worry you folks or anything, but we still have this—thing to take care of."

Everyone gathered around it.

"Wait." Violet leaned in and squinted. "Did you freeze our magic?!"

Mae peered closely at *Ice Fortress*. Runes shimmered inside it, the spells vibrant against their translucent background. She hadn't noticed them before.

She straightened and scratched her cheek, a slightly crazed chuckle leaving her. "Well, would you look at that?"

Her attempt at lightening the mood didn't work. Most of the coven sorcerers and witches were staring at her in open awe.

"You gotta teach me that spell," Violet said, resolute.

Bryony eyed the mishappen form locked inside the ice block warily. "What *is* that thing anyway?"

"From the way it behaved just now, I reckon it's some kind of parasite. It must be what turned those people into ghouls." Mae went to her duffel bag and extracted a metal canister from within it. "I bet we'll find traces of it in here too."

Vlad swore. "Is that Agnes's blood?!"

Nikolai stormed toward her. "Get away from it!"

Mae yanked the vial out of their reach. "Relax. This thing only activates when it enters the human body."

Her words failed to reassure them. She sighed and put the canister away.

Abraham was staring at the ice block. "What the hell do we do with this now?"

Mae narrowed her eyes. "We analyze it and Agnes's blood. Carefully." She rubbed the back of her neck and grimaced awkwardly. "There's only one problem. This kind of work should be done in a lab with a microbiological containment facility. Not only that, it needs to be able to operate at sub-zero temperatures."

Lines creased Nikolai's brow. "There should also be magic users on site in case it gets out of control again."

"I agree," Vlad murmured.

"There's a suitable place just outside Philadelphia," Bryony said briskly. "It's owned by the U.S. government and run by the Immortals. We can assign some high-level sorcerers and witches to be on standby while they work on the samples."

Abraham bobbed his head. "I'll make arrangements to take these with us when we leave tomorrow."

Mae startled. "I thought we weren't meant to leave until Wednesday."

"The covenstead meetings officially start on Wednesday," Bryony said. "There is an opening reception tomorrow night. We'll be expected to attend it." She narrowed her eyes slightly. "I'm pretty sure I told you about it."

Mae made a face. "You did?"

The High Priestess sighed. "You weren't paying attention, were you?"

"In my defense, it was a lot to take in." Mae's stomach sank. "Does this mean I'll be on show, like some kind of freak?"

Violet patted her shoulder. "Pretty much."

Sympathetic murmurs broke out among the coven witches and sorcerers. They'd gotten used to Mae and were relaxed enough in her presence now to treat her casually. The same could not be said of the rest of the magical community.

Mae's shoulders drooped. *I'm gonna be like one of those performing monkeys in a street circus, aren't I?*

Let's just do what the incubus suggested last night, Brimstone proposed. *Let's kill them all.*

Like I said, you guys can't just go around writing off everyone who annoys me!

You worry about the details too much, Hellreaver grumbled.

Mae was about to berate him when a sudden thought came to mind. Her eyes rounded. *"Oh God!"*

Tension thrummed the air. Vlad and Nikolai

unleashed their weapons and scanned the area for danger, the others following suit.

"What is it?" Violet's gaze swept the operating room, body braced for combat. "Are you sensing demons?!"

"It's worse than that," Mae mumbled. "I haven't told my family about Philadelphia."

Everyone froze before sagging. There was some eye rolling and indistinct muttering. Vlad shook his head and put his swords away. Nikolai sighed and retracted his spear.

"Jeez, Mae, you almost gave me a heart attack!" Violet groused.

"I'm sure they'll be alright," Bryony reassured. "Especially now that your mother is aware of your magic."

"You don't know the Jins. Holidays are a sacred topic in our household. Our trips are usually organized with military precision." Mae swallowed. "There are even...colored tabs."

"It's a covenstead, not a holiday," Abraham said sharply. "Besides, they're not on the guest list. It's not like they can just invite themselves."

"Ten bucks says otherwise."

Abraham took one look at her glum expression and pinched the bridge of his nose.

"How about I serve you a brandy when we get upstairs?" Bryony told the aide gently.

"There's not enough booze in the world for what I have to put up with," he grumbled.

"Don't worry about a dress for the reception," Vlad told Mae. "I'll take care of it."

Nikolai's face tightened.

Vlad raised an eyebrow. "What? Want me to get you a suit?"

"I can buy my own!" the sorcerer growled.

"Wait." Mae stared. "I have to wear a dress?!"

CHAPTER NINETEEN

"This is nice." Ye-Seul peered through the limo's tinted window.

The vehicle had pulled up in front of the stone and marble portico of an imposing building in Philadelphia's business district. Shallow steps rose from the sidewalk to a pair of revolving doors and a VIP entrance manned by a uniformed doorman. The guy's face lit up when he saw the car.

"Was it really necessary to take a limo?" Mae groaned.

"Of course." Vlad raised an eyebrow. "My queen needs to make an entrance."

"You mustn't berate him, Mae," Yoo-Mi protested. "He was only thinking of our comfort. After all, we barely had time to get ourselves organized."

Mae ignored her mother's faintly accusing tone and studied the spots of color on her cheekbones instead. She wasn't sure if it was a side effect of spending time in an enclosed space with an incubus or because Yoo-

Mi had raided the minibar in the back of their luxury ride. This was the first time since Mae's father's death that they'd been on a family trip. Guilt tightened her chest.

Looks like she really needed the break.

Ryu flashed her a dirty smirk. "Yeah, Mae. Vlad is only thinking of your—" she cocked her fingers into air quotes, "*comfort*."

Mae rolled her eyes at her sister. Ryu had recovered from her cold. Since they were only going to be gone for three days, they'd left Bianca in charge of the funeral home. One of Noah's men had stayed back to assist the mortician.

As for Noah, he and the rest of his team had followed the Jins to Philadelphia. It made sense to everyone that they continue their assignment during the covenstead. Abraham had welcomed Bryony's suggestion on the subject with relief. Mae could tell from the aide's harried expression that tagging them onto the coven's trip to Philadelphia was proving to be a nightmare.

Ilya, Vlad's bodyguard, helped Yoo-Mi and Ryu exit the limo. His stoic face softened when he took Ye-Seul's hand. The two had bonded over Mahjong, Ye-Seul even managing to get a smile out of the stony man. Vlad had had to punch his bodyguard Milo discreetly in the ribs when the latter had tried to make fun of Ilya and Ye-Seul's unlikely friendship.

Noah and three of his men were already waiting on the sidewalk, having gone ahead to check out the hotel and make sure everything was secure for their arrival.

The sorcerer dipped his head at Ilya and Milo as he and his team surrounded the Jins. They knew one another from Vlad's regular visits to the Jins for Sunday brunch, a state of affairs that seemingly happened without Mae having much say in the matter. Though they tolerated one another, Noah's guarded expression indicated the Russian gangsters' presence at the covenstead was an unwanted distraction they could have done without. Mae had to privately concur. She was certain the High Council would have a thing or two to say about a notorious crime lord attending their Grand Meeting.

"Are you ready?" Vlad murmured.

Mae dipped her head, stomach fluttering. *Here we go.*

Tarang jumped out of the car ahead of Vlad. Brimstone joined the tiger and looked around curiously. Noah's cocker spaniel Wayne trotted over to say hello to the two familiars, his tail wagging furiously as he sniffed them.

Vlad offered his hand to Mae. "Let's do this, Princess."

He flashed her a smile that made her libido sing.

Mae told it to calm the heck down and took his fingers. She let him guide her out of the vehicle, the royal-blue, velvet pantsuit he'd gifted her last night swishing smoothly against her body. Though she kept her expression neutral, the way Vlad's hand tightened slightly around hers told her he was as aware of the attraction sizzling between them as she was. She bit her lip.

It was a miracle she hadn't self-combusted on the drive down from New York, what with his incubus energy filling the back of the car and making her senses swim. For some reason, she was the only one who'd appeared sensitive to it, her family seemingly immune to his sultry appeal.

You have become more attuned to his demonic blood, Brimstone said.

I have?

Yes. It must be a sexual thing.

Hellreaver snorted.

Mae's mouth flattened to a thin line. *Keep yanking my chain like that and I'm gonna dump your sorry asses before we leave Philadelphia.*

The doorman rushed down the steps with a bevy of bellboys and a cordial expression. "Welcome to The Azure. I hope you'll enjoy your stay with us. May we take your luggage, sir?"

Vlad passed the guy a fifty-dollar bill. "Sure. We're in the Royal Suite."

Mae startled. "The Royal Suite?"

She became aware of a sudden hush. People on the sidewalk had stopped to stare at Vlad. The doorman's face flushed as he gazed at the incubus, a lovestruck simper stretching his mouth.

Mae leaned sideways, her voice coming out on a low hiss. "*Stop that!*"

Vlad blinked innocently. "Stop what?"

"Your—you know!" she spluttered. "Your damn glamour!"

Vlad grinned. Several women swooned.

Mae breathed a sigh of relief when the incubus dampened down his sexual aura. The doorman blinked, as if coming out from under a spell. His smile grew stilted when he saw the pile of cases Milo had unloaded from the trunk.

"I'm sorry," Mae said ruefully. "Someone got carried away with their shopping." She cut her eyes to Vlad. "What's this about a Royal Suite? That sounds like the most expensive room in this joint."

"It's a suite of rooms. There are ten of them, to be precise." Vlad raised Mae's hand and kissed the back of her knuckles. "Only the best for my queen."

She shivered. The incubus's gaze grew hot.

Noah cleared his throat discreetly where he and his men waited with the rest of her family at the top of the stairs. They joined them and headed inside the hotel, Noah's team at the head of their group while Vlad's bodyguards formed the rear guard. The noise level dropped when Mae passed the revolving doors and entered a majestic lobby.

Dozens of pairs of eyes focused on her as they started across the wide, marble floor, people moving aside hastily to make way for their party.

"It's like the parting of the Red Sea," Ryu remarked. She glanced at Mae. "I bet you wish you'd had this kind of power on Sunday, huh?"

Yoo-Mi shuddered. "No one is to mention that funeral again. Ever."

Ye-Seul grinned. "It was the best thing I've seen in ages. Well, except for the bit where Mae got punched in the face."

Vlad scowled. "Someone hit you?"

"It was an accident," Mae murmured. "And, no, before you ask, you can't kill her. She's a grieving widow."

"I heard that thing was a humdinger," Noah whispered to Ryu out the corner of his mouth.

"I'll show you the video Bianca recorded later."

A low growl left Brimstone when they reached the halfway point of the immense foyer. Hellreaver hummed on Mae's chest.

"I know," she said quietly.

She could feel magic all around. Though most of the people staring looked guarded or wonderstruck at the sight of her, a few showed faint hostility.

Bryony was right. Not everyone is happy about the revival of the Witch Queen.

Tension tightened Mae's stomach. She reached for her power. Heat bloomed from the hot core of magic inside her and spread through her veins.

"*Nullify.*"

Vlad stiffened at the spell she murmured, his gaze sweeping the foyer. It was the one she'd used a few weeks back to break the defensive shield the Sorcerer King had imprinted on his Dark Council to conceal their powers.

Her magic washed through the lobby, invisible to all. A few sorcerers and witches blinked. Mae noted their reactions with a neutral expression. She could tell from the brilliance of their cores that they were powerful.

"Anything?" Vlad said in a low voice.

"No. There aren't any black magic users in the building." Mae's skin prickled. "But there *are* a lot of demons in this city."

Brimstone huffed in agreement. Vlad's face hardened, his pupils gleaming vermilion.

"There are?" Noah asked in a guarded voice.

"Yeah. Brimstone and I could tell when we were driving here." Mae hesitated. "I don't know if it's a normal number for this place or whether it's a recent development." She grimaced. "By the way, is the entire hotel reserved for the covenstead? All the guests appear to be of a magical persuasion."

"Yes. It's the case for all Grand Meetings. In case of —incidents."

Mae flashed Noah a wary look. "What kind of incidents?"

The sorcerer's expression turned distinctly uncomfortable. "Like getting drunk. And stripping down to your underwear. Or threatening to pole dance and stuff."

Ye-Seul sucked in air. "Oooh! That sounds like fun." She turned to Ilya. "We should try that someday."

Milo's eyes bulged.

Ilya smiled regretfully. "I'm afraid my party days are well over, Mrs. Hwang."

"Nonsense!" Ye-Seul cackled. She slapped Ilya on the back. "I bet there's plenty of steam left in your engine."

Ilya's ears reddened. Milo choked on air.

"Oh God," Yoo-Mi mumbled glassily.

"I thought you meant people fought with magic," Mae told Noah.

Noah brightened. "Oh, there's that too."

Mae grimaced.

"This place is *so* cool," Ryu murmured as they made their way to the front desk.

Yoo-Mi and Ye-Seul were staring around, similarly bedazzled.

Even Mae had to admit to being impressed. The venue for the Annual Grand Meeting was the most expensive hotel in Philadelphia. Not only did it occupy a considerable chunk of prime real estate in the business district, but there was also enough marble and crystal in the place to sink a ship.

"You're finally here." Relief brightened Bryony's voice as she emerged from the group crowding the south end of the main desk.

Abraham and Nikolai appeared behind her, along with the other New York coven delegates attending the gathering. Nikolai's face grew chilly when he noticed the proprietary hand Vlad casually laid on Mae's back.

Mae peeked at the incubus from under her lashes. *He's gotta be doing it on purpose.*

Nikolai had chosen to travel to Philadelphia with Bryony. Mae suspected the main reason for this was that he hadn't wanted to be trapped in the back of a car with Vlad for two hours straight. Though they put up with each other for her sake, Mae would have had to be a fool not to be conscious of the rivalry that thickened the air whenever they were around her.

Brimstone huffed condescendingly. *They're like dogs*

with a bone. You should put them out of their misery and just choose one of them.

No one's choosing anyone.

Your loins say otherwise, my witch.

Hellreaver tittered. Mae managed not to roll her eyes.

"It seems there's a problem with our rooms," Abraham said in clipped tones.

"What problem?" Mae looked around. "Where are Violet and Miles? I thought they came with you."

"They're meeting with their family." Bryony's brow furrowed. "It appears someone switched our reservations."

Suspicion bloomed in the back of Mae's mind. She turned to Vlad. "Wait. Did you—?"

A voice cut through the brouhaha from their right.

"What do you mean, the Royal Suite is taken?!" someone snapped. "We booked it months ago!"

CHAPTER TWENTY

An immaculately dressed witch in her fifties with dark hair, gray eyes, and a raccoon at her feet was glaring at one of the front desk staff. A similar-aged sorcerer with a frog and a blonde witch with a Siamese cat stood next to her, their expressions similarly irate and a retinue of attendants hovering anxiously behind them.

Mae's pulse quickened. She could tell the two witches and the sorcerer were at the same level as Bryony from their magic cores.

"Shit." She cast an accusing look at Vlad. "You did, didn't you?"

Nikolai scowled, his distrustful gaze swinging between the two of them. "What'd the asshole do now?"

"I booked the Royal Suite for us." Vlad arched an eyebrow at their stares. "What?"

Bryony glanced at the fuming witch and leaned closer. "Did you cancel their reservation?!"

Vlad's mouth tilted in a beguiling smile. "Let's just say I overwrote it. And you're welcome."

Abraham's left eye started to twitch. The aide looked like he was close to having a meltdown.

"Ah, Mr. Vissarion."

They turned. A man wearing an expensive suit and a deferential expression had exited an elevator and was making his way toward them.

"We're so pleased to welcome you and your guests to The Azure." He dipped his head respectfully. "If you'd like to follow me, I'll guide you to the Royal Suite."

Mae stared. *Is he the manager?*

The dark-haired witch's head snapped around where she was looming over the distraught front desk employee. "Wait!" She stormed over to them. "Did you just say the Royal Suite?!"

Suit Guy flashed her an affable smile. "Why, yes. Now, if you'll excuse us, I'm sure my staff will see to your needs."

The witch bristled at his dismissive tone.

The sorcerer accompanying her joined them. "I believe there's been a mistake." His gaze swept their group, lingered fractionally on Mae, and settled on Bryony. "You know as well as I do that the Royal Suite was reserved for the exclusive use of the High Council."

Bryony lifted her chin at his supercilious tone. "I'm aware of that, Gerard. Unfortunately, this matter is out of my hands."

She indicated Vlad.

Mae squinted. *Is she gloating?*

Abraham swallowed a sigh. There was no mistaking the jubilant gleam that had darted in Bryony's eyes. The New York High Priestess was thoroughly enjoying this unexpected development.

Mae studied the sorcerer who'd spoken and the outraged witch huffing and puffing beside him.

He must be Gerard Mosele, the High Priest of the Orlando coven. And she's Ephra Erwin, the head of the Houston coven.

The blonde witch made her way over.

"What's the problem?" she said coolly.

Her face hardened when she spotted Mae. Her familiar's didn't look any better.

And she's Karin Everheart, the High Priestess of the San Francisco coven.

Mae studied the woman with a neutral expression. Bryony had warned her about the witch.

It didn't take a genius to realize there was little love lost between the New York coven High Priestess and the three High Council members facing them. Still, she hadn't expected them to be so openly hostile to Bryony outside of a private meeting.

Brimstone bared his teeth. *They're being rude!*

The witches and the sorcerer eyed the fox guardedly, their familiars shrinking at their sides.

Suit Guy's gaze darted between them. "I do apologize if there's been a misunderstanding. Rest assured I will do my utmost to make your stay here—"

"There is no misunderstanding." Ephra indicated Vlad with an accusing finger. "This man stole our suite!"

Mae winced.

"Oh wow," Nikolai muttered.

Abraham's eyes looked like they were about to roll up into his head. Even Bryony started to look worried.

Tarang snarled, jaws snapping perilously close to Ephra's finger. The witch jerked back. Suit Guy stared at the space occupied by the tiger, confused.

As a non magic user, it looked empty to him.

Karin observed Vlad with arrogant insolence.

"Who is this?" she asked Bryony.

Mae, Nikolai, and Vlad's bodyguards took a careful step back. The others looked at them and hastily followed suit.

"Hoo boy," Ye-Seul chortled under her breath. "This is gonna be fun!"

Yoo-Mi hushed the older woman. A nervous look darted across the faces of the High Council witches and sorcerer for the first time.

Crimson magic erupted around Vlad. It swept through the lobby in a violent pulse that rattled the windows and shook the chandeliers faintly. Suit Guy looked at the stained glass and trembling crystals, the color draining from his face.

Mae's stomach sank. *Shit. He's* really *pissed.*

The incubus's lips parted on a feral smile. "My name is Vlad Vissarion. I am certain Bryony mentioned me when she reported the...events that took place in New York a few weeks ago. Since your memories appear to be as short as my patience, allow me to formally introduce myself. I am the heir to the *Black Devils.*" Gerard and Ephra paled. Karin went still.

"We own thirty percent of the shares in The Azure. Which technically makes me one of the owners of this place." His pupils flashed crimson. "I am also the future consort of the Witch Queen. The woman at my side." His voice dropped to a growl. "The one you should be bowing your heads to!"

A muscle twitched in Nikolai's jawline.

Mae narrowed her eyes at Vlad. *The bastard! He just had to sneak the consort thing in there, didn't he?!*

He's clever, Brimstone observed in a disgruntled tone.

"Wait!" Yoo-Mi whispered to Ryu. "Did he just *propose* to Mae?!"

Ryu peeked at Nikolai.

"I don't think it's that simple," she murmured. "I'm more shocked by the fact that he co-owns this place."

Mae had to agree. *Why didn't he just tell me that?*

The answer came to her immediately. In all the time she'd known Vlad, he'd never flaunted his wealth and influence out loud. He preferred to use his actions instead.

A stringent voice rose behind them, cutting through the palpable tension. "What is this unsightly commotion?"

Mae twisted around. An elderly woman with silver hair and bright gray eyes was storming across the lobby, a cane in hand and an aging terrier hobbling at her side. Violet, Miles, and a bevy of sorcerers and witches followed in her wake, their expressions ranging from the mildly harried to the resigned.

Oh. Mae blinked. *She must be Barbara Nolan, the head of the Chicago coven.*

Brimstone cocked his head. *She's powerful.*

Mae had to agree. The witch's magic core was a brilliant scarlet despite her age.

Barbara stopped next to Bryony. She studied Mae for a moment before dipping her head curtly. "My queen."

Suit Guy's face glazed over.

"Er," Mae started awkwardly, "about that—"

Barbara waved a dismissive hand. "I know. Violet and Miles told me you don't like to be addressed by that honorific." Her face softened for an instant. "Allow this frail old woman to call you by the title you deserve, just this once. After all, you *are* Azazel's daughter."

Mae's shoulders loosened slightly. She nodded, a faint smile on her lips.

I like her, Brimstone said.

"There's nothing frail about you, Barb," a woman who shared Miles's features muttered. "Also, remember what the doctors said about your blood pressure."

Barbara sniffed. "There's nothing wrong with my blood pressure that a little brandy won't cure." Her eyes shrank to slits as she studied the High Council members. She waved her cane at them, her tone turning shrill. "So, is anyone going to tell me what all this fuss is about?"

Karin tilted her chin defiantly. "This is none of your business, Barbara."

Barbara straightened to her full height. "Since it appears our High Council is determined to behave like fools, I am *making* it my business, Karin. As a former head of said Council." She arched an eyebrow. "As you're well aware, that gives me certain…privileges."

Surprise jolted Mae. *Wait. She used to govern the High Council?!*

"It appears that man—" Ephra stopped and ground her teeth. "Mr. Vissarion here has claimed the Royal Suite reserved for us."

Barbara observed Vlad critically. "Is that the truth?"

"He kinda owns the place," Bryony explained.

"Oh." Barbara's eyes took on a shrewd gleam. She inclined her head regally. "In that case, thank you for welcoming us under your roof, Mr. Vissarion."

Vlad bowed his head briefly. "My pleasure, Ms. Nolan."

Barbara stared at him for a moment before cutting her eyes to Mae. "He's sharp. Watch he doesn't run circles around you." She pointed her cane at Nikolai's chest. "As for you, you need to be more ballsy. Acting like a wallflower won't serve you well when your opponent is a fierce beast."

Nikolai startled. A smug smile curved Vlad's lips.

Ephra opened her mouth to protest.

"We shall provide you with the next best alternative accommodation," Suit Guy told the witch and her companions hurriedly, sweat now beading his brow. He glanced questioningly at Vlad. "And free drinks for the entire duration of your stay with us?"

The incubus shrugged. "Fine by me." This time, his smile didn't reach his eyes. "After all, they *are* paying guests."

CHAPTER TWENTY-ONE

"WAS ANYONE ELSE SHITTING BRICKS BACK THERE?"
Abraham muttered.

His owl Shiloh let out a soft, anxious hoot where
she perched on his shoulder.

Nikolai glanced at the rearview mirror.

The aide still looked drained where he sat next to
Mae and Miles in the back of the SUV. Since the
opening reception for the Annual Grand Meeting
wasn't due to start for another few hours, they'd
decided to stick to their plans and take *Ice Fortress* and
Agnes's blood to the private research facility Bryony
had made arrangements with to analyze the samples.

"I've never seen Vlad that mad before," Violet
observed from the front passenger seat.

Nikolai drummed his hands on the steering wheel,
face tight. "That asshole needs to learn to stop
antagonizing people."

"To be fair, he was right to come to Bryony's
defense."

"Yeah, the High Council was totally out of order talking to her like that," Miles grumbled.

Nikolai acknowledged their points with a grunt. His gaze met Mae's in the mirror. He furrowed his brow. "I sure hope that bastard was joking about sharing a room with you."

Mae bit her lip.

Vlad had brazenly announced that since he was Mae's future consort, it made sense for them to stay together. Nikolai still wasn't sure if he'd been serious or not; the incubus had disappeared before he could challenge him on the matter. According to Mae, he had a meeting with his associates in the city.

More troubling still had been the notable absence of April Blackwood, the Philadelphia coven's High Priestess and a close friend of Bryony and Barbara. As the head of the coven hosting the Annual Grand Meeting, everyone had expected to see her and the more prominent members of her entourage at the hotel. There were already unpleasant rumors circulating amidst the witches and sorcerers attending the covenstead about Ephra Erwin's displeasure with that state of affairs.

Though it was his first time attending the annual event, Nikolai could tell the High Council didn't particularly get along with Bryony and her closest friends. The two witches had finally received word from one of April's aides that afternoon, just before Nikolai and Mae had left the hotel. The sorcerer had confirmed that April would be at the reception that night.

Nikolai hadn't been able to stop the sliver of dread that had taken root in his mind. *Is the reason for April Blackwood's no-show the demons Mae and Brimstone sensed in the city?*

From Mae's expression, she'd been similarly troubled by the witch's absence. None of Vlad's local contacts had reported anything untoward when he'd gotten in touch with them yesterday. Neither had the handful of sorcerers Nikolai knew in the city. Still, they were all conscious that the Dark Council going under the radar was likely a ruse to lull them into a false sense of security. His stomach tightened as he observed the thermoregulated hardcase next to Mae.

He was glad Violet, Miles, and Abraham were going to be part of the group assigned to guarding the samples. Since Violet and Miles knew the scientist they were going to meet, Bryony had suggested they stick around and provide magical assistance to the lab if required. He'd been somewhat surprised she'd suggested Abraham join them, considering the aide was meant to assist her during the covenstead.

Mae had taught them and the other witches and sorcerers going to the lab *Ice Fortress* last night, in preparation for their task. Though their versions of the spell weren't anywhere near as devastating as hers, they would do the job until reinforcements arrived.

Ten miles outside Philadelphia, Nikolai turned off Interstate 76. The road they were seeking wasn't on the map. Abraham's directions finally led him and the SUV following them to an unmarked dirt track masked by thick undergrowth and a dense canopy.

The vehicle juddered as he navigated a pothole-ridden trail carving through heavy woodland. Blacktop appeared. The lane became a smooth road that ended at a steel-reinforced, concrete wall some half a mile later.

Nikolai rolled to a stop before it. "What now?"

"Turn the engine off," Violet said.

"What?" He looked at her, puzzled. "Why?"

She pointed at the sign to their right. Nikolai stared.

It said to turn their engine off. There was another one next to it.

He squinted. "Smile at the camera? What camera?"

Movement outside made him tense. Alastair squawked out a warning.

A drone had dropped from the sky and was circling their vehicle. It roved around the second SUV before disappearing into the canopy.

"That was weird, right?" Abraham said dully.

"Yeah," Mae murmured.

Miles made a face. "Great. Trust them to go over the top."

Violet grimaced. "This is gonna be like Dimitri and Howard's place all over again, isn't it?"

"What do you mean?" Mae asked, nonplussed. "And who are Dimitri and Howard?"

Nikolai glanced at the cousins, now more than a little irate. He was about to ask them the same thing when the ground trembled. Motion in the rearview mirror caught his gaze. His eyes widened. He looked jerkily over his shoulder.

A metal wall was rising behind the second SUV,

blocking off their retreat. The section of road they were parked on started to sink into the earth.

Nikolai grabbed the steering wheel. "What the—?!"

Alastair flapped his wings in alarm. Brimstone woke up where he'd been sleeping in the footwell and growled. Magic lit the inside of the vehicle as Nikolai, Mae, and Abraham brought forth their powers.

"Relax!" Violet said hastily. She eyed the concrete walls rising around them. "There's no need to panic. We're just headed underground."

Nikolai's earpiece buzzed.

"What the hell's going on?!" barked the witch driving the other SUV.

A quick glance in the mirror showed it was similarly alight with globes of magic.

Nikolai hesitated before snuffing out his power. "It's okay. Apparently, this is the way they do things around here."

Mae and Abraham followed suit reluctantly.

"What, make us shit our pants?" the witch mumbled.

"Some kinda warning would have been nice," Abraham grumbled at Miles.

"We didn't know the place would be so heavily guarded," the sorcerer protested.

"So, you guys haven't been here before?" Mae asked suspiciously.

"No." Violet sighed. "It's just—well, the Immortals have this strange fascination with bunkers. You'll see."

Daylight faded. The elevator platform carrying their vehicles dropped into pitch blackness. Another growl rumbled out of Brimstone. Mae gently hushed him.

Nikolai had to agree with the fox. He didn't like the feeling of being caged in either.

The SUV juddered when the platform finally came to a stop. There was a moment's stillness. The wall before them rumbled and slid open.

They were faced with the mouth of a wide tunnel lit by strips of lights.

Nikolai startled when a crisp voice boomed around them.

"Please restart your engine and proceed to the checkpoint."

"This is starting to feel like a spy movie," Abraham murmured.

Nikolai pressed the ignition. Blacktop hissed under the tires as they rolled out onto the underground road. They kept to the fifteen mile-per-hour speed limit signs and soon reached a steel barricade manned by armed soldiers.

Violet brightened at the sight of the two women standing behind the rows of metal posts and barbed wire blocking the tunnel.

"Oh." Surprise widened Miles's eyes. "I thought it was just going to be Madeleine."

Nikolai pulled into the parking bay one of the soldiers directed them to. The second SUV slid into the spot beside him. They disembarked under the soldiers' watchful gazes and were checked over for weapons before being escorted to a security booth. Their fingerprints and faces were scanned and their I.D.

badges were issued. They were allowed beyond the barricade a moment later.

Violet's steps quickened as she strode toward a pretty brunette with slate-colored eyes. "Madeleine."

They hugged warmly.

"I wasn't expecting to see you this soon." The stranger scratched Trixie's head. "Hi, Miles."

"Hey, Madeleine." Millie dropped from the sorcerer's shoulders and went over to say hello. The sorcerer turned to the beautiful young woman with short, dark hair and cool, silver eyes beside the brunette. "How about a hug?"

"No, thanks," the woman drawled as she and Violet embraced. "The last time we did that, you tried to cop a feel."

Violet cut her eyes to her cousin. "You're such a douche bag. Also, Mila is taken."

"Yeah, well, that guy is so laid back it's easy to forget she has a boyfriend," Miles said without any sign of remorse. "How's life with the ditzy seraph?"

"I got him into D&D," Mila volunteered.

"You did? Is he any good at it?"

"He sucks so bad Caspian almost cracks a rib laughing every time we play."

Miles chuckled. Violet grinned.

Mae cleared her throat discreetly. The two women looked over to where the rest of them stood waiting. A strange expression flitted in their eyes.

Nikolai couldn't shake the feeling that they knew exactly who he and Mae were.

"I'm sorry, we got a bit carried away." Madeleine

came forward and shook their hands. "I'm Madeleine Godard-Black. I'm a molecular geneticist and genomic expert temporarily assigned to this facility."

"And I'm Mila Jackson," murmured the woman with the silver eyes. "I'm a synthetic biologist. I got called in when we heard what you were bringing us."

Mae's eyes widened. "I've heard your names before." She stared at Madeleine. "I'm pretty sure I read your papers when I was in medical school." Admiration brightened her face as she turned to Mila. "And aren't you the youngest recipient of the Harrison Prize?"

Mila shrugged awkwardly. "My dad beat me to it by six years."

Mae sucked in air. "Wait! You're Professor Zachary Jackson's daughter?!" She glanced distractedly at Brimstone. "Oh." She blinked. "Brim says you smell like Jared."

Nikolai stiffened. *So, they* are *Immortals.*

Abraham's expression grew cautious. Though Violet and Miles had alluded to the Immortal races as their future allies and Jared had similarly assured them they meant the covens no harm, they were still an unknown entity.

Mae didn't appear anywhere as heedful as he and Abraham were being. In fact, she looked like she trusted the Immortals implicitly. Nikolai's belly tightened.

Is it because she's Azazel's daughter, just like they are from the bloodline of an archangel?

Mae listened to something Brimstone said to her. She smiled and nudged the fox. "Go on then."

Madeleine and Mila drew a sharp breath as the familiar made himself visible to them. Alastair and Abraham's owl familiar Shiloh followed suit. So did the familiars of the witches and sorcerers accompanying them.

"It's a good thing they won't be spotted on the cameras," Madeleine said dully.

"Yeah. The guys in charge would have a fit if they saw them." Mila observed Brimstone shrewdly. "I bet you and the rabbit get on like a house on fire."

Nikolai frowned. "The rabbit?"

Mae's expression cleared. "You mean the one that belongs to the guy who made Jared's sword?"

Mila grimaced. "Belongs is the wrong word. You can't own a hellhound."

Brimstone's eyes flashed crimson. He said something to Mae, his tail swinging animatedly. Her eyes rounded.

"Wait. That rabbit is *Cerberus?!*"

CHAPTER TWENTY-TWO

Mae stared at the dress on the bed.

"Wow. That thing should come with some kind of warning label," Ryu remarked. "Like, for people with a heart condition and stuff."

The outfit Vlad had gifted Mae for the reception was a sleeveless, floor-length, black, satin number with a built-in, intricate, gold corset belt, with gold clasps accentuating the slim straps. It had side-splits that extended to the mid-thigh and a deep V front and back that left little to the imagination. He'd complemented it with gold stilettos, a black and gold choker, matching loop earrings, bangles, and a gold and crystal chignon hair piece.

"I don't know whether to kill him or recommend him to a fashion house," Mae muttered.

Ryu grinned. "You're gonna look insanely hot. It's a good thing Noah and I are taking mom and grandma out for dinner tonight."

Since they weren't witches, Ryu, Yoo-Mi, and Ye-Seul would not be attending the reception or the covenstead. Instead, Noah would be acting as their guide on a three-day tour of the city and its surrounding tourist spots. Mae was grateful to the sorcerer for having come up with the last-minute plan the night before. She wanted her family as far away from the High Council as possible, now more than ever.

The afternoon visit to the secret government facility overseen by the Immortals had proven more fruitful than she'd thought it would be. She'd had her reservations about whether the scientists Bryony had recommended would be able to get to grips with the entity that had possessed the dead sorcerer and Agnes. Having met Madeleine and Mila and seen their labs, she had no doubt she'd left the samples in the best hands possible.

"Give us twenty-four hours," Madeleine had told Mae before they left. "We should have some preliminary results by then. And Mae?"

"Yeah?"

"Welcome aboard." Madeleine had given her a quick hug and smiled warmly at Nikolai. "We're so glad to finally meet you."

Though Nikolai had still expressed some doubts about their new allies while they were driving back to the hotel, Mae was certain that what Violet and Miles had told them about the Immortals in Chicago and the others scattered across the world was true.

There was a bond between them. A thread of fate buried deep in their bloodlines that connected them to a common cause. She'd felt it in her bones, as had Brimstone and Hellreaver.

"You and Noah seem to be getting along well," Mae told Ryu presently.

"We do?" Ryu said breezily.

Mae wrinkled her brow. She was distracted by the sound of the door being nudged open. Brimstone padded inside the room.

The fox was back from exploring their suite.

"Need a hand getting dressed?" Ryu asked brightly.

Mae studied her evasive expression with rising suspicion. *Is there something going on between her and Noah?*

"I'll be fine. Have fun."

Ryu left hastily.

"How are things looking?" Mae asked Brimstone.

I cannot sense anything untoward. The closest demon is at least a dozen blocks from here.

Relief filled Mae. "Good. After everything that's happened in the last two days, we could do with an evening of R&R." She grimaced. "I say R&R, but I feel like we're about to walk into Goliath's cave."

Do we eat soon? Brimstone asked.

Mae shot the familiar a sharp look. "You had two cheeseburgers at the lab."

That was a snack, he protested.

"There'll be food at the reception. Although it's likely to be canapes."

Brimstone eyed her dubiously. *What are those?*

Oh, I know! Hellreaver perked up. *They are bite-sized nibbles.*

The fox growled. *How bite-sized?*

"How the heck do you even know what canapes are?" Mae asked Hellreaver.

The eyeball of a hellboar is one such demonic delicacy in Hell.

The fox did not look happy at that answer.

Mae wrinkled her nose. "You guys mentioned helldragons the other day. So, you have hellboars too?"

Yes. Hellreaver hummed. *There are lots of hellbeasts. And the hellboars are the tastiest of them all.*

Something grumbled loudly in the room.

Brimstone squinted at Mae. She patted her belly guiltily.

Looks like those stupid canapes won't be enough for you either, the fox grunted. *How about we skip the reception and go find an all-you-can-eat Chinese buffet?*

Mae vacillated for a second. Common sense prevailed.

"You know we can't do that. Bryony would have our heads."

She lifted the dress from the bed and headed into the bathroom-slash-dressing room, only to rock to an abrupt stop when she saw the lingerie positioned prominently on a hanger opposite the doorway.

It was black. And lacy. And wickedly sexy.

Mae gulped, fingers fisting involuntarily on the dress.

Brimstone poked his head inside the room. *What's wrong?* The fox studied the scanty pieces of material arranged on the hanger with a critical eye. *I don't think that will cover a lot, my witch. That incubus shortchanged you.*

"He's gonna give me a heart attack is what he's gonna do," she grumbled, her pulse far too fast for her liking.

She placed the dress on a second hanger and reached for the top button of her jeans. Brimstone sat on his haunches.

"What are you doing?" Mae asked stiltedly.

Brimstone blinked. *It's not like I haven't seen you or Na Ri naked before.*

Mae gaped. "Don't tell me you peep at me when I get changed?!"

Relax. I'm not lusting after you, unlike the incubus and the sorcerer. Brimstone grinned. *Na Ri had the cutest little bottom. Yours is very simi—*

Mae picked the fox up, deposited him unceremoniously outside the bathroom, and slammed the door shut.

The familiar's wheezing voice reached her through the wood. *Come now, my witch. There's no need to be shy.*

Mae scowled, undid her fastener, and had her jeans halfway down her thighs when Hellreaver spoke.

You know I'm still here, right?

TARANG'S TAIL BEAT GENTLY AGAINST VLAD'S LEGS AS they stopped in front of Mae's room. He adjusted his cufflinks and knocked on the door.

"Who is it?" Mae called out.

"It's Vlad."

"Oh great! Come on in!"

Vlad frowned at the relief coloring her voice. He opened the door, walked inside the room, and stopped dead in his tracks. His incubus blood stirred, quickening his pulse.

Mae was standing in front of the floor-length mirror, her back to him. She had her head down and was cursing under her breath as she struggled to fasten the clasp of her necklace.

"Could you give me a hand with this? I don't think I'm doing it right."

Desire tightened Vlad's belly. The dress he'd bought the witch fitted her body flawlessly, the satin clinging to her curves even as it exposed her creamy skin and hinted at what lay beneath.

Black and gold really suit her.

"Vlad?"

Mae glanced at him in the mirror. She startled and straightened, her pupils widening. Color stained her cheekbones. Vlad's body grew hot at what he read in her eyes, the hunger swirling through him turning to full-blown lust.

"You look, er, nice," she croaked, her gaze nervously sweeping his body.

The black tuxedo with gold accents and matching brogues he wore were a perfect complement to her outfit. It was by a sheer act of will that Vlad managed not storm across the room and take her in his arms. He gave her a beguiling smile instead.

"Thank you. And you look as stunning as I thought you would."

Mae flushed.

Vlad walked over to her, took the clasps from her fingers, and fastened them. The soft curls dangling from her chignon tickled his skin as he let go of the necklace. He stiffened slightly when he saw the slight tremor in his hands. If Mae noticed, she didn't say anything.

Their gazes collided in the mirror. Vlad stilled. Mae's breath caught.

He maintained eye contact and stroked her nape and shoulders with a featherlight touch. Her skin was soft and scorching hot under his fingers. She shivered but didn't move, her mesmerized stare locked on his reflection.

Vlad skimmed his hands down her bare arms and brushed his body close to hers. "How about we skip the reception?"

Her lips parted when he leaned in and coasted his mouth across her ear lobe. Hunger darkened her eyes. She angled her head instinctively to give him better access.

A faint wheezing reached them. They froze.

Tarang sat to their left, big, blue eyes unblinking and visibly enthralled. Brimstone was grinning next to the tiger, his entire body vibrating with laughter.

Vlad sighed. Mae pursed her lips.

"Am I interrupting?" someone said icily.

Nikolai stood in the doorway of the room. He was wearing a murderous look and a classic, black tuxedo that showcased his powerful frame and long legs. Alastair rustled his wings self-consciously where he perched on Nikolai's shoulder, his midnight-black feathers almost invisible against the sorcerer's jacket.

Bryony and her retinue hovered awkwardly behind them, gazes swinging between the incensed sorcerer and Vlad.

Guilt flashed in Mae's eyes. She moved.

Vlad's heart sank, instantly missing her closeness.

Nikolai stilled when he finally got a look at Mae. His pupils dilated. Vlad lowered his brows, not liking the heated expression of yearning that dawned in the depths of the sorcerer's gaze.

"You look…amazing," Nikolai told Mae grudgingly.

Mae smiled, the tension melting from her face. "You scrub up quite nice yourself."

Bryony cleared her throat. "Shall we?"

"Before we go, I have some news," Nikolai said. "Gregory called. He said Agnes remembered something from when she was possessed by the ghoul."

Mae frowned. "What did she recall?"

"Oscar mentioned the Annual Grand Meeting." A muscle twitched in Nikolai's cheek. He indicated the skeleton key next to Hellreaver with a jerk of his head. "Whatever is causing demons to appear in this city must have something to do with the Dark Council and that key."

Vlad rubbed the back of his head.

"I heard something strange during my meetings this afternoon," he confessed stiltedly. "The gangs in Philadelphia are all pretty jumpy. Thing is, they can't pinpoint what's making them nervous. They just know something isn't right."

Mae's face grew tight. "How good are their instincts?"

Vlad clenched his jaw. "As good as mine."

CHAPTER TWENTY-THREE

GIANT CHANDELIERS GLITTERED BRIGHTLY ABOVE THE ballroom at the top of The Azure. Their light washed across the cream, marble pillars framing the rich, parquet floor and reflected prettily off the French mirrors lining the upper galleries running the length of the function room. The place was magnificent. Except Mae hadn't gotten a chance to appreciate it yet.

They'd been there nearly half an hour and there was still no sign of April Blackwood, the host of tonight's reception. The High Council hadn't put in an appearance either. Though a few people had come over to greet the New York coven and pay their respects to Mae, most of the sorcerers and witches were keeping their distance.

From what Bryony had said, until the High Council recognized her as the rightful Witch Queen of prophecy, many would not swear their allegiance to her.

Mae was conscious that they needed to utilize every

resource at hand if they were to win the war against the Sorcerer King and his Dark Council. Though she was powerful in her own right, Vedran Borojevic had an ally in the form of Barquiel that could more than match her. And Nikolai's half-brother Oscar wasn't to be sneered at either.

She had initially been reticent about coming to Philadelphia for the annual covenstead. Now that she was here, she understood why Bryony would have desired her attendance even if the High Council had not commanded it. They needed to strengthen the existing partnerships Bryony had with the other covens and make new allies that would commit to their cause.

Mae couldn't suppress the disquiet knotting her belly. An expectant tension shrouded the ballroom, like the calm before a storm. The bad feeling she'd had ever since the ghouls attacked her apartment had gotten stronger since they arrived in Philadelphia.

Brimstone sat next to her, his piercing gaze carefully assessing the people around them. *Do not fret, my witch. None here poses a threat to us.*

Mae's fingers tightened on the stem of her champagne flute. *I know. But we need their help if we are to defeat Barquiel and the Sorcerer King. I would rather not make enemies of them.*

Would you like me to threaten them? Hellreaver asked in a hopeful tone.

Mae grimaced. *No.*

Brimstone huffed. *You are too hot-blooded.*

The weapon drooped dejectedly where he hung around her neck. *You guys are no fun.*

Nikolai scanned the ballroom above his champagne glass. "You could cut the air with a knife."

"Our covensteads are normally fraught affairs, but even I have never seen it this strained before," Bryony remarked in a troubled voice.

Mae carefully sipped her drink, all too conscious of the stares being leveled her way. She'd already cast a subtle version of *Nullify* and hadn't identified any black magic users in the crowd.

"Are you sure your friend is okay?" she asked.

"I got a message from April before we came here," Bryony replied. "She sounded on edge, but fine otherwise."

Movement near the entrance caught their attention. Barbara Nolan swept inside the ballroom ahead of the Chicago coven delegation. The witch wore an elegant, black dress with a matching cane. A distinguished, middle-aged man in a royal-blue tuxedo and with a ferret in a matching bow perched on his shoulder was acting as her escort. Thorn, Barbara's terrier familiar, ambled beside them, a black bow similarly tied around his neck.

Mae side-eyed Brimstone.

The familiar grunted. *Don't even think about it.*

But you'd look cute.

So would daisies, Brimstone said scathingly. *I'm still not wearing one.*

Barbara and her entourage nodded at their

acquaintances as they made their way over. Bryony introduced the Chicago High Priestess's companion.

"Mae, this is Armand Duprey, a close friend of ours. He's the current secretary of the High Council."

"*Enchanté, mademoiselle.*" Armand dipped his head courteously. "It's a pleasure to finally meet you." He glanced around the ballroom, his brow furrowing faintly. "Although I wish it were under better circumstances."

Mae didn't like the sound of that.

From Bryony's tense expression, neither did she. "Is there something we should know about the High Council meeting tomorrow?"

An awkward expression flitted across Armand's face. "I'm afraid I cannot divulge the details of the agenda. Suffice to say you need to keep your wits about you." He studied Mae guardedly. "I would like to ask for your patience and forgiveness in advance, *mademoiselle*. Know that they mean well, even if they often fail to express themselves that way."

Mae narrowed her eyes slightly. *So, he's warning us that whatever will be discussed tomorrow has the potential to piss me off.*

Brimstone growled faintly beside her.

Judging from Nikolai's pinched face, he was thinking the same thing.

Barbara perused Mae with an arched eyebrow. "That dress should be outlawed."

Mae sighed. "It wasn't my first choice of outfit."

"You didn't have any outfits," Bryony reminded her.

"Let me guess? The incubus?" Barbara drawled.

"Bingo," Mae murmured.

Barbara sniffed. "Ah, well. The dress has done what he intended it to do."

Mae gave her a puzzled look. "What do you mean?"

"You look like a queen." She indicated the ballroom at large. "I'm sure he wanted their first impression of you to leave them speechless."

Mae blinked. She hadn't thought of it that way.

Another commotion drew their gazes before she could say a word. A group of gaily-dressed, chatty people had entered the ballroom. An elderly woman with sparkling, brown eyes and chestnut hair was at the head of the rowdy delegation, her purple dress a flamboyant splash of color against the subdued monochromes around her. A black jackrabbit with a violet bow hopped at her side, his golden eyes bright with intelligence.

Mae looked pointedly at Brimstone.

The answer's still no, witch, the fox snapped.

"Great." Bryony's mouth had pressed into a thin line. "The troublemaker's here."

"Come now, she's mellowed with age," Barbara said, her tone indulgent.

"Mellowed, my ass," Bryony retorted darkly. "She tried to pole dance at the Vegas covenstead, remember?"

Oh. Mae stared. *That must be Regina Nox, the Las Vegas coven High Priestess.* Her gaze shifted to the man with dark hair, brown eyes, and a long-suffering expression lagging in the wake of the witch. She clocked his pulsing, aquamarine magic core with interest. *And that must be Erik Nox, Violet's ex-boyfriend.*

Brimstone spoke. *Miles was right. He is strong.*

The subjects of their conversation closed in on them, seemingly oblivious to the mildly disapproving looks being cast their way by the other covens in attendance. Mae swallowed a smile.

Not oblivious. It's more like they know and couldn't give a rat's ass.

Regina stopped and beamed at Barbara and Bryony. "Howdy, ladies! We're looking mighty hot tonight if I say so myself."

"Mother, we've spoken about this," Erik protested in a low voice. "You need to tone down your words in public."

Regina waved a dismissive hand. "Bah! You worry too much about the details." She studied Nikolai appreciatively. "And who's this handsome fellow?"

"This is Nikolai Stanisic," Bryony said in clipped tones.

Erik's expression grew guarded, as did the faces of most of the Vegas coven. Nikolai met the sorcerer's stare unflinchingly. He'd endured similar reactions since he'd walked inside the ballroom and had been equally indifferent to them.

Mae had to hand it to Nikolai. He had thick skin.

"Interesting." A sharp light brightened Regina's eyes as she scrutinized Nikolai. "A white magic user."

Mae's pulse quickened. *She's good.*

Nikolai blinked and raised his glass to his lips to mask his surprise.

Regina leaned closer and cocked a thumb at Mae. "Gotta admit, it's a bit bold of you to bring an escort here."

Nikolai choked on his champagne. Mae bit her lip.

"Hmm, Regina? That's Mae Jin," Armand said glassily. "The Witch Queen."

Erik blanched.

Regina didn't miss a beat.

"Your majesty," she said effusively.

She lifted the skirts of her dress and curtseyed primly.

Mae smiled. "There's no need for that. And I know what you mean about the dress." She leaned in and dropped her voice. "You should see the lingerie."

Nikolai drew a sharp breath.

Regina's eyes rounded. She burst out laughing the next instant, her cackles drawing scores of frowns.

"I like you!" she told Mae, wiping tears from her cheeks.

Mae grinned.

"You really are just like Bryony described," Armand murmured dazedly.

Mae glanced self-consciously at Bryony. "Why, what'd she say?"

"That you're without arrogance or artifice," the witch stated firmly.

Regina prodded Mae's ribs with an elbow. "Is it true you drive a Vespa?"

"Yeah. Her name's Betsy."

Regina beamed. "Cool. You gotta take me on a ride next time I'm in New York."

The little color that had returned to Erik's face drained straight away at the thought of his mother on a scooter.

Bryony sniffed. "You need to watch the corners. She tends not to slow down when she takes them."

Barbara almost dropped her cane. "You rode on her Vespa?!"

Nikolai straightened, tension roiling off him. Mae followed the sorcerer's gaze. She stiffened.

CHAPTER TWENTY-FOUR

Vlad put his cell away and stormed across the ballroom toward Mae and her companions, face locked in a scowl. Tarang chuffed softly beside him.

The people in their path scattered nervously. Word of his identity had spread through the covenstead like wildfire and everyone was trying to steer clear of him. Not that he gave a damn. He had bigger fish to fry.

Vlad stopped in front of the witch, took her champagne, and placed the flute on a passing waiter's tray. "We need to talk, Princess."

Mae's brow wrinkled at his cold tone, her shoulders tight. "Now?"

Vlad dipped his chin, a muscle jumping in his cheek. He knew he was acting like a dick but the time for pleasantries was long gone. "Now. In private."

Nikolai bristled, magic flashing in his eyes.

"You should come too," Vlad said tersely. "You need to hear this."

Bryony and her entourage watched them leave with worried frowns.

A man with a white cat in his arms bumped into Mae as they crossed the ballroom. He murmured an apology and hurried off. She stared after him.

"Everything okay?" Nikolai asked gruffly.

"Yeah."

A cool breeze washed over Vlad when he parted the curtains at the far end of the function room. He stepped out onto a balcony overlooking the city. Goosebumps broke out across his skin. He turned to give his jacket to Mae, only to find Nikolai already draping his across her shoulders. Given what he was about to tell them, he decided to let that irritating fact slide.

"Thanks." Mae pulled the material closer, her wary gaze locked on Vlad.

He could see the dark foreboding growing in her eyes. Brimstone shifted closer to the witch, as if he sensed this too.

"Are you finally going to tell us why you came to the apartment the night the ghouls turned up?" Mae asked quietly.

Nikolai gave her a startled look.

Vlad frowned faintly. *So, she knew something was going on.*

He turned his back on them and gripped the balustrade with white-knuckled fingers, angry with himself for the news he was about to give her. The news he'd just heard from his uncle. He'd thought he'd have more time to prepare Mae for what was to come.

But it seemed the powers that be weren't having any of it.

An anxious rumble left Tarang. The tiger paced the balcony and brushed against his thigh. Vlad petted his familiar's head distractedly before twisting to look at Mae and Nikolai.

"I don't know how to put this any other way, so I'm just gonna say it like it is," he said gruffly. "The Russian mob wants you."

Mae paled. Nikolai drew a sharp breath.

Brimstone bared his teeth in a low growl.

"What?" Nikolai finally said in a dangerous tone.

Vlad blew out a frustrated sigh and raked his hair with his hands.

"Someone recorded what happened at the waterfront," he said bitterly. "The video's been circulating among the *Bratvas* here and in Europe. The syndicate my uncle answers to has expressed a strong interest in…hiring your services."

Mae swallowed. She finally found her voice. "They want to hire me?"

Vlad clenched his jaw. "Yes."

"To do what? Party tricks?!"

Shock was giving way to outrage and fear.

Vlad's heart twisted. "I'm sorry, Mae. This is all my fault. If I hadn't associated with you, you wouldn't have come to their attention."

He dug his nails into his palms.

Mae watched him wordlessly, a storm of emotions flitting across her beautiful face. She took a shuddering breath, walked over, and took his hand.

"Don't say that. Dozens of people would have died had you not helped us." She stared into Vlad's eyes, resolve replacing the anger tightening her features. "I don't regret meeting you. None of us does. We'll find a solution to this. Together."

Vlad's chest tightened, relief rendering him weak.

"They're scared your alliance with Mae will make the *Black Devils* the strongest crime syndicate in the world," Nikolai said sourly. "That must be it, right?"

Vlad nodded grimly, not surprised the sorcerer had caught on to the real reason Moscow wanted Mae. He looked at the witch. "My uncle would like to meet with you. A representative of the main syndicate arrived in the country tonight. We weren't expecting him to come this soon. He'll be at the meeting too."

Mae steeled herself. "When?"

"As soon as we get back to New York."

Lines furrowed her brow. She clenched her teeth and took a ragged breath. "Okay. It sucks, but it needs to be done. You're my friend and I don't want you to get into trouble."

Vlad stared at her, his heart now knocking against his ribs for a whole other reason. "You never cease to amaze me, you know that?"

He curved a hand around her nape and took her mouth in a hot kiss.

Mae gasped. Nikolai sucked in air.

Fire burned Vlad as he tasted the woman he wished to possess. He ended the kiss reluctantly and pressed his lips against the witch's brow.

"And really, Princess? Friend?" He chuckled. "You're hurting my feelings."

Mae punched him in the ribs and stepped out of his hold.

"That was cheating!" she snapped, her flushed cheeks telling their own story.

"You're *such* a dick!" Nikolai growled.

"Ouch." Vlad's smile widened. "Oh, come on. You would have done the same."

Nikolai glanced at Mae. "I would have asked her permission first."

Vlad blinked, too stunned to speak for a moment. His lip curled back. "My God, you really are a goody two shoes, aren't you? That's why you're going to lose, choir boy."

Mae threw her arms in the air. "What am I, some kind of trophy?!"

A middle-aged man in a blue tuxedo with a ferret on his shoulder rushed out onto the balcony before they could reply. He glanced distractedly at Vlad and Nikolai, and focused on Mae.

"You'd better get in there," he told her stiffly. "Things are about to get ugly."

Magic ruffled the curtains in turbulent currents. Vlad tensed as it washed across his flesh, surprised at the potency of the powers he could sense. Mae frowned, gave Nikolai his jacket back, and led the way inside.

A crowd had gathered near the center of the ballroom. Vlad slowed when the focus of their attention came into view, tension knotting his shoulders once more.

An elderly woman with red hair and a sphere of incandescent, cerulean magic in her right palm stood facing Ephra Erwin, Gerard Mosele, and Karin Everheart. Though she looked the worse for wear, she still glowered at the High Council members, her back straight and her head held high.

"Is that April Blackwood?" Mae asked the man in the blue tuxedo.

"Yes. She just got here."

Mae's face grew troubled. "Her magic core is almost depleted. She shouldn't be using her powers like that."

The guy in the blue tuxedo shot her a shocked look. Vlad frowned.

Magic sparked at the fingertips of the scowling High Council members. Two others stood behind them. An elderly woman with blonde hair, blue eyes, and an indulgent face. And a young woman with dark eyes and short, jet-black hair. The latter pair's expressions stayed impassive as they observed the confrontation, their magic unengaged.

Bryony, Barbara, and a feisty-looking lady in a purple dress framed the redhead, their familiars at their sides and their respective delegations at their backs. The rest of the sorcerers and witches in the ballroom were giving them a wide berth, the low buzz of their furious whispers making the air hum while their bright gazes focused on the contestants of the impromptu showdown.

Vlad narrowed his eyes. *Like vultures to a kill.*

CHAPTER TWENTY-FIVE

"WE MUST CANCEL THIS COVENSTEAD," APRIL Blackwood ground out.

Nikolai's stomach tightened at the witch's words. He exchanged an uneasy look with Mae.

"Really, April," Ephra scoffed. "I know you're the host of this year's Annual Grand Meeting, but to not be here from the start and just barge in when it suits you is utterly deplorable, let alone single-handedly deciding to call off this gathering."

"You may be the High Priestess of this city, but your authority stops there." Karin eyed April haughtily. "We can override your mandate if we so wish."

"Hear, hear," Gerard said disparagingly.

Troubled murmurs broke out across the ballroom. From Bryony and Barbara's bitter expressions, it appeared Karin's assertion was correct. A frustrated scowl twisted April's brow.

Regina addressed the High Council. "Still, you

should at least listen to what April has to say. I'm certain she has a valid reason for her request."

Karin shot the Las Vegas coven witch a scathing look. "No one asked for your opinion, Regina. So, why don't you do us all a favor and keep your thoughts to yourself?"

A muted, red wave pulsed across the ballroom. Several sorcerers and witches looked around, puzzled. The group at the center of the confrontation didn't notice.

Nikolai eyed Mae warily. She was rigid but for the muscle jumping in her jawline. *She's pissed.*

Alastair concurred with a soft squawk. The tense glance Vlad flashed his way told him the incubus had arrived at the same conclusion.

Outrage darkened Regina's face. She surged forward, gold sparking in her eyes and those of the black jackrabbit at her side. Bryony and Barbara startled as a sphere of orange magic exploded in Karin's hand.

"Mother, no!" Erik grabbed Regina's shoulder and yanked her back, the rottweiler at his side picking up her irate hare by the scruff.

"Stop!" Bryony barked at Karin.

"Wait." The young, dark-haired witch Nikolai suspected was Raven Quinn reached for Karin's shoulder, her face tight. "This is going too—"

Karin shrugged her off and launched the shimmering spell bomb at Erik and Regina, her mouth a hateful sneer.

Crimson magic detonated across the ballroom.

Nikolai gasped as he was shoved back several steps. Alastair screeched, alarmed.

Devour exploded into life and swallowed Karin's attack five feet from its targets.

Nikolai stared, his heart in his throat. He glanced dazedly at Mae.

Did she just incant that spell with her mind?!

Mae lifted her arm and flexed her fingers, expression furious. Scarlet lines forked out from *Devour*. They doused the magic lighting up the fingertips of the three High Council members, leaving red wheals in their wake. The trio gasped and clutched their hands.

"I'm sorry," Mae said icily. "Did that hurt?"

She snapped her fingers. *Devour* vanished as seamlessly as it had appeared. The crowd parted hastily as she crossed the floor, the click-clack of her stilettos the only sound breaking the shocked silence.

Karin recovered first. "Know your place, witch! You have no right to interfere in this matter!" Her eyes shrank to slits. "Just who the hell do you think you are?!"

Gasps rippled the air as the witch's angry words reverberated around the ballroom. Ephra shot Karin a nervous look. So did Gerard.

Raven grimaced and sneaked a peek at Mae.

Mae's eyes had gone dead. Hellreaver hummed menacingly against her chest, a crimson aura enveloping the medallion. Brimstone's hackles rose. The fox growled, the sound too loud for his body.

"Fuck," Nikolai mumbled.

"You said it," Vlad muttered.

"We should step back a bit," Bryony advised Barbara and the others hastily.

"Why?" Regina scowled. "What's the—? Oh." Her expression turned glassy when she saw Mae's face. "Yeah, let's do that!"

Raven retreated to a safe distance. Confusion clouded Ephra and Gerard's faces. Karin jutted her chin out defiantly.

Mae put her hands on her hips and looked at the floor. A giggle left her.

Vlad grabbed Tarang's scruff and backpedaled to a safe distance. Nikolai took Armand's arm and did the same.

"What's going on?" the secretary asked, perplexed.

"She's about to blow a fuse." Vlad made a face. "And it won't be pretty."

Armand swallowed nervously.

Mae started chuckling. Soon, her shoulders were shaking uncontrollably with her mirth. She threw her head back and laughed until she cried.

The crowd stared, unsure how to react.

"Has she gone mad?" Karin said to no one in particular.

Mae finally took a gulping breath and wiped the tears from her eyes. She looked over at Bryony. "I'm sorry. I know you and Armand told me to give them the benefit of the doubt, but it's clear someone needs to do the magic community a favor and remove these people's heads from their collective asses."

Someone sniggered in the crowd. They were rapidly hushed.

"After the stunt they just tried to pull, I wouldn't blame you." Bryony narrowed her eyes at the High Council, her voice hard. "Don't say I didn't warn you."

Gerard's brows met. "What do you mean—?"

Mae's pupils flashed crimson.

The air shivered. The chandeliers tinkled. A sconce fell off the wall. Alarmed cries ripped through the ballroom. They became choked with fear when Brimstone changed into his true form, his nine tails causing a harsh wind to erupt as they vibrated savagely. Hellreaver detached himself from Mae's neck and morphed into the double-bladed dagger, his edges gleaming ominously as he exposed his fangs.

Redness blossomed around Mae, wrapping her in a scarlet aura. The gold and crystal piece holding her chignon fell as she rose amidst a storm of her own making, her hair fluttering wildly around her. Vlad lunged forward and caught the hairpiece before it landed on the floor.

"Who am I, you ask?" Mae's voice chilled Nikolai to the bone as it reverberated around them. "I am the daughter of Ran Soyun, the first witch who ever walked this Earth, and Azazel, the demon whose magic runs in all your veins. I am your queen." Her words rose to a roar. "*And you will show me the respect my presence warrants!*"

Nikolai's skin prickled. He was certain he'd heard another voice beneath Mae's. *Is that Na Ri?!*

Demonic magic blasted from Brimstone. The fox gnashed his teeth.

"It seems you have forgotten who your true master is." He took a threatening step toward Karin, flecks of drool dripping from his jowls. The witch recoiled when his shadow fell upon her. *"Shall we teach you how to bow?!"*

Hellreaver opened his jaws and let loose the voices of a thousand demons.

A savage pressure descended upon the ballroom. Nikolai grunted and widened his stance to maintain his balance. He had to draw on his magic to stop it from crushing him.

The power of the Witch Queen drove everyone to their knees bar him, Vlad, and the strongest witches and sorcerers in the room. Even then, it was clear that those still left standing were struggling to keep their legs from buckling under them. Nikolai's mouth went dry as he slowly lifted his head and stared at the woman hovering above them in all her resplendent fury, the tendons in his neck screaming.

She really is something else!

Vlad's reverential expression reflected the emotions coursing through him.

Someone dropped to the ground, unconscious. Another person threw up. Mae retracted her magic as more followed.

Nikolai gasped, oxygen flooding his starving lungs.

The witch landed nimbly on the ground, ignored the dazed stares of the swaying High Council, and scanned the ballroom with a heavy frown.

"Here's what we're going to do," she declared. "First, someone is going to bring these guys some steak before they eat some of your familiars." She cocked her thumb at Brimstone and Hellreaver. "You people have *no idea* what they've been saying about them."

A shudder shook her.

Nikolai blinked. Vlad snorted.

"Come now, my witch. You exaggerate." Brimstone bared his teeth. *"I was only going to consume some of them."*

He eyed Karin's cat pointedly. The Siamese yowled and shot behind her shellshocked witch.

Mae narrowed her eyes at Karin. "Second, we're going pretend what just happened didn't. I'm in the mood for a drink and a party. I would prefer it if you all remained civil for the remainder of this reception and generally avoided pissing me off. I can be a bitch when I'm hungry."

A loud grumble erupted on cue. Several people jumped. Mae grimaced and pressed a hand to her stomach.

"Also, what does a girl have to do to get some decent food around here?" She pursed her lips and pointed at a buffet table. "Like, seriously, these canapes aren't going to cut it. I could literally eat a cow right now."

A strangled sound broke the befuddled silence. Nikolai looked sideways. Vlad was bent over and wheezing with laughter. Others were smiling around them. Even Armand was struggling to keep a straight face.

"Wait!" Regina hissed at Bryony. "Was she just hangry?!"

"There's a hellhound in Chicago who gets like that," Barbara said in a disapproving tone.

CHAPTER TWENTY-SIX

"We've had ten sorcerers and twelve witches go missing in the last forty-eight hours."

Mae's stomach plummeted at April's somber statement. Fresh tension vibrated off Nikolai and Vlad where they stood framing her chair. Brimstone stopped chewing on his plate of fresh meat and looked up, his pupils glowing crimson.

Bryony's eyebrows knitted together. "Missing how, exactly?"

"That's the thing. I don't know." April rubbed her face tiredly. "We've been investigating their disappearance ever since we were notified by their next of kin. All I can say is that whatever happened to our coven members, they didn't leave willingly. There's evidence of a magical fight at pretty much every scene we've examined."

They'd regrouped in a private lounge off the main ballroom. A muted roar reached Mae through the closed door. Now that the strain that had plagued the reception had been broken, the party was in full swing. Judging from what she'd observed before they'd left the function room, Mae wouldn't be surprised if there were a few sore heads come the morning. She hadn't spotted Ephra, Karin, or Gerard since they'd stormed out after their confrontation.

I bet tomorrow's meeting is gonna be peachy.

Brimstone huffed at her glum tone. *They wouldn't dare try anything, I'm sure.*

I don't know about that. They looked pretty pissed when they left.

She was about to ask April to elaborate on the missing magic users when someone knocked on the door.

Armand frowned and opened it a fraction. "Oh."

He pulled the door wide open.

Raven stood on the threshold, a reserved look on her face. "Mind if I join you?"

She'd addressed the question to Mae. Mae peeked awkwardly at the four other High Priestesses in the room.

"We're at your command," April said magnanimously.

Barbara waved a dismissive hand. "This is your rodeo."

Bryony shrugged.

Regina beamed at Mae. "Why, I'm even thinking about loaning Erik to you for tonight after what you did for us out there. It's the least I can do to repay our debt."

Erik's mouth fell open. "*Mother!*"

"Er, no, thanks," Mae mumbled. "Besides, I'm sure Violet would have something to say about that."

Erik's head whipped around, his face brightening. "Vi is here?"

"Yes. She and Miles are helping us with something." Bryony turned to the witch beside her, her tone turning disapproving. "And really, Regina? Pimping out your son?"

April narrowed her eyes. "Will you two cut it out? I've had enough drama for one night!"

Armand cleared his throat discreetly.

"Sorry." Mae grimaced at Raven. "Come on in."

"Thanks." The witch closed the door behind her. She studied Mae for a moment, as if deciding something. Resolution filled her eyes. "I'm Raven."

She came forward and shook Mae's hand, the bottle-green vine snake coiled around her shoulders hissing out a hello.

"I'm Mae."

A stilted silence followed.

"Look, I'm sorry about what happened out there. Those three are stubborn as mules, but they mean well." Raven frowned. "Still, that attack was totally unwarranted."

Mae could sense the witch's genuineness. The fact that Violet and Miles had spoken highly of her meant she should trust her.

"Are you sure?"

Raven blinked. "Am I sure about what?"

"That they mean well?"

Mae's quiet words hung like a guillotine's blade in the hush that ensued.

"I know their actions haven't put them in a favorable light," Bryony said hesitantly. "But I doubt they're our enemies."

"Sometimes, the enemy is the last person you expect it to be," Barbara muttered.

Mae could tell from the older witch's brooding expression that she spoke from bitter experience.

She met Raven's strained gaze steadily. "Something is about to go down in Philadelphia. And your High Council either genuinely has no idea what's going on, or it's aware and doesn't care."

Raven flinched. "What do you mean?"

"This city is teeming with demons. I can't tell how many are ghouls, like the ones we fought in New York before we came here. The only way to know for sure would be to witness their aura in person." Mae looked at the men by her side. "Right now, only Nikolai, Vlad, and I can detect those. So, excuse me if I think your High Council is acting suspicious considering the circumstances." Her voice hardened. "Right now, they seem intent on not listening to us."

Raven put up a hand. "Hold up. Ghouls?!" She scowled. "That's the first I've heard of any of this!"

The color had drained from April's face. "Teeming with demons?"

Regina looked around, confused. "What the devil is going on?"

"I think you should start at the beginning," Vlad advised Mae.

Mae swiftly recounted the events of the last few days. Nikolai pitched in and told everyone about Agnes's exorcism. Bryony reported on what Mae had discovered inside the body of the dead sorcerer and the private research facility currently examining *Ice Fortress*. She also reluctantly told them about Barquiel and his association with the Sorcerer King.

Barbara's shrewd gaze swept over Mae, Nikolai, and Vlad. "So, the only ones who can see the ghouls' auras are the three of them?"

"Yes," Bryony said. "We're not quite sure why."

Mae avoided Brimstone's wily stare. She had a feeling Barbara suspected the truth behind the matter too.

She kinda reminds me of Mrs. Son-Ha that way.

Raven sat down heavily in a chair, her face pale. "Jesus, Bryony. Why didn't you report this to us sooner? Especially about Barquiel!"

A guilty light shone in Bryony's eyes. "I was intending to, at tomorrow's meeting. I felt it would help Mae's case if I made it known then."

A trace of sympathy colored Raven's expression as she eyed Mae. "Your best friend got possessed by an Archduke of Hell?"

"Yeah. Some days, it sucks to be the Witch Queen."

A frustrated sigh escaped Armand. "Raven is right. I wish you'd informed us of all this in advance, Bryony. It could have avoided the situation with Karin."

April's face tightened. "I doubt that. Karin was on the warpath tonight. She's up to something, I'm sure of it."

Raven and Armand exchanged a guarded glance.

Suspicion brought a faint frown to Mae's face. "What?"

Raven looked discomfited.

"You didn't tell her?" she asked Bryony.

"Not yet," Bryony murmured.

"What was I not told?" Mae said stonily.

Raven chewed her lip. She jerked her head at Bryony. "*You* tell her."

Bryony sighed and pinched the bridge of her nose. "Karin may have intimated that your only role should be to serve the needs of the High Council."

Mae blinked. Hellreaver made an angry sound.

What?! Brimstone jumped to his feet. *How dare they?!*

He snarled, magic pulsing from his body. The lights flickered.

"It's okay, Brim." Mae laid a hand on the fox, the anger bubbling in her veins controlled by the thinnest of threads. She leveled a hard stare at Raven and Bryony. "So, you're saying they want me to be their puppet?"

CHAPTER TWENTY-SEVEN

A STRAINED SILENCE FOLLOWED.

"Those people sure have a death wish," Vlad said between gritted teeth.

A muscle jumped in Nikolai's jawline. "That sounds like something my father would say."

Raven raised her hands defensively at their dark stares. "Hey, I didn't vote for it. Karin was the one who suggested it. Though Ephra and Gerard didn't openly agree, they tend to support her decisions."

"And the others?" Barbara said sharply.

"Charlotte and Derrick abstained from commenting." Raven faltered. "I couldn't tell where Linus's allegiance lay."

Barbara tapped her cane on the floor. "Still, the fact that Karin even dared suggest such a thing shows how out of tune some in our High Council are. To have so easily forgotten the threat posed by the Sorcerer King and the Dark Council means they have lost touch with what's at stake and are simply craving power." She leveled a piercing look around the room. "Which makes them no better than our enemy."

Raven lowered her brows. "Look, I know they did something shitty out there tonight, but I doubt they're on the same side as the Sorcerer King."

"Quite honestly, I don't give a rat's ass about Karin and the others right now," April said bitterly. She turned to Mae, her knuckles white where she'd fisted her hands in her lap. "Do you believe my coven members were kidnapped by the Dark Council?"

Mae hesitated.

"Yes," she said reluctantly. "As much as it pains me to come to that conclusion, it's clear Oscar and Barquiel need people with magic to bring forth ghouls from Hell. That must be why they were taken." She drummed her fingers on the armrest of her chair. "There's one thing that puzzles me, though. From what Agnes described, the facility where they were carrying out their experiments was likely in or around New York. I'm surprised they have one in Philadelphia too."

"That may not necessarily be the case," Vlad said thoughtfully. "They may have perfected their technique enough to be able to change magic users into ghouls at will."

Dread filled Mae at his words.

"I think Vlad's right," Nikolai concurred grimly. "We know Oscar and the Dark Council want something out of this covenstead. We still haven't figured out what that is. What we're certain of is that it has something to do with that."

He indicated the skeleton key dangling off Hellreaver's chain.

Raven frowned. "A key?"

"What does it do?" April asked.

"We don't know. We were hoping to find the answer here." Mae paused, her stomach fluttering with fresh unease. "Also, does anyone know a sorcerer in his late thirties with brown hair and green eyes? He has a white cat familiar."

The High Priestesses and Armand traded a surprised look.

"That sounds like Linus Jarrett." Bryony frowned. "He's standing in for Isabella West, the Phoenix coven High Priestess. She's been bedridden since last month."

"Why do you ask?" Raven said curiously.

"Because he gave me this tonight." Mae uncurled her right hand and showed them the balled-up paper fragment in her palm.

Nikolai drew a sharp breath. "Wait. He's the guy who bumped into you when we were headed for the balcony!"

Mae dipped her chin. She'd already read the contents of Linus Jarrett's note. She showed it to them.

Raven swore. Bryony and the others scowled.

NIKOLAI SPLASHED WATER ON HIS FACE AND STARED AT his reflection in the mirror above the sink. It was past midnight and they'd just returned to their suite.

They'd spent an hour coming up with a strategy in

light of what Linus Jarrett had revealed in his hastily written message to Mae. Although Mae had wanted to leave straight afterward, Bryony and the others had convinced her to join the reception. There was now a queue of people who wanted to introduce themselves to her after witnessing her showdown with the High Council.

Looks like many covens are unhappy with Karin, Ephra, and Gerard. He clenched his jaw. *Let's hope we're all wrong about tomorrow.*

A knock came at the door of his room just as he was drying his face.

He stepped out of the bathroom. Alastair was snoozing on top of the wardrobe. If there had been a nefarious magic user outside, they'd both have sensed it. He grimaced.

Plus Brimstone or Hellreaver would have had their teeth in them by now.

He went over to the door and checked the peephole. A woman stood outside, her back to the room. His pulse quickened.

Mae?!

Nikolai yanked the door open. "What's wrong? Why are you—?"

He froze when the woman turned.

It wasn't Mae.

Nikolai drew on his magic and unleashed his spear.

"I don't know who you are or how you got in here, but access to this suite is by invitation only," he said threateningly. "You should—"

He stopped, startled.

Tears had sprung to the woman's eyes. Her breath hitched. She swallowed heavily and composed herself.

"Bryony let me in." Her voice quavered. "I'm Marlena Kosek. I'm your aunt."

A buzzing noise filled Nikolai's ears. He gripped the door with white-knuckled fingers.

"What?!" he whispered hoarsely.

Marlena smiled tremulously. "I'm sure you have a lot of questions for me. May I come in?"

The black terrier at her feet let out a soft, friendly woof.

"I—sure," Nikolai mumbled.

He retracted his powers and stepped aside, his mind still reeling. It dawned on him that he was being reckless letting a complete stranger into his room. She could be lying for all he knew. Still, there was no denying what he could see in the woman's face.

She had his mother's eyes.

They gazed wordlessly at each other for the longest time. It was Alastair who broke their daze, the crow landing on the floor with a soft flutter of wings to inspect the terrier. The dog sniffed him curiously.

"You have Gabriella's features." Emotion choked Marlena's words.

Nikolai startled as she touched his cheek.

She withdrew her hand hastily, regret darkening her gaze. "I'm sorry. That was too forward of me."

"It's alright." His throat tightened. "Are you—are you my mom's younger sister?"

Marlena nodded jerkily.

Nikolai's heart twisted. "But—my father told us you

were dead! He showed us your graves when I was still a child! He said there were no Stanisics left alive!" His voice broke, rage and sorrow squeezing his chest until he could barely breathe. "He told my mother she was an orphan!"

Marlena's eyes blazed. "Whatever Vedran showed you and Gabriella was a lie. He didn't want you to have any contact with her family. We are very much alive, Nikolai. And we've been trying to find a way to reach you for decades."

Nikolai sagged, the enormity of the untruths his father had told him weighing him down so heavily he was surprised his knees didn't buckle.

Did Oscar know? Did Barquiel?!

He fisted his hands, his nails biting so hard into his palms he almost drew blood. Alastair flew up onto his shoulder and butted his cheek gently with his head, soft croons rumbling from his chest. Nikolai touched the familiar, grateful for his comforting presence.

"Did she—" Marlena stopped and inhaled raggedly. "Did Gabriella ever speak of us?"

"Yes, she did." Childhood memories swam up from the depths of his mind. "She called you Marley."

Marlena pressed a hand to her mouth and swallowed a sob.

Nikolai motioned her awkwardly to the seating area and offered her a tissue. Marlena murmured her thanks and dabbed at her eyes before perching on the edge of a chair.

"I'm sorry." Her eyes glimmered. "We couldn't stop him from taking her."

The tension tightening Nikolai's body faded. It had been a long time since he'd let go of his anger toward his mother's family. "There was nothing you could have done in the face of my father's powers."

Marlena's fingers sank into the material of her dress, her remorse all too clear.

Nikolai hesitated before reaching over and placing his hand atop hers. "If I had known you were alive, I would have reached out to you after I escaped my father's clutches. I now have a permanent target on my back, so I have to be careful about my movements."

His gut twisted as he recalled all he had sacrificed over the years to achieve his goals. He frowned, fury surging through him once more.

And I'm still nowhere near fulfilling the promise I made to my mother. I have to avenge her and punish my father for the atrocities he's committed.

Marlena turned her hand over and clasped his fingers. "How did you do it?" She studied him with a fierceness that reminded him painfully of his mother's strong spirit, before the Sorcerer King broke her will. "How did you manage to break free of his hold?"

"It wasn't easy. But I had no choice." Nikolai furrowed his brow. "Had my father gotten his hands on Mae Jin before her awakening, all would have been lost. I knew the only way to save the world of magic and to avenge my mother was to get to her first."

Marlena's fingers twitched against his. She frowned faintly. "You intend to avenge Gabriella?"

Nikolai bobbed his head jerkily. "It's why I laid low all those years and did as I was told." His voice turned bitter. "My father thought he had me under his heel. I was probably the most loyal dog he owned. But I was only biding my time, waiting for the right moment to enact my revenge. Now that Mae has awakened, I'll finally get my chance."

Marlena's gaze roamed his face.

"You are close to her," she said quietly.

Nikolai flushed slightly. "We have a…connection, yes. I'm living at her place right now."

Marlena blinked. "Oh." She bit her lip. "So, you and the Witch Queen are—?"

"No," he said hastily. "We're just friends."

Her expression turned enigmatic. She took a shallow breath, as if steeling herself. "I'm glad to hear that. I know what I'm about to tell you will come out of the blue. I want you to join the Council of the Moon."

Nikolai's heart stuttered. Marlena's gaze pierced him with an intensity that spoke of a long-held conviction.

"Gabriela was the strongest white magic user born into our family." Marlena's voice hardened. "You carry her blood and her magic. Your rightful place is at our side, Nikolai."

CHAPTER TWENTY-EIGHT

IT FELT LIKE BARELY AN HOUR HAD PASSED BEFORE MAE'S alarm went off. She blinked blearily, rolled over, and came face to face with a frowning fox. She swore and bolted upright.

"Stop doing that!" Mae clutched her chest and scowled at Brimstone. "I almost had a heart attack!"

You were gonna hit the snooze button again, weren't you? Brimstone said suspiciously.

"Why, what's it to you?" Mae snapped.

It's late. If you want breakfast before you attend that blasted meeting, you'd better rise and shine.

Mae's eyes rounded at the sunlight streaming into the bedroom. She snatched her phone from the nightstand and gasped when she saw the time.

"Shit!" She jumped out of bed and hurried into the bathroom. "Why didn't you wake me?!"

I tried, the fox said morosely. *You hit me before you pressed the snooze button the first time, remember?*

"I deeth?" Mae garbled around her toothbrush. She

poked her head out. "I'm shorry." She glanced at her sister's empty bed. It looked slept in. She took the brush out of her mouth. "Where's Ryu? I didn't hear her come back last night."

Brimstone sniffed. *Your sister went to breakfast. Although I'm not sure she'll be able to manage it.*

Mae narrowed her eyes. "Why?"

You'll see.

She showered hastily, slipped into jeans and a T-shirt, and opened the door. The smell of fresh coffee hit her. Mae followed it to the breakfast room, her grumbling stomach reminding her that it was running on empty.

Everyone was already there.

Yoo-Mi passed the butter to Vlad and gave Mae a jaundiced look when she took the seat opposite them. "Do you have a hangover too?"

"No," Mae said defensively. "Why, who has a hangover?"

"Your sister does." Yoo-Mi pointed at Exhibit A before handing plates of fresh steak to Brimstone and Hellreaver. "She insisted Noah take us to a bar after dinner last night."

Ryu pressed her fingers to her temples and groaned. "You guys are too loud."

"They did shots," Ye-Seul added helpfully. "Absinthe."

Mae grimaced. "How's Noah?"

"He's fine," Bryony reported. "He went for a run. He's always been able to hold his liquor."

Ryu paled at the L-word. "Excuse me."

She shot out of her chair and vanished in the direction of the closest restroom.

Yoo-Mi stared after her critically. "Well, there goes our plans for the morning." She cut her eyes to Mae. "Are you wearing that to the meeting?"

Mae paused, the fried eggs she'd spooned out of the serving dish slipping onto her plate with a faint splat. "Yeah." She looked down at her outfit. "Why, is it too casual?"

"I think you should wear the velour pantsuit," Vlad said.

Mae narrowed her eyes. "Which one? You bought so many."

Vlad's gaze grew heated. "Should I help you choose?"

Heat flooded Mae's cheeks. "No, thanks."

Ye-Seul sniggered into her porridge. Yoo-Mi flashed her a disapproving glance. Mae looked at Nikolai, half expecting him to berate the incubus.

The sorcerer was eating his toast with a distracted expression, oblivious to their conversation. Mae stared before leaning across the table.

"What's wrong with him?" she hissed out the corner of her mouth.

"I don't know." Vlad shrugged. "He's been that way all morning. Maybe it's his time of the month."

He lobbed a steak at Tarang. The tiger caught it and swallowed it whole.

Mae wrinkled her nose. "Period jokes? Really?"

Vlad smiled thinly. "I'd do cartwheels if it'd help

lighten your mood, Princess. Your shoulders look so tight they're almost touching your ears."

Mae bit back a sigh. The incubus had a point.

The way Bryony was surreptitiously studying Nikolai told Mae the High Priestess likely knew what had the sorcerer preoccupied. Ryu returned and managed some dry bread. They finished breakfast just as Noah turned up with his team.

"Have a nice day," Mae told her family as they got up to leave. Her smile slipped from her face after they exited the room. "Noah knows not to bring them back until we give him the signal, right?"

"Yes," Bryony replied. "He's taking them outside the city."

"Good. I'll go change and meet you at the elevator."

Vlad grinned when he saw her minutes later. "You went for the black one."

Mae rolled her eyes. She wasn't going to admit how nice the clothes he'd bought felt against her skin. Her stomach fluttered as they made their way to the sixth floor.

I hope this works.

Brimstone huffed. *If it doesn't, Hellreaver and I can always kill them.*

Mae frowned. *Killing the High Council won't solve our immediate problems. We still need to figure out what this key is for and why the Dark Council wants it.*

I know, the fox countered. *But ending those rude assholes' existence would make us feel better.*

Hellreaver vibrated in agreement.

Though Raven had been shaken by the contents of

Linus Jarrett's note, the L.A. coven High Priestess had rallied around and promised to help them. Mae chewed her lip.

Her assistance was going to be invaluable to their scheme.

They exited the elevator and proceeded to the conference room Armand had given them directions to. The secretary was standing outside when they got there. One look at his face and Mae knew things were not going well. Voices reached them through the door.

An argument was in full flow inside the meeting chamber.

Armand sighed when he saw her expression. "I'd advise you to give them a few minutes, but something tells me that's not going to work."

Mae narrowed her eyes. "Bingo."

She stepped around him, opened the door, and barged inside.

"Good morning. Are we interrupting?" she said brightly.

Karin whipped around where she stood face-to-face with Barbara and a woman Mae didn't recognize in a circle ringed by tables.

There were two other people in the room whose faces were unfamiliar to her. One was a man with a hawk whom she presumed to be Derrick Adlington, the High Priest of the Baton Rouge coven. The other was a beautiful, olive-skinned woman with a lazy expression and a desert fox familiar.

"That's Nadia Hadid, the High Priestess of the Council of the Sun," Armand murmured behind Mae.

"She landed in the country last night. The woman next to Barbara is Marlena Kosek, the High Priestess of the Council of the Moon."

Karin paled slightly when she saw Mae and Brimstone. She recovered her composure and scowled at Armand. "I told you not to let them in yet!"

This witch really hasn't learned her lesson, Brimstone growled.

Armand held Karin's angry gaze unflinchingly. "I'm afraid that was an impossible task to accomplish. It is not within my power to stop the Witch Queen."

Nadia stirred, her languid face sharpening for a moment as she scrutinized Mae. Derrick stared, equally curious.

Charlotte Brix carried on with her knitting, her demeanor relaxed.

Karin's expression turned ugly. "And what are they doing here?!" She pointed an accusing finger at Nikolai and Vlad. "They're not on the guest list!"

A threatening sound rumbled up Tarang's throat.

"Nikolai is acting as my aide," Bryony said steadily. "I entered his name as an attendee for this meeting yesterday."

"I thought you already had an aide," Ephra said suspiciously.

"He's busy."

Mae indicated Vlad. "Mr. Vissarion is here as my legal advisor."

Derrick choked on a snort. Nadia inspected her manicured nails, a faint smile playing on her lips. Charlotte looked up briefly.

A nervous look darted across Gerard's face. "He's not a lawyer."

Vlad smiled. "I am more than familiar with your coven laws. I've broken them a few times." He shrugged at Mae's pointed stare. "They're archaic."

"Right," Barbara declared briskly. "Like I was saying, Karin, you can't stop me from being here. It is my right as the previous head of the Council to attend this meeting." She ignored Karin's outraged gasp and whirled around. "Come, Marlena, let us sit down. I am sure they will consider your demands *objectively*."

Marlena eyed Nikolai worriedly.

"It's okay," the sorcerer murmured.

She hesitated, her troubled gaze swinging between him and Mae. She dipped her head and returned to her seat beside Barbara, her movements stiff.

"You know her?" Mae asked Nikolai in a low voice.

"She's my aunt."

Surprise jolted Mae. Vlad cut his eyes to the sorcerer, equally startled.

Nadia leaned her elbows on the table and dropped her chin on her steepled hands. "Where is Linus?" She arched an eyebrow. "I find it strange that you would begin this meeting without him."

"I agree." Derrick tapped a restless finger on the armrest of his chair. "It's not like him to be late."

CHAPTER TWENTY-NINE

"Linus sends his apologies. Something urgent came up." Charlotte directed a contrite smile at Armand. "I'm sorry, it completely slipped my mind."

Armand nodded curtly. "I'll make a note in the minutes."

Nadia's gaze sharpened. "Considering what's on the agenda today, I find that very curious indeed."

Karin waved a dismissive hand. "It's not that unusual." The witch had reluctantly taken her seat next to Ephra and Gerard. "This meeting wasn't due to start until 10:30 a.m. anyway. He still has a few minutes left."

Mae's skin prickled as she and Bryony took the chairs Armand indicated. She'd just cast a controlled version of *Nullify*. Though she couldn't detect any black magic in the room, there was something else there. Something that was being shielded.

Do you feel that?

Yes, Brimstone replied. *But I can't pinpoint where it's coming from.*

Hellreaver hummed faintly, equally alert.

Vlad and Nikolai took up position behind Mae and Bryony. Brimstone leapt onto Mae's lap.

Ephra cast an uneasy look at the fox and cleared her throat.

"Before we begin, I am well aware that yesterday's incident has left a sour taste in all our mouths," she started stiffly. "I will be extending my apologies to Regina and Erik later today but, for now, as the current head of the High Council, I would like to formally express my regret for what took place at the reception last night."

Mae blinked. *That's unexpected.*

There may still be hope for them yet, Brimstone grumbled.

Ephra cut her eyes to Karin and Gerard.

Karin clenched her jaw. "I will admit to losing my temper somewhat."

"Same," Gerard admitted grudgingly.

"What the hell did I miss?!" Nadia whispered to Derrick.

Derrick shrugged, his astute gaze swinging briefly to Mae and Brimstone. "I wasn't there, but I heard it was pretty spectacular."

"It was epic," Raven muttered.

Mae exchanged a look with Bryony and Barbara. They dipped their chins.

"And I apologize for my, er, reaction." Brimstone growled on her lap. She pressed a warning hand to the fox's flank. "Brim says sorry too."

I am not in the least bit sorry! the fox snarled.

Hellreaver vibrated against her chest. *Yeah, like heck we are!*

"Do you guys want lunch?" Mae threatened.

Brimstone's tail drooped. Hellreaver sulked and grew heavy around her neck.

"Who's she talking to?" Karin asked Ephra warily.

Ephra stared. "I have no idea."

Bryony grimaced awkwardly. "I forgot to mention this when we last spoke. Mae can, hmm, communicate telepathically with her familiar and her weapon."

A stunned silence befell the room.

"What?!" Karin choked out.

Gerard scowled. "That's ridiculous!"

Barbara tapped her cane sharply on the floor.

"Do you people have a short memory?" she snapped. "I explicitly told you the same thing regarding our allies in Chicago. The divine beasts can communicate with their hosts telepathically too."

Mae straightened in her seat. *Oh.*

Brimstone's ears perked up.

"They're not magic users, Barbara." Lines knitted Ephra's brow. "And their lineage is totally different from ours. I have never heard of a witch or a sorcerer who's been able to do that in all the history of our kind."

"Na Ri could," Mae stated.

Her words were greeted with a confused hush.

"Na Ri?" Derrick repeated.

"Azazel's daughter. The Witch Queen who I am the reincarnation of."

"I—" Ephra blinked and faltered. "That's a lot to

take in." She flashed a stern look at Bryony. "Some warning would have been good."

Bryony sighed. "I confess to being at fault for not telling you sooner, but you didn't leave me much choice either."

Karin's face hardened. "How do we even know what you're saying is the truth?"

Mae only got a second's warning before Brimstone sprang from her lap and landed inside the circle. Startled gasps erupted as he transformed into the nine-tailed spirit, his magic making the air throb and the curtains flutter.

"Because I say so!"

The fox's growl rattled the windows.

Mae winced. *Ah, shit.*

He's SO pissed, Hellreaver observed in a gleeful tone.

Brimstone loomed over Karin and lowered his massive head. The witch shrank back in her chair, face ashen.

"Do not make me break my promise to my bond, witch," the fox snarled. *"Hellreaver and I pledged not to harm any of you unless she gives us permission, but you are truly testing the limits of our patience."*

Hellreaver detached himself from Mae's neck and joined the fox, his blades hissing into life as he morphed. Karin's familiar burrowed into her lap.

Mae blew out a sigh. "You guys. What did I say about threatening people?"

Brimstone and Hellreaver flinched.

"You know what this means, right?" she added sharply.

"*Yeah, yeah,*" Brimstone muttered. "*No steak for lunch.*" The fox bared a fang at Karin's familiar. "*Cat meat sounds like a good alternative.*"

He shifted back to his smaller shape and returned to Mae's lap.

"He's kidding," Mae told Karin hurriedly as the witch cradled her trembling cat to her chest.

Penley let out an anxious meow.

Brimstone nudged him affectionately. *I would never eat you.*

The cat licked him, pleased.

Color returned to Ephra's face, though her expression remained somewhat wooden. "Still, none of this detracts from what we came here to do today."

Mae tensed. *Here we go.*

"Before you begin, might I say a few words?" Marlena interrupted.

Ephra lowered her brows. "If you must."

Mae studied Nikolai's aunt from under her lashes. *I assumed she and Nadia were here as honorary guests, but it looks like I was wrong.*

They are not to be dismissed, Brimstone observed. *Even their familiars are powerful in their own right.*

Mae's gaze dropped to Marlena's terrier and Nadia's fox. Brimstone was right.

Marlena looked around the room, her expression strained yet resolute. "We're all aware of the increasing activities of the Dark Council within our territories these past few years. Things appear to have died down since the incident in New York, but that doesn't mean we're out of the woods yet. The peace since Mae Jin's awakening is likely the calm before the storm. We should expect the Sorcerer King to retaliate soon." She glanced at Nikolai and Mae. "This is why I have two suggestions I would like you to strongly consider. Mae should be allowed into the High Council and Nikolai should take his place at my side in the Council of the Moon."

Mae's gut twisted. She looked jerkily at Nikolai, her pulse quickening. Vlad glanced sideways at the sorcerer, his face tight despite the triumphant gleam that flashed in his pupils.

From what Mae had learned, the Council of the Moon was based in Europe. Having the sorcerer on another continent would clear the way for the incubus to court her.

Nikolai's gaze stayed locked on his aunt.

Karin scoffed. "Besides the fact that what you've just suggested is utterly absurd, there is no evidence of this threat you all keep talking about." A reproachful look dawned on the witch's face. "I really wish the ones who stand at the top of our magic community would stop spreading lies and fear. We clearly outnumber the Dark Council. We shouldn't be afraid of them. So, no. I object to your suggestion that Mae Jin join the High Council. As for your own household, it's your business what you do with it."

Mae blinked. *Jeez, she really doesn't get it, does she?*

That woman is a fool, Brimstone grunted.

"You really do believe that, don't you?" Marlena said, aghast.

Karin shrugged, undaunted. "Of course. There are

plenty of powerful magic users in this room, let alone the rest of our covens."

Nadia was staring at Karin like she'd grown a second head. "You imbeciles have really lost touch with reality." She ignored the witch's outraged gasp and directed a scathing glare at Ephra and Gerard. "You are fools if you've convinced yourself that the Sorcerer King doesn't pose a threat to our way of life. That man would crush us under his feet in a heartbeat to rule over the world of magic."

Karin's eyes shrank to slits. "Why, you—!"

"Nadia is right," Derrick interrupted brusquely. A muscle jumped in the sorcerer's jawline. "Just because your coven hasn't had any direct confrontation with the Dark Council in the last decade doesn't mean you should be misguided about the threat they pose, Karin. This applies to you too, Gerard."

Gerard scowled.

Karin jutted her chin out, body fairly quaking with rage. "Your collective hysteria doesn't make you right! I for one believe the events in New York were grossly exaggerated to justify the prophecy about the Witch Queen." She glared at Bryony. "We're old enough to realize that that prophecy is but a children's fairy tale passed down the generations to glorify how we view the world of magic!"

A crimson aura erupted around Vlad.

"I have video evidence of that fairy tale in action!" the incubus snarled. "Wanna see it?!"

Nikolai stepped forward, his posture equally aggressive.

"None of you has ever fought my brother," he ground out. "Believe me when I say you should be afraid of Oscar. As for Barquiel, only Mae can match him."

Gerard furrowed his brow. "Barquiel?"

Karin's mouth became a thin line. "Who the hell is that?"

"He's an Archduke of Hell and the ninth leader of the Grigori," Mae stated, her voice calm despite her drumming heart and the anger bubbling through her veins. "He's the fallen angel who once went by the name *the Lightning of God*. He allied himself with the first Sorcerer King and each one who's taken the throne after him." She paused, her nails digging into her palms. "He's the reason why my father's kingdom fell."

Charlotte stirred. Ephra drew a sharp breath. Gerard blinked.

Karin opened and closed her mouth soundlessly, her face growing red.

"That's—that's preposterous!" she spat out. The witch glared at Bryony. "Is this the best lie the New York coven could come up with?! Well, it won't work." She pointed a finger at Mae. "She still has to go through the *Rites of Passage* to prove her allegiance to us!"

The hairs rose on the back of Mae's neck.

Brimstone went stiff in her arms. *Rites of Passage?*

"What the hell is the *Rites of Passage?*" Vlad said between gritted teeth.

CHAPTER THIRTY

Nikolai's heart knocked against his ribs.

He had a nasty inkling what Karin was talking about.

Bryony pressed her hands on the table and rose to her feet, eyes flashing emerald with magic. "Are you insane?!"

Penley hissed, hackles rising.

Nikolai had never seen the witch and her familiar so furious.

"How could you even suggest such a thing?" Marlena told Karin, horrified. Her terrier was growling at her side, his pupils crackling with moon magic. "That's an archaic tradition. It was banished hundreds of years ago and for good reason!" She stiffened, the color suddenly draining from her face. Her gaze swung jerkily to Ephra. "Wait. Is this why you asked me to bring the *Book of Light* to Philadelphia?!"

"Bloody hell!" Derrick swore.

Nadia flinched. "You brought the *Book of Light* here?!"

"Yes." Marlena swallowed, scowling. "Ephra insisted. But she wouldn't tell me why."

A chill coursed through Nikolai. The pieces of the puzzle were starting to fall into place. He could tell from Mae's hyper alertness that she'd come to the same conclusion as him.

"If someone doesn't tell us what this *Rites of Passage* is in the next fifteen seconds, I swear to God, heads are gonna roll," Vlad ground out.

Tarang bared his teeth at his side.

Mae laid a hand on the incubus's arm as he lurched forward. Vlad froze.

Nikolai sensed magic building up inside them. His insides twisted when he detected what they'd just felt. There was something in the room with them. Something that had just released the faintest pulse of corruption.

He reached for the core of his own power, Alastair bracing on his shoulder.

"The *Rites of Passage* is an oath which witches and sorcerers used to swear centuries past," Barbara said grimly, her furious stare locked on Ephra and Karin. "It involved making a pledge on a white magic grimoire called the *Book of Light*. The covenant was deemed a sacrilege after the magic communities realized it bound a piece of the soul of the one who entered the contract to the grimoire. It's been kept under lock and key in the Council of the Moon's secret archives since the Treaty of Argentheim."

Vlad drew a sharp breath.

Nikolai's eyes widened. *Fuck!*

"So, that's it," Mae said quietly. She turned to Charlotte Brix. "That's your end goal? To bind my soul to this book?"

Charlotte's fingers stilled on her knitting needles.

Confusion darted across the faces of the rest of the High Council.

"What are you talking about?" Ephra asked irately.

"It was Charlotte who suggested the *Rites of Passage* to us, Ephra," Raven said bitterly. "Remember, she said it would alleviate the concerns you, Karin, and Gerard expressed about Mae? And it's Charlotte who hasn't said a single word since this meeting started." The young witch glowered at the older woman, hurt darkening her eyes. "She's also the only one who entered this room without a familiar."

"Linus Jarrett will not be turning up for this gathering," Bryony said coldly while startled murmurs rose around them at the absence of Charlotte's bonded animal. "He passed a note to Mae last night, before he vanished from the hotel. He warned her that someone in the High Council was working for the Sorcerer King."

"Isabelle West isn't sick. She's been taken hostage by the Dark Council, probably to force Linus to do their dirty work. I sent a team to Phoenix last night." Raven fisted her hands. "They reported back to me at dawn today. Isabella was nowhere to be found. Her home was a mess and her butler and housekeeper were discovered buried in shallow graves in her garden.

They'd suffered injuries consistent with black magic attacks." A muscle twitched in her cheek as she studied Charlotte. "Linus was probably forced to hide all of this from his coven by the Dark Council."

Outraged gasps and cries erupted across the chamber.

Nikolai never looked away from the Atlanta coven High Priestess. Neither did Mae and Vlad.

The elderly witch sighed and put down her knitting needles. "So, that fool betrayed us, huh?"

Crimson energy burst around Mae. Brimstone and Hellreaver transformed. Nikolai unleashed his spear and a sphere of white magic. Vlad's black-diamond studs extended into a pair of swords as they dropped from his ears, incubus power pulsing violently around him and Tarang.

Panic laced Karin's voice. "What is going on?!"

Mae vaulted over the table. *"Now, Raven!"*

Charlotte cut her eyes to the young witch just as runes flashed into life on the floor beneath her. The rest of the High Council backed away from their tables, chairs clattering to the ground.

Ephra gasped. "What the—?!"

Horror rounded Karin and Gerard's eyes. Nadia cursed, the bangles on her wrists morphing into curved sabers that glowed with sun magic.

Something was happening to Charlotte. Something unreal. The old witch twitched and jerked in her chair, clothes rippling and flesh quivering with macabre eeriness.

"Bind!" Raven roared.

Her spell exploded upward, trapping the Atlanta High Priestess inside a viridescent prison. Nikolai's stomach churned as a pall of demonic energy bled the light from the room, the air so heavy with corruption it burned his eyes and throat.

Dammit! That barrier is barely holding her back!

Charlotte stood up, body growing taller and hair regaining its brightness. She snapped her fingers.

Raven's prison cracked and splintered.

Nikolai blinked. *How—?!*

Mae stiffened, pupils flaring with surprise.

"Tsk-tsk." Charlotte's voice changed, the pitch shifting to that of a much younger woman. "And here I thought we'd all have a pleasant morning getting to know one another. What a shame."

Nikolai's chest tightened as the one who had taken on Charlotte Brix's form finally shed her disguise, the remains of Raven's magic crumbling around her.

"*Rose!*" Mae hissed.

The demon in Rose's skin acknowledged her glare with a mocking smile. "Hello, Mae. It's been a long time."

She raised a leg and kicked her table violently across the chamber.

Derrick swore and jumped out of the way as it sailed toward him. The table missed him by inches and smashed into the wall. Golden light exploded in his palms and in his hawk's eyes.

"Who the hell is that?!" the sorcerer barked, his ring shifting into a double-ended spear.

"That's Rose Blake, Mae's best friend." Raven cast a

stiff look at Mae. "She was possessed by Barquiel during the incident in New York!"

Black lightning blossomed on Rose's fingertips.

She raised her hands, her smile turning savage.

MAE'S PULSE SPIKED, FURY TURNING TO ALARM. "*WATCH out!*"

Dark electricity forked out from the inky globes Barquiel had brought forth. They crackled and spat, pure malevolence in motion as they raced toward Derrick and the others.

"*Shield!*"

The word tore from the lips of every Council witch and sorcerer in the room. Defensive walls covered in runes flashed into life before them. The lightning smashed into the magic barriers.

They held.

Rose raised an eyebrow. "That's pretty good. I'm glad to see the power of the Councils has not been eroded by time." She smirked. "Let's see if you can cope with *this*."

A dark portal ripped open next to her. She reached inside the crimson-tinged opening and extracted Barquiel's demon sword from within it.

"What is that thing?!" Gerard exclaimed, ashen faced.

Light faded outside the hotel as Rose raised the obsidian blade above her head. A rumble of thunder reached Mae's ears.

Shit!

Brimstone swelled in size beside her when he grasped her intentions. Hellreaver snarled, a red aura enveloping his blades. Fire flooded Mae's blood as she drew on the sources of magic within her and their demonic energy.

Ozone tickled her nostrils. They had but seconds left before Barquiel brought black lightning down upon the building.

Mae raised one hand to the sky and called forth the only spell that could save them. *"Eclipse!"*

Thunder boomed, the sound so loud it smashed the light bulbs in the room.

The hairs rose on Mae's arms, static sparking the air ahead of the deadly bolt of electricity arrowing down from the Heavens. She gritted her teeth when she felt it strike *Eclipse* where it shielded the rooftop.

The hotel trembled. Plaster dust fell from the ceiling.

The quake passed as the spell swallowed the demonic bolt whole.

Rose's eyes flashed crimson. *"You bitch!"*

Mae bared her teeth. "It takes one to know one!"

Horns sprouted on Rose's forehead. Her skin darkened. Black wings snapped open on her back. Alarmed shouts tore across the chamber as she let loose the demon within, her eight-foot frame towering above all of them bar Brimstone.

Barquiel moved, his figure blurring.

His sword clashed with Hellreaver and Brimstone's claws in a shower of sparks. The impact rattled Mae's bones and drove her back a step where she grasped the dagger, her shoes leaving dark marks on the floor.

Barquiel scored her arm with his talons. Mae bit her lip at the sharp sting.

Brimstone snarled and sank his teeth in the demon's shoulder.

Barquiel's eyes flared at the sight of two figures darting toward him at blistering speed. Roars left Vlad and Nikolai's throats as they leapt into the air and attacked, fury distorting their features. Barquiel froze when their magic sizzled across his skin. Shock widened his pupils as the diamond blades and the spear scored his flanks.

The demon snarled. Dark scales sprouted from his flesh and drove out the incubus and the sorcerer's weapons as well as Brimstone's fangs. He staggered back a step, his scowling gaze dropping to the obsidian blood trickling from the wounds the two men had inflicted.

"How?!" He glared at Mae. "Is this your magic, witch?! These two weaklings should never have been able to touch me!"

Even Nikolai and Vlad looked stunned as they retreated to Mae's side, Tarang growling and Alastair squawking along menacingly.

"That's because my witch's soul has acknowledged these two as her potential mates," Brimstone proclaimed, his nine tails agitating the currents of corruption swarming the chamber. *"Their magic grows stronger because of her bond with them."*

Mae flushed as she met Vlad and Nikolai's stares. "What? It's not like I can control this stuff, okay?!"

Their expressions grew heated.

"Sure, cupcake." Vlad's lips tilted in a smile that made Mae's mouth go dry. He cut his eyes to Nikolai. "Does this mean you're thinking of a threesome? Not that I mind." He shrugged, still smirking. "I mean, he's kinda passable for a human."

The sorcerer recoiled. "Fuck no! Keep your incubus dick away from me, you hear?!"

Barquiel's enraged snarl focused their attention. Magic charged the air as the Council members prepared to join the attack.

The power of Hell prickled Mae's skin with her next heartbeat.

CHAPTER THIRTY-ONE

SHE LOOKED UP IN TIME TO SEE THE CEILING RIP APART. A dark portal opened in the concrete. It discharged a horde of black-magic users and demons.

"Dammit!" Mae scowled at the witches and sorcerers behind her. "You guys deal with them! Barquiel is ours!"

They nodded, their familiars' eyes aglow with their magic.

"*You think me so easy to defeat, witch?!*" Barquiel spat, incensed.

Mae's gaze clashed with the demon's. She gritted her teeth. "I don't doubt your strength. I just think it's a shame you're playing for the wrong side. That's why you and the Sorcerer King will lose."

Her veins swelled with magic in response to the anger burning through her. She jumped, twisted in mid-air, and back-kicked the demon viciously.

Barquiel's eyes bulged. He flew off his feet, sailed

across the chamber, and smashed through the wall. A harsh grunt left him as he crash-landed inside an empty conference room.

Vlad grimaced. "Ouch."

"Did you just strike a demon in the balls?" Raven asked Mae woodenly.

She deflected a Dark Council witch's attack and slashed the woman's throat with her magic-wreathed, twin short blades, her vine snake hissing where he coiled around her arm.

Mae slowly lowered her leg. "The bastard had it coming."

The conference door slammed open. Violet and Miles stormed inside.

"What'd we miss?!" Miles asked jovially.

Millie bobbed enthusiastically around his shoulders.

Miles's smile slipped as he scanned the room. "Well, shit. Leave some for us, won'tcha?"

He unleashed his saber and a sphere of golden, crackling magic.

Violet narrowed her eyes at the sight of Barquiel. "I see the scumbag of the Underworld is back." Purple light flared on her fingertips and in Trixie's pupils. "Is that Redheaded Toad here too?"

"Redheaded Toad?" Derrick asked, confused.

"She means Oscar," Miles explained.

Nikolai lowered his brows. "No, we haven't seen my brother."

Barquiel rose from the pulverized remains of the

table he'd destroyed. He shook his head dazedly and leveled a crimson glare at Mae. He headed for the hole in the wall, his claws clinking resolutely on the floor as he closed the distance to them.

Mae startled, feeling Brimstone's sudden agitation.

The demon fox stepped in front of her. "*Get back, Mae!*"

A grunt of pain tore from the familiar the next instant. The floor shuddered as he collapsed, his massive body almost filling the circle. Fear squeezed Mae's heart.

Brimstone was being forced down by something she couldn't see. Hellreaver crashed next to him with a snarl, similarly immobilized.

"Brim! Hell!"

She dashed toward them, only to rock to a stop at their desperate pleas.

"*Stay away, my witch!*" Brimstone groaned.

Don't come closer! Hellreaver grunted. *Please!*

Blood pounded in Mae's ears, her heart racing so fast it was almost a continuous drumming. She could feel Brimstone and Hellreaver's souls struggling against a power greater than them.

Panic dulled her senses. *What is this?!*

Na Ri's voice came to her faintly. *It's—*

"That's Charlotte's magic!" Karin shouted. She pointed at the shimmering, blue light escaping Barquiel's right fist. "I'd recognize it anywhere!"

Nausea churned Mae's stomach. The demon bared his teeth in a feral grin and unfurled his hand, exposing a shivering, pale globe laced with crimson and dark threads.

Is that how he managed to shatter Raven's spell?! With magic?! But how did he get his hands on—?!

The truth came to her in a flash. Mae pressed a hand to her mouth and swallowed down bile. *Oh God! What have they done?!*

"That's not just her magic!" she mumbled. "That's her soul!"

Bryony gasped. Barbara cursed.

The implication of Mae's words leeched the blood from the face of every Council witch and sorcerer in the room.

"Charlotte's dead?!" Raven said numbly.

Invisible bands squeezed Mae's arms to her body before she could answer, snatching a startled cry from her lips. She fell to her knees. The restraints choked the air from her lungs as they tightened savagely around her ribcage. Dozens of invisible whips flogged her flesh. Redness bloomed on the cuts. She screamed, the cocktail of corrupt magic and demonic energy Barquiel wielded attacking her nerve endings.

Whiteness exploded in Nikolai's eyes and hands. "*Mae!*"

The heat of his magic washed across her skin in a powerful wave. A second wave followed as Vlad's incubus energy rippled across the room in a crimson tide.

"You bastard!" Vlad snarled. "*Let her go!*"

The two men charged Barquiel, only to be viciously cast aside by the demon before they even reached him. Horror drained the strength from Mae's limbs as she watched them slam into the wall. A spiderweb of cracks exploded outward from the points of impact. They slid to the floor, half dazed and bleeding.

Tarang's snarl cut off abruptly as he crashed down beside the incubus, his large form growing deathly still. Alastair screeched and thudded into the sorcerer's chest, left wing drooping.

Violet and Miles went after Barquiel. They were thrown back brutally by the demon's newly acquired powers, the only thing saving them from injury the shield Barbara and Bryony cast to cushion their fall.

Barquiel raised his face to the sky and bellowed, his features twisting in triumph. Despair drenched Mae in a cold sweat.

No! Black spots filled her vision as her oxygen-starved brain started to falter. *Not like this! IT CANNOT END LIKE THIS!*

She didn't realize she'd screamed the words out loud until they reverberated around her, drowning out all sounds to the point she thought even the city grew still. Barquiel faltered, wariness replacing the victorious glow in his pupils. He startled as the floor started to tremble.

Na Ri's presence filled Mae with the next beat of her heart, their souls shaking the very foundations of the building. Mae's breath stuttered.

There was another there. A light she had never glimpsed before, hidden within Na Ri. The agony crippling Mae's body faded on a soothing wave that smelled like a bright, summer day. She blinked, cognizance exploding into a singular truth.

Ran—Ran Soyun?!

Tears dripped down her cheeks.

"Mother?!" Mae mumbled weakly, the word underscored by Na Ri's tortured voice.

Ran Soyun whispered through her mind. *Invoke the spell, my daughters...*

Fire blazed inside Mae's heart at the first witch's command. It ignited her magic core and sent bright lines of power through the bond connecting her to Brimstone and Hellreaver.

The demon fox trembled and shifted, one leg unbending. The weapon snarled and slowly tipped himself onto a pointed blade, metal vibrating under the pressure still weighing him down.

Mae's brows met, the power of three binding them once more. She bared her teeth and barked out the conjuration rising from the depths of her subconscious.

"Negate!"

Charlotte's soul quivered, the pale orb flaring with brightness.

Barquiel cursed as the cage of black magic and hell power containing it broke. He took a step back, bewildered.

Brimstone slowly climbed to his feet, his energy returning. Hellreaver howled and exposed his fangs, a scarlet aura detonating along his blades as he levitated off the ground.

The bands holding Mae prisoner fell away. She

rose, the blood dripping down her arms and legs slowing as her wounds healed. She lifted her right hand, fingers trembling.

"*Soul Shield!*"

Barquiel recoiled as a crimson sphere covered in pale runes wrapped around the only thing that remained of Charlotte Brix. He let go jerkily, the white magic burning him.

Mae drew the orb to her, her heart seething with fury.

She caught movement out the corner of her eye.

A portal tore open next to Hellreaver. Oscar emerged from it, an inky globe in one hand and his sword in the other, his lynx Drabek coiling sinuously around his legs. The sorcerer grabbed Hellreaver.

"*No!*" Mae screamed.

Oscar blurred across the floor and slammed the weapon into the distant wall, his eyes obsidian with black magic. Darkness swarmed Hellreaver as he struggled in Oscar's grip, his scarlet aura dampening under the magic assault.

Mae's stomach lurched. "*Hell!*"

She and Brimstone moved as one.

Barquiel blocked them with his broadsword, wings spreading wide and a powerful demonic aura pulsing around his body as he braced.

"*Let him go, you foul man!*" Brimstone snarled at Oscar over the demon's head, thick flecks of drool falling from his jaws.

The sorcerer snatched the bronze skeleton key dangling off Hellreaver's knuckle guard and cast the weapon to the far side of the room. "We have the book, Barquiel." He returned to the portal at lightning speed, smirked at Nikolai's semi-conscious form, and frowned at the demon. "Did you get what you came here for?"

Barquiel's eyes flashed crimson. He sprang back and glared at Mae, his hand curling into a fist. "Yes."

"Then, let us leave."

Oscar vanished inside the gate.

Barquiel followed.

Hellreaver snarled and arrowed toward the closing rift.

"No!" Mae barked.

"*Don't!*" Brimstone warned.

Hellreaver froze at their shouts, his rage making the air shudder. The Dark Council magic users and demons still standing retreated rapidly to the portal they had appeared from, leaving their fallen comrades behind.

A breathless stillness descended as the rift closed. Distant screams punctuated the sudden silence. The blare of sirens rose from the street below.

"Nikolai!" Marlena rushed to the sorcerer's side, her face drained of all color.

"They have the *Book of Light?!*" Nadia said numbly, her sabers dangling limply in her grasp.

Derrick retracted his spear, jaw clenched tight. "I can't think what else they'd be talking about." He looked questioningly at Mae. "What was that key?"

Mae ignored him and headed over to Nikolai and Vlad, her steps leaden. Though the two men and their familiars were still breathing, they hadn't moved since Barquiel attacked them and were bleeding heavily from their wounds. Fear consumed her, dragging her down into a pit of despair.

Please! Please be alright!

Marlena stiffened, terror rounding her eyes. "Oh God! *Klara!*"

CHAPTER THIRTY-TWO

"I'M ALRIGHT, MOTHER," KLARA KOSEK SAID FOR THE tenth time while Marlena fussed over her.

A grimace flitted across her face as she shifted her broken arm. Her anxious gaze locked on the unconscious man lying on a couch across the room.

Linus Jarrett's rib cage shuddered with his ragged breathing as three healers worked on his injuries. He had lost a lot of blood and was covered in a sheen of sweat. His cat pressed against his flank, fur trembling and pupils wide with panic.

Penley sat next to the shaken familiar and licked her from time to time, comforting rumbles vibrating from him.

Linus had been with Oscar when the Dark Council had ambushed Klara in her room. As the future High Priestess of the Council of the Moon, she had been tasked with guarding the *Book of Light*. Seeing as the only people who'd known the grimoire would be at the hotel were Marlena and the High Council, the Council of the Moon had refrained from putting a strong security detail in place in case it drew unwanted attention.

Instead of killing Klara like Oscar had ordered him to do, Linus had rebelled and protected her instead. Oscar had timed the attack so that Mae and the Councils' attention would be focused on Barquiel rather than on what was happening two floors below them. With *Nullify* only being active at the time of its casting, Mae had failed to detect their black magic when they'd rifted inside the hotel. Brimstone had been similarly distracted. Barquiel's demonic presence had been yet another confounding factor that had helped mask the presence of other demons in the building.

Mae stood by a window, her nails scoring her palms. The turmoil outside The Azure had finally died down. Considering what had passed, the hotel and the rest of the city were remarkably unscathed. Bar some broken glass littering the pavements outside the hotel and minor structural damage to the building, there wasn't much to see. The whole thing was being put down as a freak accident of nature, the clouds that had briefly darkened the sky adding to the story.

It was thanks to *Eclipse* swallowing Barquiel's black lightning that they weren't looking at the same level of devastation that had rocked New York upon her awakening. April's relationship with the local mayor and the city's police chief meant they'd managed to keep the press away from The Azure. No one had been allowed to see the destruction wreaked upon the conference chambers on the sixth floor or Klara's room.

A shudder raced down Mae's spine as she thought of what could have been had she not acted when she did.

So many lives would have been lost.

Hellreaver lay heavily on her chest. The weapon had been subdued since the attack. Despite her and Brimstone's reassurances, Mae knew he was blaming himself for what had happened in the conference room.

Her gaze swept the main sitting room of the Royal Suite and the dozen or so injured witches and sorcerers who were being treated by various coven healers. It was the largest place where they could assemble away from the curious eyes of those attending the Annual Grand Meeting, as well as from normal humans.

Mae had no doubt news of what had happened that morning would spread through the covenstead like wildfire. She was coming to realize that there was no bigger gossip than a witch. Even Mrs. Son-Ha would be impressed.

She studied Linus with a faint frown. *He must have known he was signing Isabelle West's death warrant when he decided to switch sides mid-battle.*

Or he believed in you, Brimstone said quietly where he sat in his small fox form beside her. *All of you.*

Raven was talking rapidly to someone on her cell

phone, brow furrowed and voice low and tense. They had found Isabelle an hour ago, moments before the injured High Priestess was about to be executed by a group of Dark Council sorcerers and witches.

It was thanks to Jared that they'd managed to locate the missing witch. The Immortals had the most advanced satellite network in the world and Jared had called in a favor to use their tracking system last night. He'd managed to pick up the last place where Isabelle's cell phone had been active several weeks ago.

Once they'd been made aware of what was happening behind their backs and their most senior witches and sorcerers had been shown the graves in Isabelle's garden, the Phoenix coven had helped Raven's team comb every square foot in a five-mile radius around the location Jared had identified.

Linus hadn't been the only one who had come to Klara's defense that morning. April, Regina, and Erik had been on the same floor at the time of the attack and had sensed the demonic energy and black magic coming from her room. Mae clenched her teeth.

Still, none of them had stood a chance against Oscar and the Dark Council.

A lump formed in her throat as she gazed at Nikolai and Vlad.

Just like they didn't stand a chance against Barquiel once he activated the magic he'd stolen from Charlotte Brix.

Nadia and a host of healers were working on the two men. Tarang and Alastair's injuries had already been healed by Marlena and they lay sleeping on the floor next to their masters, still exhausted from the fight. Though April's coven headquarters had a hospital less than a mile and a half from the hotel, Nadia and Marlena had deemed most of the injured too unstable to move yet.

Mae still wasn't sure how Barquiel had been able to wield Charlotte's soul magic and why it had made him so strong. She clenched her jaw.

We need to find out the answer to that question or else we may never be able to defeat him and the Sorcerer King.

There was something else that puzzled her. And that was what Oscar had said to Barquiel before they escaped through the portal.

I thought Barquiel was just there as a distraction so Oscar could get his hands on the skeleton key. Mae chewed her lip. *What did I miss?*

It didn't help that *Nullify* hadn't worked when she'd cast the spell shortly after the battle ended. It had failed to detect black magic users in the vicinity of the hotel.

They had to be close. Mae knitted her brow. *Which means they've either found a way to counter my spell or there's something else at play.*

The golden light blazing from Nadia's hands and the pale illumination coming from one of Marlena's sorcerers caught her eye. The magics the Councils of the Moon and the Sun possessed were the best at healing among all the covens. Moon Magic and Sun Magic, Bryony had called them. She could sense their difference from conventional magic.

I should study them in more detail when I have time.

Bryony appeared in the doorway of the lounge. Her

face tightened as she looked around the room, her gaze lingering on Nikolai and Vlad.

She crossed the floor to Mae. "Ephra wants a word."

"How are Violet and Miles?"

"They're okay." Bryony sighed. "They're just upset they couldn't be of more help."

Relief loosened the knot in Mae's belly. She was glad some of them had escaped the encounter with Barquiel relatively unscathed.

"And April and Regina?"

Bryony rolled her eyes. "Don't worry about those fools. It would take an act of God to kill them."

Mae swallowed a smile. She could tell Bryony was hiding her relief.

Raven joined them as they exited the room.

"Any news on Isabelle?" Bryony asked the young witch.

"Her injuries aren't life threatening. She's being treated by her coven healers. She asked after Linus." Raven gritted her teeth. "I can't believe we missed the signs. They were there all along!"

"We all missed them, Raven. Linus was never the most talkative person in the first place. His silence at High Council meetings was nothing out of the ordinary."

"Still, the fact that he slipped Mae that note and was brave enough to fight Oscar in the end speaks volume for the kind of man that he is." Raven faltered. "I'm not sure I could have done the same in his place if the life of someone I cherished was at stake."

The witch's stilted words hung awkwardly between them.

They reached Bryony's room. Ephra, Karin, Gerard, and Derrick were inside. They hadn't moved from the table where *Soul Shield* hovered, the light of the spell painting their pale faces with shades of crimson as they stared at the soul orb floating within it.

Ephra turned. Mae met the witch's stricken gaze.

"How long?" she asked numbly.

Mae swallowed a tired sigh. "How long has she been dead? I wouldn't know without seeing the body." She hesitated, raking her hair with her hand. "But the brightness of her soul tells me it was likely in the last seven to ten days. Before you guys had that meeting with Bryony."

"I spoke to her delegation." Karin's voice was dead, all the vim and vigor Mae had witnessed since she'd met the witch drained by the reality of what they had witnessed. "They didn't mention anything untoward happening recently. But her aide did bring up one thing. Charlotte disappeared for three hours, about a week ago. No one could reach her. She claimed she had a private medical matter to attend to and hadn't wanted to make a fuss."

"Then her body is still in Atlanta," Mae said flatly. "If it's there, I'll find it. Probably."

"How?" someone said behind Mae.

She looked over her shoulder.

Barbara had entered the room, a glum-looking Violet and Miles at her side.

"Hey," Mae murmured.

"Hi," the cousins mumbled back.

Mae narrowed her eyes slightly at Barbara. "By the way, has anybody ever told you that you move like a cat? I swear there's some kind of hover spell on your cane and shoes."

The elderly witch's solemn expression did not change. "You haven't answered my question."

Her terrier Thorn woofed gently beside her.

Mae looked at Brimstone.

The fox shrugged. *Might as well show them.*

Mae walked over to the table and touched *Soul Shield.*

Magic sparked against her skin. The white runes converged to form a dazzling line that connected to her index finger. Gasps sounded as she stretched the pale thread away from the spinning, red sphere. The orb inside it flickered.

Mae's stomach curdled as she relived the suffering Charlotte had experienced in her final moments on this Earth. She'd only glimpsed it before, when she'd cast *Soul Shield.* There was no point torturing the witch's friends with the harrowing details of her demise.

She clenched her teeth and kept her voice steady by a sheer act of will. "There's a lingering connection between a soul and their mortal coil. How long it remains after death is anyone's guess. As long as it still exists, I can locate the body."

A stunned hush followed.

"When did you..." Karin stopped and swallowed, "when did you realize you could do this?!"

Mae let go of the bright cord. It snapped back onto the scarlet globe, the runes expanding once more to cover the surface. "When I broke the spell suppressing Nikolai's powers. And when I freed the soul of a possessed sorcerer two days ago, in New York."

Gerard sat down heavily in a chair, shellshocked.

"I get the feeling there's a lot we still haven't talked about," Derrick said stiffly.

CHAPTER THIRTY-THREE

THE DOOR SLAMMED OPEN BEFORE ANY OF THEM COULD say another word.

Marlena stormed in. "They're dying! Nikolai and Linus!" Her voice broke. "Nadia can't help them and neither can I! She doesn't know if Vlad will—"

Mae stormed past the witch, Brimstone running by her side. Her heartbeat roared in her ears, the terror within her so overwhelming she wanted to throw up. Ice prickled her skin as she skidded to a stop in the doorway of the sitting room.

Linus's bleeding had worsened and he had started to gasp his last breaths. Nikolai was as white as a sheet and Alastair's feathers grew duller by the second as he shuddered on the floor next to the sorcerer. The blueness was fading from Tarang's irises. The tiger lifted a trembling paw and laid it on Vlad's limp hand.

"Brim! What can I do?!" Mae's breath hitched. "There must be something I can do!"

Tears blurred her vision and fell down her cheeks.

Brimstone's shadow fell upon her as he morphed into his nine-tail spirit form.

The fox's voice was tortured. *"My witch."*

Hellreaver transformed. *There's a spell! I saw Ran Soyun use it once, when Na Ri was still a babe and had a fever. Ran took on the burden of Na Ri's illness!*

"No!" Brimstone snapped his jaws close to Hellreaver. *"That was a fever! Mae could die if she tries to absorb these men's wounds!"*

Hellreaver's aura swamped them, his frustration making the air tremble. *And she will never recover if she loses them, you dumb fox!*

"What's the spell, Hell?!" Mae asked grimly.

She wiped her face angrily, determination filling her bones. Bryony and the others had followed her inside the room and were staring at her in confusion. Brimstone gnashed his teeth.

Mae laid a hand against his leg, her entire body vibrating with tension and dread. "I *have* to do this! Help me! *Please!*"

The fox's face swam before her as more tears welled up. He lowered his head and licked the salty drops.

"Alright." Brimstone looked at Hellreaver, resigned. *"Tell her the spell."*

Hellreaver hummed. *Ran Soyun called it Assimilate. It will use up your own magic fast, so make sure to pace yourself.*

"We'll reinforce your healing abilities," Brimstone promised.

Mae heeded their warnings and squeezed her eyes shut. She searched the archives of spells that resided deep within her consciousness frantically, her thoughts a mess.

Come on, where are you?!

Light sparked in the shadows. The spell floated up toward her, insubstantial at first. The runes making it up coalesced.

Mae analyzed the spell, took a deep breath, and drew on her magic. *"Assimilate!"*

Fire lanced her left flank as the incantation resonated across the room. She gripped her side hard, blood blooming under her fingers and soaking her top. The matching wound that had ripped open Nikolai's stomach and spleen started to close.

The power of three bubbled through her veins and started to heal her body from the inside out, blazing bright.

A gasp left her as her rib cage caved in. Her right thigh snapped with a loud crack, severing her femoral artery. Mae cried out and fell on one knee. A hot, coppery taste filled her throat. She spat out a mouthful of blood just as Linus's breathing started to normalize and the swelling in his leg subsided.

"Mae?!" Violet mumbled, horror lacing her voice. "What are you doing?!"

"My witch," Brimstone moaned woefully.

He leaned heavily into her. Hellreaver whined and worked himself under her hands where she clutched the floor.

Mae's fingers spasmed and closed around him, heart thundering and breathing ragged. The spell was consuming her magic at the same speed the weapon and the familiar replenished her core.

Pain gripped her skull next, so fierce it felt like she'd been struck by lightning. Color seeped into Vlad's face as his cerebral bleed dissipated, relieving the pressure on his brain. Tarang's irises started darkening to a vivid blue.

"Stop!" Marlena barked. "*You will die!*"

Nadia clutched Marlena's arm as she went to grab Mae's shoulder. "Don't! That spell will annihilate you if you touch her right now!"

Brimstone's giant shape was shrinking, his body unable to maintain his full form. "*Mae!*"

"Her hair," Miles said hoarsely. "What's happening to her hair?!"

Mae's heartbeat boomed in her ears, her nerve endings seared by a thousand suns as the spell continued to take its toll on her body. She blinked and caught a glimpse of her hair where it hung past her face.

It was turning white.

She gritted her teeth, her soul and magic core warping at speeds she'd never experienced before, her body healing itself over and over again even as she absorbed the injuries of the three men.

Realization dawned at the same time the other healers cried out in alarm, wrenching her breath from her lips.

Not just them! The room tilted around her. *Assimilate is healing everyone in the room! And their familiars too!*

Mae fell face down on the floor amidst a cacophony

of shouts. She blinked. Brimstone and Hellreaver lay quivering beside her in their smaller forms.

"Thank you," she whispered.

Brimstone licked her face feebly. Hellreaver pulsed with the faintest red light. Mae's heart thumped heavily against her ribs, each tortured pulsation dragging her down into a darkness from which she feared she might never return. Relief sighed through her mind. She had saved the people who had risked their lives to fight the Dark Council, including the two men who mattered the most to her. And she would do it all over again if she had to.

A hand touched her back, warming her cold flesh.

Tendons screamed in Mae's neck as she turned her head a fraction.

It was Violet. Tears dripped down the witch's furious face, her pupils and those of Trixie blazing with purple magic. Miles and Millie followed, the snake coiling around Mae's leg while Miles pressed his fingers to her back. Barbara, Bryony, Raven, and everyone else joined them along with their familiars, their powers burning her skin as they touched her.

"Take it!" Karin snarled. "Take our magic, dammit! *We will not have you die, you hear?!*"

Na Ri's voice reached Mae faintly. *It's okay, Mae. They are our people.*

Mae shuddered. She was aware she had the ability to absorb the magic of others. It had always been an unconscious act in the past, one over which she had zero control. Except there was a spell that could help her do it in a restrained manner, without sucking dry every magic core in the vicinity. It had come to her moments ago.

She had refused to incant it, too scared of what it would do.

Na Ri's words gave her the courage she needed to voice it. Mae called on her last remaining reserves of magic and incanted the spell, the word a whisper on her numb lips.

"*Absorb...*"

Heat exploded inside her, bright and incandescent. It soaked her flesh and her bones in all the colors of the rainbow, the magic of the witches and sorcerers around her surging toward the cores of power in her heart and belly. She sucked in air as her strength returned with every beat of her worn-out heart, her hair darkening to inky black once more. Brimstone raised his head weakly, his fur regaining its richness and shine. Hellreaver's aura reignited with a scarlet flash.

"Mae?"

Vlad had opened his eyes. He rose on one elbow, his face still pale.

Nikolai sat up slowly and groaned. "What the hell happened?" He clutched his head and froze when he saw her. He lunged from the couch and fell on his knees, eyes wide with fear and hand reaching out to her. "*Mae!*"

Mae clenched her jaw and ended *Absorb* before it could drain the cores of everyone who had gifted her their magic. They stepped back to give her space as she pushed up onto her hands and knees, their heaving chests and flushed faces signs of the toll her spell had exerted on their bodies.

Mae swallowed heavily. Though her mouth tasted like ash and her head still throbbed, she felt like herself once more. Strong hands pulled her to her feet. She swayed and blinked.

Nikolai and Vlad looped their arms around her and steadied her.

The incubus glanced around the room, suspicion furrowing his brow. "Why do I get the distinct feeling that you just did something foolish, Princess?"

The wounded sorcerers and witches were coming to slowly.

Violet scowled. "You scared the shit out of us!"

She punched Mae lightly in the ribs.

"Ouch." Mae grimaced when Violet blanched. "I'm kidding. I'm all healed up, see?"

She pulled up her top and showed them her unblemished skin.

Vlad sucked in air. "Whoa there. We should do that in private, cupcake."

Mae narrowed her eyes. "You have a one-track mind, you know that?"

"Are you just permanently horny?" Nikolai snapped at the incubus.

Abraham stormed the sitting room with Mila. "What the hell happened?" The aide's eyes rounded as he observed the bloody mess around him. He slowed to a stop, the color draining from his face. "Shit! Was it the Dark Council?!"

Bryony sighed. "It's a long story."

Mila looked around curiously. "Did you guys fight demons?"

Abraham startled. "How did you know that?"

"I have angel blood, remember?" A golden light bloomed across Mila's skin briefly. "I can smell them from a mile away. Besides, a bunch of them regularly visit us in Chicago." The Immortal made a face. "I'm familiar with *Eau de L'Enfer.*"

Ryu, Yoo-Mi, and Ye-Seul sauntered in behind her, Noah in their wake.

Ryu looked around. "Wow. You guys look like you had a wild party. Maybe we should have stayed for this meeting."

Mae pursed her lips. "It was a riot."

"Is everyone okay?" Noah asked tersely.

Derrick looked from Mae to the sorcerers and witches she had healed. "We are now."

Ryu stiffened, concern clouding her face.

"I'm alright," Mae said quietly.

Linus stirred. He blinked his eyes open and froze.

"Am I dead?" the sorcerer groaned.

They followed his stilted gaze to the tall, hooded, skeletal figure with the scythe standing quietly next to his couch. Half the room gasped and shrank back.

Alicia's orbits flared crimson as she met a sea of horrified stares. "I'm sorry. You seemed to be having a touching reunion. I didn't want to interrupt."

Karin swayed. Gerard clutched her shoulder and steadied her.

"I kinda forgot to tell you guys about Alicia," Bryony announced glassily. "Alicia, these are my friends. Everyone, this is Thod, the Queen of Soul Reapers. She goes by the name of Alicia Calvarro in this, er, guise."

Ye-Seul sniggered.

Yoo-Mi sniffed. "Your bones are showing again, lady."

Alicia blinked. "Oh." She looked down and frowned. "Dammit, I always forget to switch."

She snapped her fingers and morphed into her human appearance.

The room sighed in relief. The sound was drowned out by an almighty rumble.

Mae made a face at their stares. "Sorry."

Yoo-Mi narrowed her eyes. "Not that I disapprove of your healthy appetite, but I really don't know where you put all that food." She indicated the bloodied couches with a vague wave. "Also, these are going to be a bitch to clean. I hope we have insurance."

CHAPTER THIRTY-FOUR

"The ghouls are being actively recruited by Barquiel and his minions," Alicia said.

Mae's hand stilled on the piece of fried chicken she'd just picked up. Tension knotted her shoulders. "Any idea why?"

They'd cleared the sitting room for an impromptu, late-lunch meeting. Heavy crunching rose from where Brimstone, Hellreaver, and Tarang were inhaling entire bowls of fresh meat. A serving trolley with plenty more stood next to them, with another one on its way.

Brimstone had made space for Nadia's desert fox and Derrick's hawk. The rest of the familiars were eating primly on the clean stretch of floor beside the hungry carnivores.

"It took a while to corner one of them," Alicia grumbled. "They're slippery little shits, especially down there. The one I captured wouldn't speak at first, but I can be pretty persuasive."

Her scythe glinted at the base of her throat.

Gerard shifted uneasily in his chair.

"According to the ghoul, Barquiel promised them some kind of redemption in return for their sacrifice," Alicia continued.

Vlad frowned. "Redemption?"

"What kind of absolution could an Archduke of Hell offer other demons?" April said, puzzled.

Crimson flared briefly in Alicia's pupils. "That's the thing. I can't think of anything. And as far as what kind of sacrifice Barquiel meant, he didn't know the details."

Frustration gnawed at Mae. Linus hadn't been able to reveal more than they already knew before he'd left to join his coven in Phoenix. Oscar and Barquiel had never confided in the sorcerer. His only task had been to act as their spy in the High Council and help them infiltrate the hotel.

We're nowhere closer to figuring out their end game. She knitted her brow. *It evidently wasn't about trapping my soul in that book, or they would have done their damnedest to take me with them.*

"What was that skeleton key?" Derrick asked. "The one Oscar stole?"

Bryony filled in those in the room still not in the know on the recent incidents in New York and what they had learned from Agnes. Abraham reported on the entity Mae had discovered inside the dead sorcerer possessed by a ghoul and what they had done with it.

Regina's eyes gleamed shrewdly as she observed Nikolai and Vlad. "So, you two stud muffins are the only ones who can see the ghouls' auras besides Mae?"

"*Mother!*" Erik wailed.

Mae couldn't help but note the surreptitious looks the sorcerer kept stealing at Violet. The Chicago witch was doing her best to pretend she hadn't noticed and kept up a frosty mien. Mae masked a wry smile.

Ten bucks says those two end up locking lips before we leave Philadelphia.

Vlad slipped his arm lazily atop the back rest of their couch, distracting her. The smile that curved his mouth quickened Mae's pulse. "According to the fox, our energies are starting to sync. We're soon to be lovers after all."

Mae sucked in air before elbowing the incubus sharply in the side.

"Ouch." Vlad chuckled and rubbed his flank. "I didn't know pain was your kink, Princess." He arched an eyebrow, smile widening. "Seeing as you healed my injuries, I'd be more than happy to oblige if you want to get rough in the bedroom."

Mae blushed to the roots of her hair and spluttered incoherently.

"How about we take this outside?" Nikolai growled.

The spare rib he was holding snapped in two, his fingers clenching in a way that suggested he wished they were wrapped around the incubus's neck.

The three of them became aware of a battery of leaden stares.

Violet wrinkled her nose. "Is it me or is their flirting getting worse?"

"You obviously haven't spent enough time in Chicago lately," Mila muttered.

The Immortal had sat in on the meeting and had kept her silence so far.

Alicia's jaw set in a hard line. "You guys should just get it over with and have sex."

Mae groaned. Nikolai's brows met in the middle of his forehead.

Vlad shrugged nonchalantly. "Like I said. I don't mind a threesome if that's what Mae wants."

"*It is not!*" Mae barked.

"I will cut you," Nikolai grated out.

Ephra drummed her fingers impatiently on the armrest of her chair. "Can we get back on topic?"

Mae sighed and rubbed the back of her neck. "We were aware the key had something to do with this covenstead from what Agnes revealed to Nikolai last night. But we didn't know what Barquiel and the Dark Council might intend to do with it." She made a face. "A fact that hasn't changed."

"Maybe we're overcomplicating this," Raven said pensively.

"What do you mean?"

Raven met her puzzled gaze. "Oscar mentioned the key in the same breath as the *Book of Light*. Could it have to do with the grimoire itself?"

Mae blinked. *Damn! I didn't think of that!*

Brimstone's ears perked up.

Mae turned to Marlena, muscles tensing. "Does the book have a lock of sorts?"

The witch shook her head. "No. It has intricate metal covers, but nothing that remotely resembles a keyhole."

Mae deflated.

Brimstone transformed, startling them. "*I recall something I heard Azazel tell Ran Soyun once.*" He came over and plopped down beside Mae. "*Does anyone know the story of the first Sorcerer King?*"

There was a general shaking of heads.

Mila shrugged with a clear this-is-not-my-rodeo expression.

"The only ones who have knowledge about that man are the Sorcerer Kings who came after him," Nikolai said bitterly.

Surprise jolted Mae at that. "Does that include your father?"

A muscle jumped in Nikolai's jawline. "I would bet my life on it."

"*Azazel would never utter his name.*" Brimstone's eyes grew distant. "*Even Ran Soyun did not know it. But my master did disclose one thing to his wife. The pact he made with the first man he granted magic to involved sealing his mortal soul in a grimoire.*"

Mae's heart stuttered. "What?!"

The Councils exchanged stunned looks.

"Are you certain?" Derrick said in a strained voice.

"*Yes, I am.*"

Mae could see cogwheels turning in everyone's minds at the familiar's bombshell statement. *Is this something we could use to defeat the Sorcerer King?!*

Brimstone lowered his head on his paws and side-eyed Mae. "*He was meant to do the same with Ran, but he could only bring himself to enslave half her soul in the end.*"

"Wait." Mae lowered her brows, confused.

"Wouldn't that make the Sorcerer King weaker? I thought a soul was necessary for a magic core to exist."

Crimson flared in Brimstone's pupils. "*The power Azazel granted the Sorcerer King went beyond that. Which is why his betrayal makes it impossible for me to forgive him.*"

"Are you implying the *Book of Light* is that grimoire?" Marlena mumbled, ashen faced.

"*No. Azazel referred to the text as the* Book of Shadows."

Mae's chest tightened. "But you think the *Book of Light* and that key have something to do with the *Book of Shadows*?"

"*I cannot say for certain. But, if the current Sorcerer King is after the grimoire Oscar stole today, it might be as powerful as the* Book of Shadows *in a way we are yet unaware of.*"

Marlena's knuckles whitened on her lap. "But—the *Book of Light* has never been used as a weapon in all of its history."

"You said it's absorbed a piece of the soul of every magic user who ever made a pledge upon it." Vlad clenched his jaw. "Could that be what they're after?"

Surprise widened Marlena's eyes.

"I doubt those fragments of soul are what they're after," Mae muttered. "They're incomplete and wouldn't be of much use to them."

She fisted her hands. She couldn't help but feel they were missing something.

She looked over at Mila. "What did you and Madeleine find in the samples we gave you? It must be the reason you came here with Abraham, right?"

The Immortal exchanged a guarded glance with the aide.

"The pineal gland inside *Ice Fortress* and the blood you took from that witch contain a virus," Mila said quietly.

Dread squeezed Mae's heart.

Karin frowned. "A virus?"

"A modified one." Mila's face hardened. "The technique used to make it undeniably originated from an Immortal."

Mae's mouth went dry. "Is Agnes going to be okay?!"

"I only found fragments of the virus in her blood." Mila indicated Nikolai. "Whatever he did to her destroyed the infection."

Karin looked troubled at that. The High Council had been informed of Nikolai's abilities with relation to ley lines. Mae could tell it worried not just them, but the Council of the Sun too.

Is that why Marlena wants him? Because of what he can do?

Mae instantly chastised herself for her suspicions. It was clear how much Marlena cared for Nikolai. Whatever her motivations were for wanting him at her side, it wasn't because she sought power.

"What does this virus do?" April asked stiffly.

"We can only extrapolate from what Mae and Nikolai described to us, but Madeleine and I believe it allows a ghoul to enter the body of a magic user and control it." Mila sighed at their blank expressions. "The virus acts a primer. It makes the body of the host ready to receive a parasite. We think it only works on magic users." The Immortal knitted her brow. "One thing we couldn't decipher was the genetic material it contained. We've never seen anything like it. And there was something bound to it." The look Mila gave Mae made the hairs rise on her nape. "Something that resembles the spells you froze inside *Ice Fortress*."

Ephra looked between them, confused. "What?"

Bryony paled.

Violet drew a sharp breath. "Magic? You're saying there's *magic* in that thing?!"

Mila grimaced. "It's our first time analyzing something like that, so we can't say for sure. But as scientists, all Madeleine and I can tell you is that the core characteristics of your spells match what we found inside those samples."

Mae's mind raced. She scowled at the floor. "So, they need magic users to act as recipients for the ghouls."

"And they want the ghouls to be sacrifices for something," Alicia said slowly.

"The ghouls were guarding the key," Nikolai murmured.

Vlad frowned. "They came to Philadelphia to get their hands on the key and the *Book of Light*."

Bryony clenched her jaw. "A book of power that contains fragments of magic souls."

"They combined magic with a new kind of DNA," April said stiffly.

A ringing sounded in Mae's ears. Her breath locked

in her throat, the pieces of the puzzle finally falling into place.

Nikolai straightened, his eyes fierce. "What is it, Mae?"

Mae's heart thudded painfully against her ribs as she turned to Vlad.

"You're wrong," she said numbly.

Vlad stared. "What do you mean?"

Mae shuddered, the enormity of their mistake sinking into her bones like shackles. *Oh God! How could I have been such a fool?!* That's *what Oscar meant!*

"They weren't just after the book and the key."

Brimstone growled when her thoughts reached him. Hellreaver hummed dangerously and came over to her side.

Mae touched the unblemished skin on her right arm, her fingers trembling. The wound Barquiel had inflicted on her that morning had long healed.

"They were after my blood too," she said leadenly. She met their worried stares. "Whatever they're trying to do with that book and that key, they must need my blood to make it work."

Vlad swore.

CHAPTER THIRTY-FIVE

Mae opened the door to Bryony's room and barged inside.

The Atlanta coven magic users Ephra had tasked with looking after Charlotte's soul orb startled and jumped to their feet, magic flaring in their hands. Dread widened their eyes at the sight of her.

"It's okay." Bryony rushed in behind Mae. "We mean no harm."

The witches slowly relaxed, faces pale and eyes red-rimmed from crying. Apprehension tightened Simon Roth's face as he studied the other figures piling inside the room behind Mae and Bryony.

Charlotte's aide didn't look like he believed Bryony's words at all.

Mae approached the table.

The aide blocked her, his stance defensive as he guarded the last remnant of his High Priestess. He clenched his jaw. "Look, I know you think Charlotte betrayed the High Council, but I won't let you—"

"She did not betray anyone. And I'm not here to destroy her soul." Mae masked her impatience behind a level tone. "I would have done that this morning if that had been my goal."

The sorcerer pressed his lips together, gaze probing. "Is it true?"

Mae looked at him blankly. "Is what true?"

"I told him you would help them find Charlotte's remains after this is over," Ephra explained.

Mae bobbed her head curtly at the sorcerer. "Yes. I promise to do whatever is in my power to find her."

He sagged and swallowed. "Okay."

The sorcerer stepped aside so Mae could get to *Soul Shield*.

Mae's pulse raced as she reached for the crimson sphere. She retracted the spell and let the bright orb that was Charlotte Brix's soul drift gently into her hands.

Even though this was her idea, it seemed crazy now that she was about to do it.

"Will this work?" Raven said tightly, mirroring her thoughts.

"There's only one way to find out," Mae murmured.

She closed her eyes and drew on her powers.

Sound faded. Soon, the only thing she could detect was the pounding of her heart, the faint hum coming from the orb, and the bond connecting her to Brimstone and Hellreaver, their magic dancing brightly between them.

Show me.

Nothing happened.

Mae chewed her lip. *Well, it's not like I was expecting it to work right away.*

She slowed her breathing and focused internally. Even though there appeared to be an endless repertoire of knowledge and spells buried in her very DNA, it wasn't as if she could easily decipher it or even tap into it at will. The only times she'd successfully accessed the repository she appeared to have been born with were when she'd been desperate to save someone or herself, as had been the case after her awakening.

Technically, we're all screwed if Barquiel and the Sorcerer King win, so there's that.

Something glimmered in the depths of her consciousness at that thought. Mae tensed. She broadcasted her intent and reached out toward it.

Runes sparked in the shadows. They floated up toward her, as if rising from a deep ocean. The spell took shape hazily.

Mae forced herself to stay calm, not wanting to rush the process. It finally crystallized into something she could grasp. Cognition blazed through her mind. Her pulse quickened.

She inhaled and voiced the incantation she had just learned. *"Reveal!"*

There was a sensation of movement.

Mae blinked. Her breath locked in her throat.

She was floating in the air high above a city, Charlotte's soul fluttering gently inside her cupped palms.

I dislike heights, Brimstone groaned.

Mae's head snapped around. The fox was levitating next to her, a distinctively green tinge on his furry face.

Hellreaver was doing cartwheels through a thin bank of clouds to their left, faint *whoopee* noises leaving him.

The fox eyed the weapon darkly. *He is such a child.*

"Wait!" Mae's heart pounded heavily as she looked at the metropolis spread out beneath her feet. "Is this real?!"

Brimstone heaved a sigh of relief as he found purchase on her shoulder. *It's as real as you want it to be, my witch.*

The cool breeze ruffling her hair and the moisture soaking into her skin reaffirmed her suspicions that this wasn't an illusion.

"Did we just—teleport above Philadelphia?!" she squealed.

There was movement to her right.

Alicia's reaper form blurred into view. "There you are! We wondered where you'd gone." She glanced at the city below and made a face. "You better return soon. They're all freaking out down there. I'll go tell them you're okay."

Mae nodded jerkily and watched her vanish.

She focused her attention on Charlotte's soul and what she had intended to do.

VLAD PACED THE FLOOR OF BRYONY'S ROOM, HIS stomach a tight knot. Tarang walked back and forth beside him, the tiger brushing against his leg and letting out comforting rumbles.

It had been several minutes since Mae, Brimstone, and Hellreaver had vanished along with Charlotte's soul, leaving the rest of them in a blind panic as to their fate.

"I can't believe she just did that!" Nikolai scowled, jaw so tight the incubus was surprised he hadn't cracked a molar. "Barquiel and Oscar are still out there, dammit!"

Alastair nudged the sorcerer's cheek gently.

Vlad's nails dug into his palms. Their familiars were doing a damn better job at keeping cool than they were.

He stopped and glowered at Alicia. "Are you sure she's fine?"

"The only one who looked like he was having a hard time was the fox." Alicia sighed at their sour stares. "I don't think she'll be long."

"Maybe we should put a leash on her," Violet suggested bitterly.

"Don't tempt me," Nikolai growled.

A cool wind swept the room. They stiffened.

Mae, Brimstone, and Hellreaver reappeared in a whoosh of air.

Vlad's breath rushed out of him. He crossed the floor and took Mae in his arms, his legs weak and his heart knocking violently against his ribs.

"You're gonna make me age before my time, Princess."

Mae tensed at his trembling voice. She stepped out

of his hold, Charlotte's soul orb flickering in her hands. Guilt darted across her face when she noticed Nikolai's angry glare and the others' worried expressions.

"Look, in my defense, I didn't know that was going to happen," she protested.

"Did it work?" Violet grumbled.

"Kinda. I got a general sense of where they are, but not their exact location."

"Damn." Raven's brow furrowed. "I guess we're back to square one."

A fierce smile split Mae's mouth. "Not quite."

Vlad could see the excitement in her eyes. It stirred his incubus blood.

She turned to him and Nikolai. "I need to see your weapons."

Vlad blinked and opened his mouth.

Mae's eyes shrank to slits at his grin. "No, Vlad, I don't mean *that*."

CHAPTER THIRTY-SIX

"Why is this taking so long?" Oscar snapped.

Dietrich Farago's gaze stayed locked on the complex array of machines before him. "Good science takes time, Oscar."

The harsh light from the digital screens bleached the color from the Immortal's handsome face and made his lab coat glow in the shadows. Oscar had never been able to figure out how the guy kept it so pristine, considering his hobbies. He narrowed his eyes. He knew Farago didn't mean it intentionally, but everything he said came out patronizing.

Once he's outlived his usefulness, I will kill him myself.

A faint smile stretched Farago's mouth, like he'd read Oscar's mind. Oscar didn't know how many deaths the scientist had survived throughout his existence to date. As one of the Immortal races, he possessed the ability to reanimate over and over again, until the end of his seventeenth and final life.

Whatever. Even if I have to rip his heart out seventeen times, he'll die by my hand.

Chains clinked feebly in the gloom, the sounds echoing against bare rock walls and a distant ceiling. The witches and sorcerers they'd kidnapped to serve as hosts for the ghouls moaned incoherently where they lay strapped to gurneys, magic cores weakened and senses overridden by the drugs Farago had injected them with to keep their minds and bodies locked in a chemical haze.

Oscar didn't spare them a glance as he headed for the altar holding the *Book of Light*. The Dark Council magic users guarding the grimoire moved silently out of his path, their wary gazes on the lynx by his side. Drabek had a nasty attitude toward everyone bar Oscar and the Sorcerer King, and had disfigured many a witch and sorcerer who'd vexed her.

Lines creased Oscar's brow when he stopped before the tome. The grimoire had ornate, metal covers and a thick binding. He'd already taken a look inside and had barely managed to hide his disdain at the spells it contained. They were child's play and nowhere near as powerful as the ones his father had taught him.

Oscar's face tightened.

He had done his best to mask his doubts about their current plans from the Sorcerer King and Barquiel. As far as he was concerned, they should have stuck to their original scheme of seizing Mae Jin and binding her to him with a *Marriage of Magic*. His father had unfortunately disregarded his pleas on that subject and chosen to take Barquiel's advice instead.

The Witch Queen's face rose before Oscar. Lust stirred his blood. He wanted nothing more than to degrade her and make her a slave to his will.

More so now that I know how much my brother likes her. His mouth twisted in a savage smirk. *Those fools have no idea what we have planned for her. By the time our men are done with her, she'll be begging me to kill her.*

It didn't matter to him what happened to Mae's body or her mind. As long as the Dark Council kept her breathing and had control over her magic and the power of Azazel that flowed through her veins, she was disposable meat that would fetch a high price amongst those who would get a thrill out of violating the offspring of a demon.

The air pulsed with an aura of corruption. Distant footsteps rose from the direction of the stone staircase spiraling down from the entrance to the catacombs. They grew closer, their cadence familiar as they echoed through the tunnel leading to the vault. Barquiel emerged from a shadowy opening a moment later, his guise that of Rose Blake.

Oscar's gaze skimmed the beautiful face and cool, gray eyes belonging to Mae Jin's best friend.

He had to hand it to the demon. Possessing Rose Blake when she was on the brink of death had been a genius move and one that no doubt caused the Witch Queen endless sleepless nights. If it hadn't been for the fact that he knew how much of a monster Barquiel was, he would have suggested the demon lend him her body to have some fun with. Rose Blake was definitely more to his taste than Mae Jin.

He didn't want to risk courting the demon's wrath, however. He'd seen what Barquiel had done to the women he'd rutted with. They had not survived the ordeal.

I wonder where he went off to this time.

Not even the Sorcerer King himself had any idea where the demon disappeared to during those hours when he entered a rift on his own. Oscar recalled the first time he'd gone through one of Barquiel's portals like it was yesterday. It had not been the most pleasant of experiences and the better half of the sorcerers who'd accompanied him on the short trip had thrown up during their passage through the hell gate.

It wasn't so much the smell of sulfur or the evil miasma that drowned the air or even the hints of the horrors that lay beyond the walls of the rift. It was the feeling of utter disorientation. Of being detached from one's own consciousness and pulled in a hundred different directions. Of not knowing whether you were alive or dead and trapped in a purgatory from which there was no escape.

He'd never glimpsed the final destination of the portal.

"How close are you to finishing?" Barquiel asked Farago.

The Immortal turned from the table where he was working and bowed his head respectfully. "It will be done imminently, master."

Oscar narrowed his eyes. *So, he's okay dissing me but not his overlord.*

No one knew the backstory between Farago and

Barquiel, not even the Sorcerer King. The Archduke of Hell had brought the Immortal to his father's court ten years ago and promised the man would deliver results like they'd never seen before. And he had.

Alchemist was not a word commonly used in modern times, but it was one that fit Farago, a man who had lived longer than the Sorcerer King, perfectly.

Who knew modern science would allow the essence of magic to be combined with demon DNA? And that it would grant us the ability to control creatures from Hell as a result?

Oscar was aware his father valued Farago's work as much as he treasured Barquiel's counsel. He lowered his brows.

Still, I am to be the next Sorcerer King and it will be up to me to decide whether he will continue to be of use to us in the future.

Change was coming to the Dark Council and the world of magic. And he would be leading it with his enslaved queen at his side.

And that pig will die. Oscar clenched his fists at the thought of Nikolai. *It was only luck that allowed him to defeat us in New York. I will feast on his heart and his liver and make Mae Jin watch.*

A beep sounded from one of Farago's machines, distracting him from his dark thoughts. The Immortal's eyes brightened. He opened the device carefully and extracted several racks of vials from inside. The content of the tubes was thick and dark, the substance within roiling and twisting in turbulent currents.

It was evil alchemy brought to life.

Barquiel lifted one of the vials, pupils gleaming crimson. "You managed all this with only a few drops of her blood?"

Farago nodded. "Yes. It was enough to make what we needed."

A hard smile stretched Barquiel's mouth. "Good. Let us proceed immediately."

Oscar's pulse quickened. A buzz of excitement filled the catacombs, the Dark Council sorcerers and witches glancing at one another in jubilation. The end of their mission was in sight.

Soon, they would have the compass that would lead them to the *Book of Shadows* and the soul of the first Sorcerer King.

CHAPTER THIRTY-SEVEN

Mae's stomach churned as their SUV barreled down South 18th Street. "We should set up a barrier around that place!"

Raven's reply came through the state-of-the-art comm piece she'd given them before they'd left the hotel. "I'm on it!"

"We'll help," Violet said behind Mae. "Miles and I have learned a trick or two about shields from our friends in Chicago."

"It's a good thing the covenstead was under way." Raven's voice hardened. "There'll be enough of us to manage an area that large."

The L.A. witch was in a van somewhere behind them with Abraham and Derrick. They were being followed by a procession of vehicles full of sorcerers and witches. The Councils had just held an urgent meeting with all the coven heads in attendance and updated them on Oscar's attack and Charlotte Brix's fate. Every one of them had offered reinforcements to the team currently en route to the enemy's location. The rest would be staying put and protecting the city from any fallout resulting from their clash with the Dark Council.

"Has April spoken to the mayor and the chief of police?" Nikolai asked stiffly beside Mae.

"She just got off the phone with them," Raven replied. "They're clearing the area and will shut down the roads around it once we're inside. Go on ahead. We'll meet you there!"

"Okay." Mae tapped the earpiece. Her eyes widened.

She grabbed on to the dashboard and almost bit her tongue as Nikolai took a corner without slowing, the tires leaving black marks on the asphalt. Alastair braced his wings on the sorcerer's lap. Brimstone grunted in the footwell by her legs.

Muffled thuds rose from the backseat. They were followed by cussing and growling.

"Are you trying to get us killed?!" Vlad barked.

"I told you to put your seatbelt on," Nikolai snapped.

"There're none for our familiars," Miles groaned from under Tarang.

They passed a park and joined a main avenue. Nikolai swore and slammed on the brakes. Mae's belt snapped hard against her chest as the SUV skidded to a stop inches from the rear bumper of a bus. Tension knotted her shoulders.

It was rush hour and the boulevard was jam packed.

"Shit!" Nikolai draped an arm atop Mae's backrest and started reversing.

A horn blasted behind them. There was a fuel truck right on their ass.

"Dammit, we're hedged in!"

Mae wound her window down and stuck her head out. There were too many vehicles in the way for her to get a clean line of sight.

Her pulse quickened. "How many lights?!"

Nikolai flashed her a puzzled look. "What?"

"How many stop lights do you see to the river?!"

"Seven!" Vlad called out from the backseat.

Nikolai scanned the avenue ahead and confirmed the same with a curt nod.

"Vi, tell Raven and everyone to keep to this route." Mae narrowed her eyes. "I'm gonna clear us a path."

Nikolai stiffened. "How?"

"Just be ready to go when I tell you!"

Magic swirled inside her. Brimstone's pupils flared with power. She ignored Nikolai's protest and raised her right hand. Redness bloomed on her fingertips. She gritted her teeth, adjusted the strength and visibility of the spell, and let loose.

"*Wind Fury!*"

Air whooshed violently ahead of their SUV, driving the vehicle back a couple of inches. The palest crimson and black wave exploded into view. It crashed and surged along the boulevard, a forceful tide invisible to all but those who possessed magic.

Nikolai sucked in air as a cacophony of metal

groans rose up ahead. The smell of scorched rubber filled Mae's nostrils. Startled shouts and screams erupted from the vehicles being shifted aside by *Wind Fury*. Side mirrors snapped. Fenders bent. Scratches bloomed on paintwork.

The stop lights finally came into view. Mae curled her fingers, blood pounding in her ears as she finetuned the spell further. *Wind Fury* wrapped around the poles. Sparks sizzled on metal. The lights went out as the electrics were disabled.

"*Go!*" Mae barked at Nikolai.

The sorcerer engaged gears and floored the gas. The SUV lurched forward, driving them all back into their seats.

The people tumbling out of the vehicles lining the sides of the avenue jumped back as they zoomed past, mouths agape and wild-eyed stares following their passage.

"What the hell did Mae just do?!" Abraham yelled on the comm line.

Violet grimaced. "She cleared a path for us."

"You call this clearing a path?!" the aide spluttered.

"Stop bitching and drive, Owl Boy!" Raven snapped.

"We're gonna make the six o'clock news, aren't we?" Derrick grumbled.

Mae turned a deaf ear to their objections, the last location of the demon she had tracked pulsing inside her mind like a beacon.

Do you feel it too, Brim?!

Yes. The fox bared his teeth. *I can almost smell him!*

It was the blood Barquiel had left on Vlad and Nikolai's blades that had allowed her to successfully unleash *Reveal* and pin down his latest whereabouts. The signal grew stronger when they crossed the river. Mae's gaze swung to the treetops on a low hill to the left.

They shot under a railway bridge and took another turn. The shallow elevation came into view, abutting rail tracks and the waterway.

The place the Dark Council had chosen as their hidey hole was a cemetery and park enclosing a historical Georgian mansion and an arboretum. They navigated the police perimeter that had been set up in readiness for their arrival, raced around to the north entrance, and stormed the incline beyond the gates.

Mae jumped out of the SUV the second it came to a stop. "Brim!"

The fox leapt onto her shoulder as she rose from the ground, Hellreaver humming against her chest.

Vlad and Nikolai joined her, the incubus wrapped in a crimson haze of demonic energy while the sorcerer's enhanced abilities allowed him to levitate within an aura of white magic. Alicia's scythe flashed in the light of the setting sun as she stepped out of a rift beside them.

Mae looked from the shadows lengthening across the park and the cemetery to the sorcerers and witches disembarking from the vehicles that had just pulled up onto the driveway.

"Get ready. I'm going to shield everyone's core!"

Raven and Derrick tensed. Abraham nodded stiffly and spread the word.

Heat rushed through Mae, power flowing from the sources of magic deep within her body. Brimstone and Hellreaver's energies brushed against her soul, the threads connecting all three of them blazing bright.

She raised her hands to the sky. "*Soul Shield! Multiply! Guard!*"

The air rippled violently. Leaves rustled and branches swayed in the treetops as a giant, red sphere swarming with pale runes exploded into life above her head. It split into scores of smaller globes and arrowed toward everyone around her bar Alicia.

There was a collective indrawing of breath from all those who had yet to experience *Soul Shield*, the spell sinking inside them and locking their magic cores within a protective cage. Derrick pressed his hand hesitantly to his stomach, his face pale.

Mae's focus shifted to the leftover traces of the demonic soul she could sense. The signal was hazier now that they were close to it.

"I can smell Hell's taint," Alicia observed. "It's weak, but it's somewhere below us." The reaper frowned. "It's almost as if it's hidden behind some kind of wall."

Mae blinked. *Wait! Could it be—?!*

Her gut twisted, her instincts telling her she was right.

"I think I know why *Nullify* isn't working!" She met their puzzled stares, her own eyes wide. "It's a rift. Barquiel is hiding their location by putting up a portal all around the place! That's why *Nullify* couldn't find their black magic. It would literally have to travel through Hell's dimension to track them down!"

"They must have done it knowing how your spell works," Nikolai said grimly.

"That bastard is putting everyone's lives at risk," Alicia cursed.

Mae's nails bit into her palms. "No. From what I'm sensing, Barquiel has complete control over it. I think he's done this before. I doubt that portal poses a risk to Earth!"

Nikolai turned to Alicia, hope brightening his gaze. "Do you think you can find a safe passage through that thing?"

The reaper shook her head, orbits flaring crimson with frustration. "Each portal is unique to the one who creates it. And a reaper's gate is very different to that of a demon. Barquiel wouldn't be able to use mine, nor I his unless we granted each other permission to do so."

Lines furrowed Vlad's brow. "Then how come *Reveal* worked?"

Mae knitted her brow, equally confused.

Because blood doesn't lie, Brimstone growled.

Her breath locked in her lungs at the fox's words. The factor that she had overlooked burst to the forefront of her mind like a firework.

Brimstone's right!

Her stunned gaze found Nikolai, the truth sinking into her consciousness sending her heart thundering against her ribs. "You're the only one who can break through Barquiel's portal!"

The sorcerer's eyes widened. "What?"

"The *Book of Light* has white magic. And you're the strongest white magic user I know!" Conviction brought a fierce expression to her face. "I can use *Reveal* to try and connect you to it. But you'll have to use a ley line to find its physical location beyond that barrier!"

CHAPTER THIRTY-EIGHT

THE MALODOROUS MIASMA OF ROTTING MEAT FOULED the dry air of the catacombs.

Screams bounced off the rock walls as the sorcerers and witches strapped to the camp beds writhed and convulsed, the black-magic and demon-DNA modified virus now carrying Mae's blood searing their veins and rewriting their magic cores and will.

Oscar watched with bated breath as Barquiel acted as a physical conduit to Hell, the gateway he'd opened channeling the ghouls he'd recruited to possess the magic users.

The Dark Council kept their distance, wary gazes locked on the gruesome shapes and ochre eyes of the monsters materializing out of the portal. Though they'd fought by the side of their demon-infested brethren and quite a few carried fiends in their own souls, ghouls were something else.

The last of the creatures piled out of the hell gate a moment later. They tilted their heads to the side, listened to the silent command Barquiel issued, and moved as one. Their claws clinked on metal as they climbed upon the beds.

One of the Dark Council sorcerers gagged as the monsters invaded the bodies of their intended victims, their shadowy manifestations whooshing inside mouths, eyes, and noses like they were made of black mist.

The men and women stilled, fits abating with an abruptness that sent a chill down Oscar's spine. Their pupils brightened to yellow. Auras of darkness burst into life above their heads.

Barquiel bared his teeth in satisfaction. Farago smiled triumphantly. This was the first time no one had died during the process of being turned into a ghoul. It seemed Mae's blood had been the crucial ingredient required to stabilize the virus the Immortal scientist had created.

The straps holding down the possessed prisoners snapped as they sat up. They moved off the camp beds and followed Barquiel docilely as the demon guided them across the catacombs to the altar holding the *Book of Light*.

Oscar fell into step behind them. Something sparked up ahead, catching his eye for an instant. He frowned faintly.

Did that come from the grimoire?

If Barquiel noticed, he gave no indication of it.

Runes sizzled under Oscar's feet as he entered the black magic circle he'd drawn out earlier. The ghouls crowded around the dais, oblivious to the complex symbols on the floor.

Their sulfurous eyes stayed locked on the grimoire.

Drabek growled beside Oscar, her irises darkening. An inky aura exploded around the lynx. Power surged through him as the familiar augmented his magic.

He raised his hand and incanted the spell his father had taught him. *"Corrupt!"*

Shadows filled the crypt. The air hummed with evil.

The ghouls' new bodies started to distort, losing their material form.

Oscar's eyes widened. The monsters were dissolving into millions of black threads swarming with Mae's crimson magic. Though he'd been warned what to expect, it was still shocking to witness.

Only three people knew about the power hidden inside the *Book of Light* and how it could be unlocked. Azazel, Barquiel, and the Sorcerer King, the latter's knowledge passed down by his predecessor.

Oscar clenched his jaw gleefully. *And now me, as the future Sorcerer King!*

The grimoire shook and rattled as the creatures dove inside it, their insubstantial shapes vanishing through the metal with faint whines. The tome fell silent after the last ghoul was absorbed within it.

There was a moment of breathless stillness. The pressure inside the catacombs dropped, tugging at Oscar's stomach and making his ears pop.

The grimoire imploded with savage silence.

The *Book of Light* was now an intangible, bubbling

mass, magic arcing through its shifting eruptions with a brightness that scored their shadows on the walls of the crypt. A pale sphere emerged from within the crackling storm cloud. It contracted down into a circular object.

Farago's eyes shone with a zealous light where he stood staring at the transmuted artifact from beyond the circle.

It was a metal compass covered in complex runes. One without a needle.

A keyhole opened up in the center of the smooth surface.

The ground started to shake. Barquiel flinched.

Oscar's pulse stuttered. *This isn't part of the spell!*

Dust rained down upon their heads, the particles igniting before darkening to ash as they struck the magic circle. They looked up.

Pale cracks were forming in the ceiling of the catacombs. Oscar's eyes rounded. The lines smelled of white magic and his brother's powers.

Rage tightened his chest and flooded his mouth with bitter acid. *How?!*

"The key!" Barquiel barked. He spread his wings and shot up into the air. "Use the key! *Now!*"

He indicated the levitating compass above the altar. A rift opened beside him. He drew his sword from within it.

Oscar unfroze. He snatched the skeleton key from inside his coat and stormed the dais. The artifact felt cold to the touch when he grabbed it, the metal smoother than he'd thought it would be. He jammed the key inside its matching opening just as a section of the roof collapsed.

BLOOD ROARED IN NIKOLAI'S EARS AS THE GROUND GAVE way beneath them, forming a fifty-foot-wide crevasse in the middle of the park. The world tilted around him.

Mae grabbed his arm as he started to fall. She clocked the sweat beading his forehead and his ashen face with a worried frown.

"Are you gonna be okay?!"

Nikolai nodded weakly, nausea churning his stomach. He raised a trembling hand to Alastair where the crow drooped on his shoulder.

This was the worst either of them had felt after using a ley line.

Is it because we had to navigate Reveal and that portal?!

Somehow, he sensed there was another reason why his magic core felt so depleted. One that had to do with the *Book of Light* and what he'd experienced when his powers had connected to it.

"I'll be fine," he mumbled. "Go!"

His words failed to reassure Mae. She lowered her brows. "Alicia, guard him!"

The reaper hooked a bony arm around Nikolai where they floated above the chasm. Mae let go and drifted off to join Vlad and the others.

Surprise jolted Nikolai when she returned, a determined expression on her face. She clasped his face and kissed him, her fingers hot against his cheeks and her lips scorching his.

Fire filled his belly. He tugged her close and deepened the kiss. She matched him beat for beat, body shuddering as she pressed against him.

Alicia cleared her throat discreetly. Mae blinked and ended the kiss. She stared into his eyes, the emotions in them so strong and clear he didn't think he would be able to let her go. Though it was difficult to tell in the shadows, he was certain her cheeks were flushed.

"You did good," Mae mumbled.

She twisted around and darted to their waiting forces, leaving him to press his fingers dazedly to his tingling lips.

"How about my kiss?!" Vlad protested.

"You stole one yesterday, remember?" she snapped.

The incubus grumbled and followed her inside the crevasse.

CHAPTER THIRTY-NINE

THE BREACH NIKOLAI HAD CREATED IN THE GROUNDS OF the cemetery was some eighty feet deep and tapered down to a funnel. Mae smashed the exit wide open with Hellreaver, magic and the power of the demon who had sired her singing through her veins.

Shadowy catacombs with recesses full of skulls and bones appeared beneath them. A large, winged figure rose out of the gloom to meet her, dark sword in hand and pupils crimson with displeasure.

Brimstone sprang from Mae's shoulder and transformed mid-leap.

Barquiel grunted as the nine-tailed spirit demon smashed into his chest and drove him down with his sheer weight. They crashed into the ground with a boom. It cracked, sending deadly shards arrowing through the chamber.

One speared the eye of a Dark Council sorcerer. Another punctured the throat of a witch. A man with fair hair and striking looks ducked behind a worktop crowded with laboratory equipment as the fragments peppered the spot he had just occupied.

"Protect him!" Barquiel roared.

Mae's eyes shrank to slits as she studied the stranger in the white coat. He was soon surrounded by a group of black magic users.

That must be the Immortal helping them!

Her gaze shifted, seeking Oscar. She found him standing by a stone altar.

A savage sneer twisted the sorcerer's face as he met her eyes. "You're too late!"

He twisted the skeleton key he'd stolen from Hellreaver inside a smooth, metal compass. Mae stared, pulse racing. She couldn't help but feel that the object had been something else before. And she sensed her own magic within the thing.

Is that the Book of Light?!

Oscar froze. The key wouldn't turn. Confusion clouded his face.

"I told you to use the key, dammit!" Barquiel barked where he struggled under Brimstone.

"I am! It's not working!"

Mae flashed them a mocking grin where she hovered above them. "Did you really think I'd be dumb enough to bring the real one to Philadelphia?"

The truth dawned in Oscar and Barquiel's eyes. The sorcerer cursed.

Corruption swamped the catacombs as the demon released a strong pulse of hellish energy. The hairs rose on Mae's arms when she picked up on something within it. Something that made her stomach curdle.

That's black magic!

Barquiel shoved Brimstone off him, grabbed his broadsword, and wielded it at the beast rising to his feet. Mae moved.

Sparks erupted as Hellreaver clashed against Barquiel's blade.

Vlad's crimson-tinged, diamond-edged swords sliced into the demon's wings from behind.

Barquiel bellowed. The catacombs trembled.

Rifts opened all around them, the portals ripping the air asunder. Demons poured out of the hell gates and converged on Mae and Vlad.

Colored magic bombs crashed into the fiends, stopping them in their tracks. Abraham, Raven, and Derrick had entered the catacombs ahead of the rest of the cavalry.

"Man, those are some ugly MOFOs," Abraham mumbled.

"I hope you'll clean your mouth out with soap before we go on our first date," Raven told the aide.

Abraham almost dropped his sword. His owl's head spun around in shock.

"We're going on a date?!" the sorcerer squeaked to the witch.

"For the love of God, people, time and place!" Derrick barked. His gaze found Mae and Vlad. "We've got this! You take care of those assholes!"

Mae nodded grimly. Heat washed across her skin as Vlad let his powers loose.

A feral expression stretched the incubus's face. "Shall we, Princess?!"

Brimstone stepped up beside Mae, nine tails quivering with unholy energy and magic. She narrowed her eyes, her familiar's bloodlust and that of the man her soul had acknowledged resonating fiercely with her own.

"Yes!" she growled.

She caught movement out of the corner of her eye.

Oscar was running away, the compass in hand.

Alarm squeezed her chest. She opened her mouth to yell out a warning, saw the figures descending inside the catacombs, and stopped. Relief surged through her.

Nikolai's pulse thrummed as he landed on the stone floor with Alicia.

He scanned the shadows, found the man he was searching for, and pointed. "There!"

Alicia drew her arm back and threw her scythe. The weapon hummed as it sailed across the crypt, spinning edge gleaming with a sinister light. It decapitated three demons and lodged into Oscar's right shoulder with a meaty sound. He cried out and dropped the object in his hand. Drabek hissed by the sorcerer's side as he spun around and cast a black magic globe at them, the lynx's eyes brimming with darkness.

Nikolai raised a shield and blocked the attack.

"Looks like you're feeling better," Alicia said with an appraising glance.

He bobbed his head, frowning. He'd known his brother would attempt to flee the battle, just like he'd done in New York. Rats always abandoned a sinking ship.

His gaze found the item on the floor behind Oscar. It was a metal compass. The invisible white magic it contained throbbed with Nikolai's heartbeat.

Something told him he was looking at the *Book of Light* in a different guise. And the transformed grimoire was slowly replenishing his core and that of Alastair, returning the magic it had sucked out of them.

Oscar yanked Alicia's scythe out of his shoulder and cast it aside. The weapon stopped an inch from striking the floor. It rose, shot across the catacombs, and returned to the reaper's grip, handle striking bone with a clunk. Black magic detonated around the sorcerer. He charged them, sword in hand and Drabek spitting at his side.

Nikolai unleashed his spear.

Oscar's eyes rounded when he countered his strike.

Alastair dropped from his shoulder and aimed his claws at Drabek's eyes, angry caws leaving him.

Nikolai glanced past his brother to where Mae and Vlad fought Barquiel. He could sense magic inside the demon. Magic that tasted of his father's powers.

"Go!" he told Alicia. "They need your help!"

Outrage distorted Oscar's face. "You think you can defeat me on your—"

Nikolai elbowed him in the nose.

Oscar grunted and stumbled back, almost

swallowing his tongue in shock. He clutched the broken, bleeding appendage.

Fury filled Nikolai's heart and belly. "I'm not the man I used to be, brother!"

CHAPTER FORTY

VLAD WIPED BLOOD FROM HIS MOUTH AND RETREATED TO Mae's side, his chest heaving with his pants.

The witch glowered at Barquiel, her breaths coming equally hard and fast. "How the hell did you manage to acquire magic?!"

Surprise jolted the incubus. *Damn! Is that what I've been picking up from this asshole?!*

A continuous growl rumbled out of Brimstone and Tarang where they braced beside them. Crimson pulsed around Hellreaver, the weapon baring his fangs in Mae's hands.

However much they tried, they couldn't get past Barquiel's defense.

Nikolai's shout reached them across the catacombs. "That's Vedran's magic!"

Mae sucked in air. Vlad swore.

A victorious expression washed across Barquiel's face.

Mae cut her eyes to the Immortal who'd been

helping the Dark Council from the shadows. "It's gotta be him! He must have found a way to infect Barquiel with Vedran's magic!"

She froze the next instant, the blood draining from her face.

The tension coiling through Vlad tightened like a spring. "What is it?"

Revulsion distorted Mae's face. "It's your DNA." She stared at Barquiel. "The DNA we couldn't identify in that virus. *It's yours!*"

Vlad's pulse stuttered.

Barquiel smiled viciously. The demon's left arm flashed with Vlad's next blink. His hand locked around the scythe curving toward his neck.

"Don't think I didn't see you!" Barquiel sneered at Alicia.

The reaper's orbits blazed with anger, her knuckles blanching on her weapon as she pushed down with all her might. A gasp left her as Barquiel hurled her aside. She flew past them and smashed into the altar, splitting the stone in two.

Vlad deciphered Barquiel's intention a millisecond before Mae. Fear squeezed his heart. He darted in front of the witch and deflected the broadsword arrowing toward her right eye with his diamond blades.

Stone crumbled beneath his feet, Barquiel's strength making his legs buckle.

Vlad's lips curled back in a savage grimace. *He's one strong son of a bitch, I'll grant him that!*

He drew on the demonic power that lived in his incubus blood and the magic core his mother had gifted him. Heat scorched his soul. He roared and pushed back, Tarang's eyes and body exploding with power beside him.

Barquiel swung a hand, talons gleaming. Fire lanced Vlad's flesh as the demon's claws scored his chest and punctured his right lung.

Tarang howled in rage. Brimstone chomped down on Barquiel's wrist. Black magic erupted on the demon's skin. It swarmed the fox's jaws. He winced and let go.

Violent tremors shook the catacombs. Cracks tore across the rock walls. Skulls and bones tumbled from cavities.

A red mist filled the crypt.

Mae rose, the power pulsing from her tasting of death and destruction. "*Negate!*"

Vlad's ears throbbed, the spell detonating around him with a force that cast people to the ground. Alicia's arm steadied him as he stumbled. He clamped a hand to his whistling wound and followed the reaper's gaze to the witch whose magic thickened the very air.

A MURDEROUS FEELING CHOKED MAE'S THROAT AS SHE stared at the garish wound disfiguring Vlad's flesh.

"Your spell won't work against me, witch!" Barquiel jutted his jaw out. "I have the power of the Sorcerer King running through my veins!"

"Oh yeah?" Mae bared her teeth. "Well, this is what I think about *that!*"

She flipped him the middle finger.

Vlad snorted before groaning in pain. Alicia grinned.

Fury darkened Barquiel's face. He spread his wings and rose, only to freeze an instant later.

Mae smiled fiercely as she watched awareness dawn on his face.

"What did you do?!" the demon bellowed.

"*Negate* doesn't just disable external magic and demonic energy."

Barquiel's eyes widened.

"That's right, asshat," she ground out. "It's destroying the magic and power inside you!"

Crimson ignited along Hellreaver's blades, the weapon vibrating with power. Brimstone's tails raised a violent windstorm across the catacombs.

They attacked Barquiel as one.

Nikolai countered Oscar's strike, ducked beneath his next swing, and swiped his legs out from under him. Motion flashed to his left as his brother fell. Drabek sprang for his throat, all claws and fangs and madness fueled by dark magic.

Nikolai knocked the lynx aside with the blunt end of his spear before impaling her hind haunch with the sharp end. The lynx yowled in rage.

"Drabek!" Oscar jumped to his feet and charged Nikolai, his eyes full of barbaric intent.

A dark miasma flooded the crypt.

Oscar rocked to a halt. His gaze rose, jubilation brightening his face. Horror wrapped an icy hand around Nikolai's heart. He knew this corruption.

A black sphere exploded silently into existence some twenty feet above the floor. It expanded and lengthened, forming an inky doorway.

Only one person Nikolai knew possessed a black magic portal.

The Sorcerer King stepped out of it.

Bile filled the back of Nikolai's throat. *Oh God!*

"MAE!"

Vlad's warning shout reached her faintly above the clashing sounds of blades. She ignored him, her focus on the demon before her. Though Barquiel had been weakened by *Negate*, and Hellreaver and Brimstone had inflicted many a wound upon him, he was still strong enough to hold his ground against them.

This bastard did use to be an angel, after all!

A savage snarl left Brimstone. Mae startled as the fox whirled around sharply.

"*Watch out, Mae!*" Nikolai roared across the catacombs.

Someone grabbed the back of her neck with enough raw strength to break her spine, the only thing saving her from instant death the demon power and magic flowing through her flesh.

Her invisible assailant moved at lightning speed, taking her along with him. Mae glimpsed their final destination, gritted her teeth, and managed to shield her head with her arms a millisecond before she was forcibly smashed into the wall.

The impact rattled her bones. Pain bloomed through her body.

"No!" Alicia snarled somewhere behind Mae. "You don't stand a chance against him!"

"*Let me go!*" Vlad bellowed, voice full of rage.

"Stay back, you fool!" Nikolai barked at the incubus.

Fear sent black spots dancing across Mae's vision.

Barquiel's voice reached her dimly through the blood pounding ferociously in her ears. "Thanks for coming."

The demon's tone was full of grudging relief.

Mae choked for air where her face remained pressed into the shattered rock. Every muscle in her body froze when the man behind her spoke.

"I did not think you would need me, Barquiel."

CHAPTER FORTY-ONE

ICE SKITTERED THROUGH MAE'S NERVE ENDINGS. NA Ri's presence filled her consciousness with her next tortured breath. She knew instinctively from the fury saturating the soul of her first incarnation that the man who held her in his grip was the Sorcerer King.

Hellreaver and Brimstone attacked her assailant.

Black magic throbbed across the crypt, the air so dense with evil Mae could barely get oxygen into her starving lungs. Horror dulled her mind when she heard the fox yelp and the weapon whine out of sight. She dug her nails into her palms and called out to them.

Together!

Brimstone and Hellreaver heeded her command. Fire rushed through her veins from the bond that connected them. Her magic core detonated.

The spell left her on a snarl. *"Wind Fury!"*

The storm that swept the catacombs brought debris down onto their heads.

Vedran's hold loosened slightly.

It was all the breathing space Mae needed. "*Devour!*"

The wall she was pressed against crumbled as the spell consumed the rock, giving her leeway to move. She twisted around, body wrapped in a thick, crimson haze.

"*Eclipse!*"

A black hole detonated near the ceiling. Screams sounded from the Dark Council as they were dragged relentlessly up into it, bodies lifting off the ground even as they tried to cling to the floor. The demons followed, howling and screeching. Abraham, Raven, Derrick, and the others stayed put, eyes wide.

Mae had perfected the spell so it would focus on only those she deemed her enemies.

Her heart knocked against her ribs as she met the cold, blue gaze of the man who wanted to rule the world of magic. She could see where Nikolai had inherited his looks from.

Vedran Borojevic was handsome as sin and barely looked old enough to have two grown sons.

She swallowed, bitterness turning her mouth to ash.

Not just two. He killed eighteen of them during the Trial of Blood *and God knows how many before that. He's a monster!*

The Sorcerer King appeared remarkably calm considering what was above his head. Mae's pulse stuttered at the realization *Eclipse* wasn't having any effect on him.

He cocked his head to the side, his stare one of a scientist watching a lab rat. "Did you know there's a spell that allows a magic user to increase the density of their body to the extent that nothing can move them?"

Alarm twisted Mae's insides. *Shit!*

Vedran sighed. "Let's end this." He lifted a hand lazily, as if he didn't really want to be there. "*Contain.*"

A black cage exploded around Mae, its surface covered in crimson runes. Nikolai and Vlad shouted out her name, their voices reaching her as if traveling across a vast ocean.

Mae gnashed her teeth, moved back a couple of feet, and bolted for the wall of her prison. She smashed into it with her shoulder.

It held, solid as concrete.

"Come, Oscar." Vedran's voice echoed clearly in her head, the spell obviously making it easier for her to hear him. He turned, expression bored. "We'll take her back with us. I'm sure we'll bring her around to our way of thinking eventually."

Brimstone howled in rage. An inhuman sound left Hellreaver.

She met their tortured gazes through the hazy barrier. "*No!*"

Go to Nikolai! Tell him to do what he did in New York! Tell him this time, the circle is you two! He'll understand what I mean!

The fox and the weapon hesitated, their distress churning across the bond that linked them to her. They retreated reluctantly.

"Giving up so easily?" Vedran drawled.

Mae's head whipped around.

The Sorcerer King was studying her with faint curiosity.

"No." She bared her teeth at him. "Just getting ready to wipe the floor with your ass."

The Sorcerer King blinked. A bark of laughter left his throat. "I like your sense of humor. Your company might amuse me."

Mae's eyes shrank to slits. "Shame. I think yours would bore me to tears."

Vedran's smile faded. The pressure of his presence pressed against her prison. "You should bow to me while you still can, little girl." His tone raised goosebumps on her skin. "Who knows, I might grow tired of your attitude and slice your head off." He turned his attention to Oscar. "Where is the compass?"

The sorcerer shook his head, brow furrowed. "I lost it earlier. It should still be here!"

I ate it, Brimstone said triumphantly.

Mae blinked and kept her face blank.

Vedran frowned. His gaze landed on the fox.

Mae's stomach lurched. *No!*

She inhaled and laid her hands on the wall of black magic separating them. "*Absorb!*"

The red runes flickered. The cage trembled.

Vedran stared, his attention successfully diverted. "Now, there's a spell I have yet to witness."

Mae glanced past his shoulder. A savage smile split her mouth. "Unfortunately, you won't see the end of it!"

Vedran spun round, alarm flickering in his eyes for an instant.

Magic arced across the floor of the catacombs, sizzling lines of dazzling power. The Sorcerer King's gaze found the son who had fled his court. Anger darkened his face, the first true emotion he had shown since he'd appeared before them.

The radiance blazing from Nikolai's eyes and hands and sparking from Alastair's pupils scorched everyone's shadow onto the walls. The white magic they had drawn from a ley line powered through Brimstone and Hellreaver's souls and arrowed straight to hers inside the black prison.

The Sorcerer King's spell exploded into nothingness.

"*Ice Fortress!*" Mae barked.

The temperature inside the catacombs plummeted. Whiteness raced across the ground and up the rock walls, what moisture there was inside the catacombs and on their breath solidifying instantly into crystals. An ice cage grew around Vedran, the layers thickening and melding together at dizzying speed.

The Sorcerer King watched it close around him with the faintest frown.

Mae blinked. *Wait! Why is he so composed?!*

Angry shouts answered her question. Nikolai and Brimstone missed capturing Oscar by inches as he vanished inside a rift with his injured lynx. Vlad swore as his blades, Alicia's scythe, and Tarang's claws raked the empty air Barquiel had occupied, the portal the demon had used to escape closing behind him.

Mae's gut twisted. A black-magic doorway had appeared inside *Ice Fortress*. Vedran headed toward it at a leisurely pace. He paused on the threshold and directed a cold stare at Nikolai.

"I look forward to your return, my son. Know that I shall treat you as Oscar's equal from this day forth." He cut his eyes to Brimstone. "As for the *Book of Shadows*, there are other ways to find it."

He stepped inside the rectangle of darkness, his shocking words resonating in Mae's ears. The door faded to nothingness. Stillness descended around them.

Her heart thumped heavily against her breast. *Is it over?!*

For now, Brimstone said grimly. *For now.*

The fox and Hellreaver made their way over to her, a pale-faced Nikolai in their wake. Mae detected the toll accessing the ley lines had taken on the sorcerer and his familiar in his haggard complexion and the crow's dull wings. She could also see the fresh shadows clouding his eyes.

His father's words had rung with a veracity that had surprised even Mae. She couldn't stop herself from wondering what the Sorcerer King's intentions were toward his second heir.

Vlad was the first to reach her as she drifted to the ground. The incubus embraced her tightly in his arms, his hands trembling on her back.

She stiffened, alarmed. "Don't! You're hurt!"

"It's nothing," he murmured in her hair.

"Your lips are blue!"

"That's the color of love," he said drowsily, growing heavy against her.

Tarang chuffed agitatedly, his tail sweeping the air as he paced the floor around them.

"Give me a hand!" Mae asked Alicia.

The reaper transformed back into a human and helped her lower Vlad to the ground.

"You're so pretty," the incubus mumbled.

He lifted a handful of Mae's hair and kissed it.

Alicia raised an eyebrow. "Is he high?"

"No, he's just hypoxic," Mae said grimly.

She examined Vlad's wound, made a makeshift dressing with a strip of her top, and partially applied it to the incubus's open pneumothorax.

The color slowly returned to his lips and face. He blinked, his pupils constricting on a crimson flare. Tarang licked his face ardently.

"Did I just embarrass myself?" the incubus groaned, gently pushing the tiger away.

"You do that just by flapping your lips, dumbass," Nikolai said darkly.

Alicia shrugged. "It's nothing we've not seen before."

Vlad grimaced. "Thanks."

Brimstone shrank to his small fox form and leapt into Mae's arms. She hugged him and Hellreaver's medallion shape to her chest, their bond blazing brightly through her soul.

Abraham, Raven, and Derrick joined them. Violet and Miles weren't far behind.

"Next time, you're doing the shield," Violet grumbled at Raven.

"You realize I have authority over you, right?" Raven said tartly.

"Our childhood friendship trumps your status as a High Priestess," Violet scoffed.

"So, what'd we miss?" Miles asked. "We felt some pretty awful black magic from where we were standing."

"Vedran was here," Derrick said.

Miles's eyes rounded. Millie grew limp with shock around his shoulders.

"You mean, the Sorcerer King himself put in an appearance?!" Violet spluttered.

"It was a touching family reunion," Nikolai said bitterly.

Derrick and Raven exchanged a guarded look. Confusion clouded Violet's face.

Mae's gaze swept the catacombs. "Did anyone see the Immortal?"

"You mean the guy in the lab coat?" Abraham grimaced. "He made his getaway during the fight."

Mae scowled. "Dammit!"

"Jared is gonna be pissed," Alicia observed.

A clunk sounded next to Mae. Brimstone had regurgitated the metal compass.

Miles wrinkled his nose. "What is that?"

CHAPTER FORTY-TWO

"It's demon DNA alright," Mila confirmed.

Mae's stomach sank as the Immortal corroborated the truth she'd realized during last night's clash with Barquiel.

She had given Mila a sample of her blood after they'd returned to the hotel. She'd wanted the Immortal to analyze it and compare it with the unknown genetic material they had identified in the specimen inside *Ice Fortress* and Agnes's blood.

Mila lifted her cup to her mouth and took a sip of her tea, her silver gaze calmly sweeping the noisy breakfast room.

It was the morning after. The Councils had gathered in the Royal Suite, the hotel providing an extra table to fit everyone. Karin and Gerard kept glancing nervously at the morsels and crumbs flying through the air where Brimstone, Tarang, Hellreaver, and several smaller carnivores feasted on various meat dishes.

"Are they always that—keen?" Ephra enquired politely, staring at the fox and the weapon.

"You mean do they make a goddamn mess all the time?" Mae munched gloomily on her bacon sandwich. "Never at my mother's."

Yoo-Mi smiled smugly. Ryu offered a piece of her bagel to Raven's snake and Abraham's owl.

Ye-Seul leaned sideways and nudged Bryony's aide in the ribs with a bony elbow. "A little birdie told me you and the L.A. witch are shacking up."

Abraham spat out his coffee. Bryony's buttered toast fell on her plate with a splat. Violet choked on air.

Half the table gaped at Raven. She made a face. "Was that birdie Mae?"

"Hey!" Mae blurted out.

"It was the hoochie with the scythe," Ye-Seul admitted.

Bryony turned to her aide, her expression pinched. "You're not leaving the coven, are you?"

"Why, are you jealous?" Raven teased.

Bryony scowled. "No! Do you know how long it took me to train him? I don't want to go through that again for a long time."

"I hear you," Derrick muttered.

Abraham narrowed his eyes at Bryony. "I'm just a dog to you, aren't I?"

"Good aides are hard to come by these days." Barbara glanced at April and pushed a croissant onto the witch's plate. "You should eat. Your coven needs you."

Mae's chest twinged at the Philadelphia High Priestess's glum mien.

They hadn't been able to save the local sorcerers and witches who had been kidnapped by the Dark Council. It was Mae who'd had to tell April that they had been sacrificed to transform the *Book of Light* into a compass.

Her stomach knotted. *A compass that can find the* Book of Shadows.

Irritated voices rose in the passage outside the breakfast room.

"Why are you back?" Nikolai snapped. "Did they kick you out of the coven hospital?"

"I'm all healed up, Choir Boy," Vlad responded in a patronizing voice.

"Here come your future husbands," Violet drawled.

"Shut up," Mae muttered.

Her heart skipped a beat at the sight of the two men entering the room.

Vlad greeted her with a smile that was probably visible from the next city. "Good morning, Princess,"

"Hey," Nikolai murmured sulkily.

Mae chewed her lip. It was getting harder to ignore the hot incubus and the brooding sorcerer.

Maybe you should have a chamomile tea, like the Immortal, Brimstone suggested.

Yes, Hellreaver contributed. *It might help with your sudden case of lust.*

Mae's brows met. *I swear, I will* cut *you!*

She drank her coffee, the breakfast conversation

washing over her while she mulled over what else they had learned last night.

The Immortal scientist's name was Dietrich Farago. Madeleine had called a friend after Mae had given the Immortals a description and had received confirmation of his identity within the hour.

Farago was apparently a well-known, rogue scientist who rose to infamy in the 18th century for performing cruel experiments on animals and children. He was spotted a couple of times in different countries around the world before finally fading into obscurity in the early 19th century.

I wonder where Barquiel and the Sorcerer King came across him?

It was Karin who had solved the other puzzle. The question why Charlotte Brix had been preyed upon by the Dark Council. Charlotte specialized in transmutation magic. Mae could only speculate that Barquiel had utilized the witch's abilities to access the full power of Vedran's magic.

Ephra had brought them news of Isabelle West that morning. The witch was on the mend and wished to pay her respects to Mae at the earliest opportunity.

As for why the Dark Council was after the *Book of Shadows,* Mae and Brimstone had surmised Vedran wanted to mitigate any future threat to his reign by recovering the soul of the original Sorcerer King.

It's a good thing we left the real key in New York.

Noah buzzed Simon Roth in. Charlotte's aide hesitated when he reached the threshold of the breakfast room.

Mae pushed her chair back. "What time's the flight?"

"Not until eleven." Guilt flashed across the sorcerer's gaze as it swept the chamber. "You still have half an hour."

"It's okay." Mae gave him a sad smile. "I want to find her as much as you do."

Simon swallowed convulsively, his eyes glittering.

Ye-Seul passed him a tissue. The sorcerer mumbled his thanks.

Vlad raised an eyebrow. "Want us to come with you?"

Nikolai looked similarly interested in accompanying her.

Mae made a face. "You two, in a confined metal space thousands of feet in the air? I don't think my ulcer will cope."

"We're not five," Nikolai protested.

"Don't forget our date when you return to New York," Vlad said lightly, the warning in his eyes a reminder of what they'd talked about on the ballroom balcony two nights ago.

Jeez, was that really only two nights ago?

"What date?" Nikolai snapped.

Ryu grinned, her shrewd gaze swinging between Vlad and Mae. "Yeah, what date?"

Vlad sneered at Nikolai. "Did you hit your head during the fight? You were there when we talked about it!"

"I have business with his uncle," Mae explained at everyone else's confused expressions.

Abraham sucked in air. "You're seeing the *Black Devils'* boss?!"

Derrick and Gerard's eyes filled with respect.

"Our Mae's a regular gangster," Ye-Seul said cheerfully.

CHAPTER FORTY-THREE

THREE DAYS LATER AND MAE WAS STARTING TO SUSPECT her grandmother's words were going to become a reality. She stepped out of Vlad's car and eyed the gleaming mansion rising before them with a sliver of dread.

"This is where you used to live?"

"Only after we came to the U.S." Vlad closed the door of his Bentley. "I grew up outside St. Petersburg."

Brimstone brushed against Mae's legs as they climbed the steps to the front door. She was wearing the black, velour pantsuit Vlad had bought her for their trip to Philadelphia and matched it with some of the jewelry he'd gifted her for the reception. Tarang chuffed excitedly beside the fox, keen to show his friend his territory.

It had taken her a couple of days to recover from all that had happened in Philadelphia and their subsequent findings in Atlanta. As promised, Mae had used Charlotte's soul orb to locate her body. To everyone's relief, the witch's remains bore no visible external injuries. Mae speculated from this that the agony she had felt from Charlotte's soul orb had to do with Barquiel tearing her magic core out of her body.

Nikolai's words from last night weighed heavily on her mind.

It had taken him a day to tell her the decision he'd come to concerning Marlena's invitation to join the Council of the Moon. Though he hadn't accepted her offer, he had agreed to go to the Council's headquarters to meet the rest of his family. More importantly, Bryony had informed Marlena about the disabling side effect Nikolai and Alastair experienced after accessing a ley line. As the New York coven High Priestess had suspected, Marlena had told them there was a solution to the problem. It would, however, require Nikolai to physically practice his white magic with her and other senior members of the Council of the Moon.

He didn't have a date in mind yet for his departure. Only that it would be in a matter of weeks.

The mansion door opened, distracting Mae from her gloomy thoughts.

A tall, wiry, middle-aged man in an impeccable suit stood in the entrance. "Please, do come in."

Vlad introduced Mae to his former tutor and Yuliy Vissarion's current secretary as the latter closed the door behind them.

Gustav Luchok greeted Mae with a gentlemanly bow. "It is a pleasure to finally meet you, Ms. Jin." He smiled. "I've heard a lot about you."

Mae cut her eyes to Vlad. "I hope they were all good things."

Vlad smirked.

A stylish older woman in an elegant black dress appeared from inside the mansion, her eyes bright as she studied Mae. "Oh my."

"Mae, this Lena Dubravac," Vlad said.

Mae startled when Lena clasped her arms and pulled her in to kiss her cheeks.

The older woman stepped back and beamed at Mae and Vlad. "You shall make beautiful babies."

Hellreaver sniggered on Mae's chest.

"I doubt that's going to happen anytime soon," Mae said politely.

Vlad slipped a hand on her lower back. "I would like three."

Mae ignored his heated touch and curled a lip. "Oh, please! You've not even gotten to second base yet."

Lena sucked in air. Gustav inspected his shoes.

"Would you like me to get one of my former girls to show you the ropes?" Lena asked Vlad perfunctorily.

Vlad shuddered. "No, thanks."

Mae headed down the corridor to their right.

"How do you know my uncle's office is over there?" Vlad said, surprised.

"Because Tarang went that way and I can hear him scratching and yowling at a door."

"Don't kill anybody," Lena called out. "You know that white rug is a bitch to get blood out of."

"She'd get along with my mom," Mae observed as Vlad caught up with her.

"Maybe I should invite her and Gustav over to Sunday brunch."

Noah's face popped up in Mae's mind. "I think Noah might get another ulcer."

They came abreast of the door where Tarang waited impatiently, the tiger looking mighty miffed that his paws were too big to twist the handle.

They have guns in there, Brimstone told Mae.

She shrugged. *It's a crime lord's house. I'd be surprised if there weren't any.*

Brimstone huffed. *You're being very nonchalant about this.*

That's because I know you and Hell have my back. As does Vlad.

Damn right we do, Hellreaver gloated.

Mae frowned. *Besides, after the shit we just went through, this is gonna be a pleasant interlude.*

Vlad opened the door.

The man who rose from the Chesterfield sofa next to the fireplace couldn't be anyone but Yuliy Vissarion.

"Welcome," the Black Devils' crime lord said in a neutral voice.

Mae noted the warning in his eyes and dipped her chin respectfully. "Hi, it's nice to meet you." Her gaze swept the armed bodyguards fanning the room before focusing on the man in the suit who had yet to rise from the other couch. "Let's make this quick. I have a lunch date I don't want to miss."

The main Russian syndicate rep's gaze grew arctic.

"I am afraid this meeting will take as long as it needs to, Ms. Jin," he said in a heavily accented voice.

Mae shrugged. "It's your funeral." She cocked her thumb at Brimstone. "He'll get hungry in about two hours. I can't take responsibility for his actions if he eats some of you." She indicated Hellreaver's medallion form next. "And this guy is as uncivilized as they come. I'm talking a thousand demons' worth of uncivilized."

Hey! Hellreaver protested.

Confusion washed across the representative's face.

"Who is she talking to?" he asked Yuliy suspiciously.

"Oh." Mae scratched her cheek. "I guess you can't see them." She glanced at Vlad. "Can we?"

The incubus dipped his chin, the lines around his eyes and mouth telling Mae he was trying really hard not to laugh.

Mae looked at Brimstone. "Mind the ceiling."

Brimstone grinned.

Gasps sounded around the room as Brimstone and Tarang made themselves visible, the fox growing into his nine-tailed spirit form. Hellreaver detached from Mae's neck and shapeshifted with a pulse of crimson energy.

Admiration filled Yuliy's eyes as he eyed the nine-tailed spirit and the demonic weapon. Several guards dropped their guns in shock. The representative shrank back on the couch.

"Like I said, we should make this quick," Mae muttered, deadpan.

She strode up to the nearest armchair, sat down, and crossed her legs.

Several of the men stumbled back as Brimstone curled up beside her, his giant head dominating the space. Tarang jumped up on the fox and plopped down on his back with a happy rumble. Hellreaver zoomed around the office, oblivious to the ashen-faced guards watching his gleaming blades as he inspected various knickknacks curiously.

"Don't break anything," Mae warned the weapon.

"You should put a ring on her," Yuliy murmured to Vlad as the incubus settled beside him.

CHAPTER FORTY-FOUR

Bryony's eyes bulged. "They just agreed to let you be?!"

"I can be very persuasive."

The High Priestess looked unconvinced by Mae's words. She gave Vlad a jaundiced stare. "What really happened?"

The incubus smirked. "Brimstone and Hellreaver got hungry."

They looked to where the fox and the weapon were inhaling the steaks on a serving trolley, Tarang helping them clear the giant order of meat the coven had prepared.

Mae was conscious the crime syndicate Yuliy and Vlad answered to would continue to try to get her to work for them. Her little demonstration today had been intended with only one purpose in mind.

To show them who had the upper hand in this negotiation.

Hopefully, they'll decide messing with a Witch Queen is too much trouble and leave me alone.

She could tell Vlad and Yuliy had greatly enjoyed her interaction with the poor guy who'd traveled from Moscow to meet with her, even if they hadn't shown it at the time. The way Yuliy kept patting her back in a fatherly way and inviting her over for dinner was a surefire sign she now featured the crime lord among her friends.

Abraham strolled in with Violet and Miles just as lunch was served. Nikolai turned up halfway through the meal.

"Did you get the key?" Mae asked.

Nikolai shuddered. "I can't believe that's where you hid it."

Mae shrugged. "No one would have thought to look there."

Nikolai grimaced. "I bet Mr. Ho-Nam was scowling at me from Heaven."

Mae made a face. "I suspect Mr. Ho-Nam is enjoying his current whereabouts far more than Earth. Mrs. Son-Ha said his widows are fighting over his will."

She'd put the skeleton key Agnes had given them in Mr. Ho-Nam's urn, in the columbarium at Fairhill Funeral Home. Since it was surrounded by the remains of the dead, she'd been pretty confident the Dark Council wouldn't be able to detect it. She'd bound it inside a shield as an extra precaution.

"How are things between you and Raven?" Violet asked Abraham.

The aide flushed. "It's—okay."

He peeked guiltily at Bryony.

The older witch sighed. "I'm not stopping you from having a love life."

Abraham relaxed.

"You're just going to have to accept that it will be a long-distance relationship," Bryony crowed.

The aide's expression grew pinched.

Mae leaned sideways.

"You owe me ten bucks," she whispered to Miles.

The sorcerer heaved a morose sigh and fished out a ten-dollar bill from his wallet.

"What's that about?" Violet asked suspiciously.

Mae wrinkled her nose. "I won a bet."

From Vlad's reports, there had been definite lip locking between Violet and Erik prior to their departure from Philadelphia. Mae couldn't help but feel a little sorry for the Vegas sorcerer. Violet was on a mission to rid him of his chastity and was undoubtedly going to win.

"Fifty bucks says they're doing the dirty by Valentine's Day," Mae murmured to Miles.

He grinned. "You're on."

They finished lunch in record time and gathered around the main conference table while Abraham brought out the compass from the coven's vault.

Excitement thrummed the air as the aide carefully laid it down. Mae's heart started to race. Nikolai removed the skeleton key from his pocket.

He looked over at her.

She shook her head. "You should do it. Your magic has a stronger affinity with that thing."

"Are you guys sure you want to open that artifact here?" Vlad indicated the coven's official meeting chambers with a skeptical expression. "We have no idea what could happen."

"Yeah," Miles said. "What if it opens up a doorway to another dimension?"

Everyone stared.

The sorcerer grimaced. "Okay, I just heard what I said and it sounded ridiculous. We've already seen portals to Hell, ha-ha."

Brimstone approached the table. *If this leads to the* Book of Shadows, *we should take the risk and use the compass.*

"Brim says to go for it," Mae stated.

Nikolai grasped the compass, inhaled, and placed the skeleton key inside it.

Everyone held their breath.

He turned the key. It wouldn't budge.

Nikolai frowned. "It's not working."

"Let me try." Mae took the compass off him and attempted to twist the key. It grated against the keyhole. She took it out. "Why is it not—?"

Her stomach dropped at the sight of the grooves on the shank and the bit. Suspicion bloomed in her mind. Her accusing gaze locked on Hellreaver where he was sucking on a bone.

"Hell?"

Yeah?

"Did you chew on this?!" Mae spluttered.

Brimstone groaned. Nikolai drew a sharp breath. Vlad looked disgusted.

"You cannot make this shit up," Violet said leadenly.

Horror drained the color from Bryony's face. "He didn't?!" Her head whipped around, her eyes shrinking to slits. "Why that little ass—!"

The little asshole had stopped sucking on his bone and was looking distinctively uncomfortable in the face of their glares.

I only nibbled on it a little to see what kind of magic it had inside it, he protested.

"And?" Mae snapped.

"What'd he say?" Nikolai asked grimly.

"He chewed it to test its magic."

"Did he find anything?" Vlad asked tensely.

Hellreaver squirmed. *Er, no.*

"No!" Mae growled for everyone else's benefit.

I'm sure it can be fixed. Hellreaver started to sweat. *I mean, someone made it, right? So, whoever it is can fix it!*

Mae scowled. "Do you know who made it?"

"What's he saying now?" Nikolai asked.

"He says it can be fixed."

Vlad made a face. "By whom? I thought Brimstone told us Azazel created that thing."

Your father wasn't a metalsmith. Brimstone huffed. *He would have outsourced this to someone else.*

"Either of you got an address or a phone number?!" Mae snapped.

Brimstone sniffed. *It was thousands of years ago. I haven't a clue who was around at the time.*

Mae pursed her lips. She came to a decision.

Crimson pulsed across the room.

Calm down, my witch, Brimstone warned.

Mae cracked her knuckles and headed over to Hellreaver. "I'll calm down after I rough him up a little."

The weapon squeaked and shot across the room.

"*What* is going on?!" Abraham barked.

"Come here, Hell," Mae crooned with a glassy smile. "It'll only hurt a little."

The red haze filling the room thickened with her magic.

Everyone blanched, including Hellreaver.

"Shield!" Abraham gurgled. "*Shield, dammit!*"

THE END

Mae, Brimstone, and Hellreaver's adventures
continue in
Of Flames and Crows.

ACKNOWLEDGMENTS

To my friends and family. I couldn't do this without you.

To my readers. Thank you for reading Rites of Passage. If you enjoyed my book, please consider leaving a review on Goodreads or on the store where you purchased it. Reviews help readers like you find my books and I truly appreciate your honest opinions about my stories.

Make sure to sign up to my store newsletter for special deals on my books and new release alerts. Or you can sign up to my author newsletter to get upcoming release notifications, sneak peeks, and giveaways.

BOOKS BY A.D. STARRLING

Legion

ABOUT A.D. STARRLING

Visit Shop AD Starrling and buy all of AD's ebooks, paperbacks, hardbacks, audiobooks, and exclusive special edition print books direct.

Want to know about AD Starrling's upcoming releases? Sign up to her author newsletter for new release alerts, sneak peeks, giveaways, and more.

Follow AD Starrling on Amazon.

Join AD's reader group on Facebook
The Seventeen Club.

Check out this link to find out more about A.D. Starrling
Linktr.ee/AD_Starrling.

www.ingramcontent.com/pod-product-compliance
Lightning Source LLC
Chambersburg PA
CBHW060750190726
48285CB00002B/370